THE YEAR OF THE VIRGINS

In the autumn of 1960 Winifred and Daniel Coulson presented a highly acceptable façade to the outside world, living at Wearcill House in Fellburn with their three sons. Stephen, the eldest, remained at thirty the man-boy he would always be, utterly dependant on others, especially his two siblings, the staunch and self-reliant Joe and young Donald, on whom Winifred doted to the point of obsession. Now Donald was to be married. But could his mother face up to letting him go? And was he entering marriage with the unbesmirched purity of body and spirit that mattered so much to her? This might be the second half of the twentieth century, but amidst the strange workings of Winifred's mind much older conceptions of morality and the teachings of the church still held sway. There was something potentially explosive just below the surface of life at Wearcill House, but when that explosion came it was in a totally unforeseeable and devastating form.

THE YEAR OF THE VIRGINS

Catherine Cookson

CHIVERS PRESS
BATH

First published 1993
by
Bantam Press
a division of Transworld Publishers Ltd
This Large Print edition published by
Chivers Press
by arrangement with
Transworld Publishers Ltd
1993

ISBN 0 7451 7613 5

British Library Cataloguing in Publication Data available

Photoset, printed and bound in Great Britain by
REDWOOD BOOKS, Trowbridge, Wiltshire

THE YEAR OF THE VIRGINS

PART ONE

CHAPTER ONE

'I just can't believe my ears. I just can't.'

'It's a simple question for a man to ask of his son.'

'*What!*'

Daniel Coulson bent over and looked at his wife's reflection in the mirror, and he saw a round flat face, the skin of which was still as perfect as when he had married her thirty-one years ago. But that was all that remained of the girl who had got him to the altar when he was nineteen, for the fair hair piled high above the head was bleached and her once plump, attractive shape had spread to fat, which now looked as if it were trying to force its way out at various points of her taffeta gown, an evening gown with a neckline just below the nape of her neck; it would be indecent to expose the flesh leading to her breasts. But any ardour those breasts would or should have aroused had died in him long ago. His attention was now focused on her eyes: pale grey eyes which at most times appeared colourless, except as now when rage was boiling in her. And as he stared into them he ground his teeth before saying, 'You expect me to collar him and ask him that?'

'It's what any ordinary father could ask of his son. But then you've never been an ordinary father.'

'No, by God! I haven't. I've fought you all the way, because you would have kept him in nappies until he left school. You had him at the breast until you were shamed out of it.'

3

When her arm came out and her elbow caught him in the stomach, he stumbled away from her, the while thrusting out his hand, for she had gripped the lid of a heavy glass powder-bowl and was holding it poised for aiming. 'You let that out of your hand, missis,' he growled, 'and I'll slap your face so hard you'll have to make an excuse for not attending his wedding.'

As he watched her hand slowly open and the lid drop back on to the dressing-table he straightened his back as he said grimly, 'You can't bear to think you're losing him, can you? Even to the daughter of your best friend. You tried to link her up with Joe, didn't you? But she had grown out of her schoolgirl pash and wanted Don. And, let me tell you, I saw that she got what she wanted, and what Don wanted. Although if there was anyone she could have had apart from Don I would have picked Joe.'

'Oh, yes, you would have picked Joe. You saddled me with a retarded son, then you inveigled me into adopting a child...'

'My God!' He put his hand to his head and turned from her and walked down the long, softly carpeted room towards the canopied four-poster bed, a bed he had not slept in for more than fifteen years, and he bumped his head against the twisted column of one of the posts. Then in the silence that had fallen on the room he turned slowly; but he did not move towards her, he simply stared at her for a long moment before he said, 'Me inveigled you into adopting a child? It's well seen it wasn't *my* father who ended up in an asylum.'

When he saw the muscles of her face begin to twitch he told himself to stop it, he had gone too

4

far, it was cruel. But the cruelty wasn't all on one side. No. By God! No. If she had been a wife, just an ordinary wife, instead of a religious maniac and an almost indecently possessive mother, then he wouldn't now be carrying the shame of some of the things he'd had to do because of his needs; and all on the sly, because one mustn't lose face in the community, the community of the church and the visiting priests and the nuns in the convent and the Children of Mary and the Catenians and all the paraphernalia that must be kept up...

He must get out. He must have a drink. He drew in a long gasping breath. He'd better not; he'd better wait until the company came, because if he started early his tongue would run away with him.

He was walking down the room towards the far door when her voice hit him almost at screaming pitch: 'You're a low, ill-bred, common swab, like your father was, and all your lot.'

He didn't pause but went out, pulling the door after him; only to stop on the wide landing and close his eyes. It was amazing, wasn't it? Simply amazing, calling him common and a low, ill-bred swab, she who had come from the Bog's End quarter of Fellburn! He could recall the day she came to the office looking for a job. She was fifteen, and Jane Broderick set her on. But after three months Jane had said, 'She's no good, she'll never be able to type; the only thing she's good for is putting on side. She's got the makings of a good receptionist, but this is a scrap-iron yard.' And it was his father who had said, 'Give the lass a chance. You said she had a good writing hand so let her file the orders like that.' And his father nearly killed himself laughing when it was

5

discovered she was taking elocution lessons from a
retired schoolteacher in town. It was from then
that he himself began to think there was something
in her, that she was different. And my God, he had
to learn just how different she was. But there was
one thing he could say for her; her elocution
lessons had been put to good use, for she could
pass herself off in any company. Even so, she chose
her company: no common working-class
acquaintances for her. Look how she had
chummed up with Janet Allison because, although
the Allisons didn't live in a blooming great
mansion like this, they were middle-class down to
their shoe laces. Catholic middle-class. Oh yes;
Winnie could not have tolerated Protestants even if
they *had* supported a title. She was faithful to one
thing, at any rate, and that was her religion.

He went slowly down the stairs and as he walked
across the hall the far door opened and there stood
his adopted son, Joe.

Joe was as tall as himself, and they were very
alike, only his hair was black, not just dark, and his
eyes were a warm brown, not blue. Daniel had
always felt proud that Joe resembled him, because
he had thought of him as a son even more than he
did of Stephen, or even of Don.

As he approached him he glanced at the two
books Joe had in his hand, saying, 'What's this?
Starting to do a night shift?'

'No; not quite; just something I wanted to look
up.' They stared at each other for a moment, then
Joe said simply, 'Trouble?'

'What do you mean, trouble?'

'Well, unless it slipped your mind, the bedroom
is placed over the library. It's a high ceiling in

6

there,' he jerked his head backwards, 'but it's not soundproof.'

Daniel now pushed past him to go towards the library, saying over his shoulder, 'You got a minute?'

'Yes; as many as you want.'

Joe closed the door after him, then followed Daniel up the room to where a deep-seated leather couch was placed at an angle facing a long window that looked on to the garden. But when the man whom he thought of as his father did not sit down but moved to the window and, raising one hand, supported himself against the frame, he walked to his side and said, 'What is it now?'

'You won't believe this.' Daniel turned to him. 'You'll never believe what she's asked me to put to Don.'

'Well, not 'til you tell me.'

Daniel now turned from the window, walked to the couch and dropped down on to it. Then, bending forward, he rested his elbows on his knees and, staring at the polished parquet floor, he said, 'She's demanding that I ask Don if he's *still a virgin*.'

There being no comment forthcoming from Joe, Daniel turned his head to look up at him, saying, 'Well, what do you say to that?'

Joe shook his head as he said, 'What can I say? Nothing, except to ask what you think she would do if you came back and gave her the answer that he wasn't.'

'What would she do? I just don't know; me mind boggles. She'd go to some extreme, that's sure, even perhaps try to stop the wedding, saying he wasn't fit to marry a pure girl like Annie, or

7

Annette, as her mother insists on calling her. These people! Or she'd try to yank him along to Father Cody. Oh no, not Father Ramshaw; no, he'd likely laugh in her face, but hellfire Cody would likely call up St John The Baptist to come and wash her son clean.'

'Oh, Dad.' Joe now covered his mouth with one hand, saying, 'That's funny, you know.'

'Lad, I can see nothing funny in anything I say or do these days. To tell the truth, and I can only talk about it to you and one other, I'm at the end of me tether. I've left her twice, as you know, but she's hauled me back through pity and duty, but when I go this time, all her tears and suicide threats and for the sake of the children ... Children!' He pointed at Joe. 'Look at you. You were twenty years old when she last named you among the children. That was five years ago and she still had her child with her, because she still considered Don, at sixteen, to be a child. It's a wonder he's turned out the decent fellow he is, don't you think?'

'Yes; yes, I suppose so, Dad. And he *is* a decent fellow. But ... have you thought, if you were to go, what would happen to Stephen, because *there's* someone who is a child for life. You faced up to this a long time ago. And you couldn't expect Maggie to take him on if there was no other support. And if you went, you know what Mam would do with him; what she's threatened many times.'

Abruptly, Daniel thrust himself up from the couch, his shoulders hunched, saying, 'Don't go on. Don't go on, Joe. Stephen will never go into a home; I'll see to that. But one thing I do know: I

8

can't stand much more of this.' And moving his feet apart and stretching his arms wide, he said, 'Look at it! A bloody great room like this, full of books that nobody apart from you bothers to read. All show. Twenty-eight rooms, not counting your original prehistoric annexe. Stables for eight horses; not even a damned dog in them. She doesn't like dogs, just cats. Six acres of land and a lodge. And for what? To keep five people employed, one for each of us. I've lived in this house for fifteen years but it's seventeen years since I bought it, and I bought it only because it was going dead cheap. A time-bomb had gone off close by, and the soldiers had occupied it, and so the owners were glad to get rid of it. Funny, that. They could trace their ancestors back two hundred years, but they were quite willing to sell it to a taggerine man who had made money out of old scrap that was helping to kill men.' He nodded. 'That's how I always looked at it, because when my Dad and old Jane Broderick were blown up together in the works towards the end of the war, I thought it was a sort of retribution. And yet it's strange, you know, for even though it was going cheap, when I saw it I knew I had to have it. I can't blame your mother for that, for like me she jumped at it and then took a delight in spending a fortune furnishing it; and wherever she got it from, I don't know, but that's one thing that can be said for her; she had taste in furnishings. But it's funny, you know, lad, this place doesn't like me.'

'Oh.' Joe now pushed Daniel on the shoulder with his fist, saying, 'Come on, come on, don't be fanciful.'

'It doesn't. I have feelings about things like this.

It doesn't. I'm an intruder. We are all intruders. The war was supposed to level us all out. Huh . . . ! But these old places, like some of the old die-hard county types, keep you in your place, and mine isn't here.'

For the first time a smile came on to his face and he turned and looked towards the window again, saying, 'Remember our first real house, the one at the bottom of Brampton Hill? It was a lovely place, that; cosy, a real home, with a lovely garden that you didn't get lost in. Do you remember it?' He turned to Joe who, nodding, said, 'Oh yes, yes, very well.'

'Yet you like this house?'

'Yes, I like it. I've always liked it, although when I was young, the "cill" part of it, Wearcill House, always puzzled me. Yes, I've always liked it, but at the same time I know what you mean. There's one thing I must point out to you, Dad: you're lucky, you know, that it takes only five people to run the house, and that's inside and out. When the Blackburns were here, I'm told there were twelve servants inside alone. And *they* had only three sons and a daughter.'

'Aye, three sons; and they were all killed in the war.'

'Come on, Dad, cheer up. I'll tell you what.' He again punched his father in the shoulder. 'Go on; go and ask Don if he's a virgin.'

Watching Joe shaking with laughter, Daniel began to chuckle, and characteristically he said, 'Bugger me eyes to hell's flames! I'll never get over that. Anyway'—he now poked his head towards Joe—'do you think he's a virgin?'

'Haven't the slightest idea. But on the other

hand ... well, I should say, yes.'

'I don't know so much. Anyway, where is he?'

'The last time I saw him he was in the billiard-room, playing his usual losing battle with Stephen. He's very good with him, you know.'

'Aye, he is. And that's another thing she can't get over; that her wee lamb has always found time for her retarded and crippled first-born. Aw, come on.'

They went out together, crossed the hall to where a corridor led off by the side of the broad shallow staircase, and at the end of it Joe opened the door and almost shouted at the two people at the billiard table, 'I knew this was where you'd be. Wasting time again. Chalk up to the eyes and company coming'—he glanced at his watch—'in twenty minutes' time.'

'Joe! Joe! I beat him. I did. I beat him again.'

Joe walked round the full-sized billiard table towards a man who was almost as tall as himself, a man thirty years old, with a well-built body and a mass of brown unruly hair, but with a face beneath it that could have belonged to a young boy, and a good-looking young boy. Only the eyes gave any indication that there was something not quite normal about him. The eyes were blue like those of his father, but they were a pale, flickering blue. It was as if they were bent on taking in all their surroundings at once. Yet there were times when the flickering became still, when his mind groped at something it could catch but only momentarily hold.

'I ... I made a seven ... break. Didn't I, Don?'

'Yes. Yes, he did, and he made me pot my white.'

'Never!' said Daniel. 'He made you pot your white, Don? In that case you're getting worse.'

'Well, he's too good for me; and it isn't fair; he always wins.'

'I'll ... I'll let you win next time, Don. I will. I will. That's a promise. I will. I will, honest.'

'I'll keep you to it, mind.'

'Yes, Don. Yes, Don.'

Stephen now put his hand up to his throat and, pulling a bow tie to one side, he said to his father, 'It hurts my neck, Dad.'

'Nonsense. Nonsense.' Daniel went up to him and straightened the tie.

'Dad?'

'Yes, Stephen?'

'Can I go in the kitchen with Maggie?'

'Now you know that Maggie's getting the dinner ready.'

'Then I'll go with Lily.'

'Not now, Stephen; we won't go through all this again. You know what the pattern is: you say How do you do? to Mr and Mrs Preston and Mr and Mrs Bowbent and, of course, to Auntie and Uncle Allison and Annie ... Annette. Then after you've done that and had a word with Annette, as you always do, you can go upstairs and Lily will bring up your dinner.'

'Dad.' Don was signalling to his father as he turned away to walk down to the end of the room where a wood fire was burning in an open grate, and when Daniel joined him he stooped and, picking a log from a basket, he placed it on the fire, muttering as he did so, 'Let him go up, Dad; he had an accident earlier on.'

'Bad?'

12

'No, just wet. But he's all nerves.' He stood up now and, looking at his father, said, 'It's hard for him. I can't understand why you make him keep it up.'

Daniel lifted his foot to press the log further into the flames, saying, 'You know fine well, Don, why I keep it up. I'm not going to hide him away as if he were an idiot, because he's not an idiot. We know that.'

'But it isn't fair to him, Dad. Let him go tonight. It would upset Mum if he were to have another accident, and in tonight's company. It's happened once before, you know it has.'

'That was a long time ago. He's learned better since.'

'Dad, please.'

Father and son stood looking at each other; neither spoke, even though in the background there was Joe's voice still forming a barricade behind which they could talk, until Don said, 'Look upon it as an extra wedding present to me.'

'Aw! you; aren't you satisfied with what you've got?'

'Oh, Dad, don't say that, satisfied. I've told you, I can't believe it, a house of our own and such a grand one. And—' He paused as he now looked deep into his father's eyes before adding, 'a good distance away.'

'Aye, lad, a good distance away. But there's one thing I've got to say, although I don't want to. But it must be said: don't cut her off altogether; invite her often, and come back here whenever you can.'

'I'll do that. Yes, yes, I'll do that. And one more thing from me, Dad: thank you for everything, particularly for bringing me through.'

13

He did not have to explain through what, nor did Daniel have to enquire; they both knew. Turning quickly, Daniel walked towards Stephen, crying, 'All right! You've got the better of me again. You're not only good at billiards, you're good at getting round people. Get yourself away up to your rooms; I'll get Lily to go up with you.'

'No need. No need, Dad.' Joe put his arm around Stephen's shoulders. 'We've got to get things straight here; he's backing Sunderland against Newcastle. Did you ever hear anything like it? Come on, you! Let's get this worked out.' And with that the two tall men left the room, Stephen's arm around Joe's waist now and a deep happy gurgle coming from his throat.

On their own now and with the opportunity for more talk, it would nevertheless seem that the father and son had exhausted all they had to say to each other, until Don asked, 'Like a game, Dad? We've got fifteen minutes; they always arrive on the dot, never before.'

'No thanks, Don. I'd better slip along to the kitchen and ask Maggie if she can send something upstairs before she gets the dinner going.' And with this he turned and abruptly left the room.

A baize door led from the hall into the maze of kitchen quarters. He'd had the main kitchen modernised, putting in an Aga, but leaving the old open fire and ovens, which were still used and baked marvellous bread. It was an attractive kitchen, holding a long wooden table, a delf rack on one wall, a sideboard on the other, a double sink under a low wide window that gave a view of the stable yard. There was a long walk-in marble shelved larder, and next to it a door leading into a

14

wood store and from this into a large covered glass porch, where outdoor coats and hats were hung and, flanking one side, a long boot-rack.

The kitchen was a-bustle. Maggie Doherty, a woman of thirty-seven, stood at the table decorating with half cherries and strawberries a trifle which had already been piped with cream, and she glanced up at Daniel for a moment and smiled as she said, 'They'll soon be here.'

'Aye. Yes, they'll soon be here ... That looks nice. I hope it tastes as good.'

'Should be; there's almost half a bottle of sherry soaking itself downwards.'

'Eeh! we mustn't let Madge Preston know, must we?'

'Tell her it's cooking sherry. It makes all the difference; you wouldn't believe.'

'Aye, I would. Is it duck the night'?

'Yes; with the usual orange stuffing and the odds and bods.'

'What soup?'

'Vichyssoise.'

'Oh aye? That's something to swank about.'

'Or shrimp cocktail.'

'Oh, Betty Broadbent'll go for those.'

He stood for a moment watching Maggie's hands putting the finishing touches to the trifle, then said, 'I've sent Stephen straight up. He hasn't been too good the day, I understand. Would you see that he gets a bite?'

Maggie Doherty lifted her eyes to his, then looked down on the trifle again before saying, 'Why you insist on putting him on show, God only knows; he suffers agony with strangers. How can you do it?'

15

'Maggie, we've been through this; it's for his own good.'

The top of the trifle finished, she took up a damp cloth from the table and as she wiped her hands with it, he said under his breath, 'For God's sake! don't you an' all take the pip with me, Maggie, 'cos it's been one of those days; a short while ago I just staggered out of another battle.'

Again she looked at him, but her gaze now was soft as she said, 'You know better than that,' before turning away and calling out to a young woman who had just entered the kitchen, 'Peggie! set the tray for Master Stephen and take it up. You know what he likes.' Then she added, 'Is everything right on the table?' And Peggie Danish replied, 'Yes, Miss Doherty. Lily's just put on the centre piece; it looks lovely.'

At this Maggie said, 'Well, I'd better go and see if I'm of the same opinion,' but she smiled at the young woman; then taking off a white apron and smoothing her hair back, she went from the room. And Daniel followed her. But once in the passage they both stopped and he, looking down into her face that was neither plain nor pretty yet emanated a soft kindness, said, 'I'm sorry, Maggie, sorry to the heart of me.'

'Don't be silly. I've waited a long time for that and I don't feel brazen in saying it.'

'Aw, Maggie; but after twenty years, and me like a father to you.'

'Huh! I've never looked on you as a father, Dan. Funny that'—she gave a soft laugh—'calling you Dan.'

'You won't go then?'

'No.' She turned her eyes from him and looked

16

up the passageway. 'I thought about it, then knew that I couldn't. But I'll have to watch my tongue and my manners, won't I? And that's going to be hard, because whenever she's treated me with a high hand I've felt like turning on her many a time and walking out. I never knew what kept me at first'—she was looking at him again—'and when I did I knew I was stuck here. But I never thought it would be for twenty years. Early on I used to imagine it was just because of Stephen because he was so helpless and in need of love, and still is'—she nodded at him—'more than any of us I think.'

'I wouldn't say that, Maggie.'

When she turned abruptly away he caught her arm and was about to say, 'Don't worry; it won't happen again,' when she forestalled him by looking at him fully in the face and saying, 'As you've known for years, I go to me cousin Helen's on me day off. You'll remember it's at forty-two Bowick Road.' She made a little motion with her head, then went from him, leaving him where she had left him, dragging his teeth tightly on his lower lip.

CHAPTER TWO

The dinner was over. The guests had spoken highly of the fare and congratulated Winifred on the achievement, and once again she had been told how lucky she was to have such a cook as Maggie Doherty.

As usual, the ladies had left the men to their cigars and port in the dining-room and had adjourned to the drawing-room. This was a custom that Winifred had inaugurated when they had first come into the big house, and this aping of a bygone custom had made Daniel laugh at first; but just at first.

Annette Allison sat on a straight-backed chair to the side of the grand piano and she looked from her mother to her future mother-in-law, then from Madge Preston to Betty Bowbent and, not consciously directing her thoughts as a prayer, she said to herself, 'Dear God, don't let me turn out like any of them.' And she did not chide herself for her thinking, nor tell herself that when next she examined her conscience she must repent for her uncharitableness to others, especially for not wishing to grow even like her mother; and she should have done for, educated in a convent, she had been trained under the nuns since she was five years old, and so such thoughts should be anathema to her.

Her mind wandered to Don, but she knew she wouldn't be allowed five minutes' privacy with him tonight; not only was her own mother like a gaoler, but Don's was too. Oh, yes. When she thought of Don's mother she became a little afraid of the future because, once married and with the added status of a wife, she might not be able to hide her feelings or curb her tongue.

When she heard Mrs Bowbent mention the name Maria and her mother put in quickly, 'Wouldn't it be nice if we could order the weather for next Saturday?' she saw an outlet for her means of escape and, standing up she said to Winifred, 'Would you mind if I went up and had a chat with Stephen?'

After a slight hesitation Winifred smiled at her and answered, 'No, no; not at all, Annette. He'll be delighted to see you.'

The four women watched Annette's departure; then Madge Preston turned to Janet Allison and said, 'Why put a taboo on the subject, Janet? She knows all about it; in fact everybody does.'

'No, they don't.' Janet Allison almost bridled in her chair. 'And anyway, they moved, didn't they?'

'Yes; but not until Maria's bulge couldn't be hidden any longer.'

'Oh, Madge, you are coarse.'

'Don't be so pi, Janet. What if it had happened to Annette?'

Rising to her feet, Janet Allison said, 'You have gone too far this time, Madge.'

'Oh, sit down, Janet. I'm sorry. I'm sorry.'

Winifred had not spoken throughout this discourse, but now, putting her hand on Janet's arm, she said quietly, 'Do sit down, please, Janet, and we'll talk about something else. This is most distressing.' And she cast a glance at Madge and made a small reprimanding motion with her head. Then, looking towards the door, she said, 'Ah, here are the men,' and sank back heavily into her chair, at the same time almost pulling Janet Allison back into her seat.

They filed into the room, led by Daniel: John Preston, round, grey-haired, and smiling; Harry Bowbent, thin and weedy, and looking like an old parochial Mormon father; then the tall, imposing, big pot-bellied figure of James Allison. Joe was the last to enter, closing the door behind him, and as he passed Winifred she screwed round in her chair and asked him under cover of the babble of voices,

19

'Where's Don?'

'Oh, he just slipped upstairs to say good-night to Stephen.'

She had to force herself not to get to her feet, but when, turning her head, she caught Janet Allison's eye tight on her she knew they were of the same mind...

In Stephen's sitting-room on the second floor Don and Annette stood locked in each other's arms. When their lips parted he said, 'I feel that I cannot live another minute without you,' and she answered simply, 'Oh, me too, Don, especially now.'

'Yes, especially now.' Then holding her face between his two hands, he said, 'Can you imagine any couple having mothers like ours?'

'No, I can't; and I'm riddled with guilt at times. But you've been lucky; your father's on your side, whereas I've got two to deal with. And, you know, the only reason I was allowed up here on my own was because the ladies were about to discuss Maria Tollett once more. Honestly, Don, poor Maria. I remember her as a shy, quiet little thing. I could put a name to twenty that might have done the same thing, but not Maria. But then Maria did, and her people had to take her away and hide her some place because of the shame. I thought we were in a new world, a new era, and that kind of thing couldn't happen in nineteen-sixty. But, I suppose while there are people like your dear mama and mine, it could still be happening at the end of the century.'

Suddenly she put her arms around him and gripped him tightly to her, and in a voice that seemed to be threaded with panic she muttered,

20

'Oh God, bring Saturday soon.'

'It's all right, darling, it's all right. And just think'—he stroked her hair—'three weeks in Italy. But of course we must go and see the Pope while we're there.'

Her body began to shake, her head moving backwards and forwards on his shoulder, and, although laughing himself but silently, he said, 'Shh! Shh! You let that laugh of yours rip and they'll be taking the stairs three at a time.'

Her eyes were wet as she looked into his, and she had to swallow deeply, saying, 'I promised faithfully we would go to Vatican City and to Mass every morning ... both of us.'

'You didn't!'

'I did.'

'Oh, why didn't you tell her we'd be cuddling in bed until twelve?'

She giggled and hugged him as she said, 'Oh, Don.'

'Listen'—he pressed her gently from him—'there's someone coming. I'll go next door and see if Stephen's asleep and you make for the door.' But as he went to move away from her he suddenly stopped and, putting his arm swiftly around her waist, he said, 'No! by God, no! We'll do no such thing. Come on. There's a limit, and if I'd had any sense I'd have reached it a long time ago.'

But when they reached the door, defiance expressed in their faces, it was Joe who confronted them, saying quietly, 'I'm ahead of the search party. Come on you two, there's departures in the offing. They're all in the morning-room looking at the presents, but conversation has been forced.'

21

He now asked of Annette, 'Was there a battle?' And she, shaking her head said, 'No, I left to leave the way open for more condemnation of Maria Tollett, which I imagined would be opposed by Mrs Preston because she's a close friend of theirs.'

'O ... oh! I see. But look'—he nodded at them—'take my advice and get that look off your faces, and don't go down entwined like that because there's been a fire smouldering all day and we don't want a conflagration, do we?'

As they laughed he pushed them both before him. And when Don said, 'Come Saturday. Come Saturday,' and Annette added, 'Amen! Amen!' they would have been surprised to know that big Joe, their friend and ally, was longing for Saturday equally as much as they were, if not more.

*   *   *

It was just on eleven o'clock. The house was quiet. Winifred had retired to her room. Joe and Stephen were also upstairs. Lily had gone down to the lodge half an hour before, and Peggie had just said good-night to him as she made her way to her attic room. There was only Maggie in the kitchen and he knew he'd be welcome there, and he needed that welcome. Oh, how he needed that welcome. But he couldn't take it, for his mind was in a turmoil: if he encouraged that, where would it end? The situation in the house would become unbearable, for he wasn't a great hand at hiding his feelings.

He wasn't feeling tired. He never felt tired at night; it was always in the morning when he had to get out of bed that he felt tired.

He went into the cloakroom and took a coat from a peg and, having put it on, he went quietly from the house and on to the drive. There was an autumn nip in the air; the long dark nights would soon be upon them. And this description, he thought, had been very like his life, one long dark night. But now a fire had been lit and he longed to warm himself at it. Yet in some odd way he was feeling ashamed of his need of it.

He walked slowly down the drive. He could see, in the distance, that the gate-lights were still on. That meant Bill and Lily hadn't yet retired.

He was near the lodge when the side gate opened and Bill White stepped out, paused, then said, 'You gave me a bit of a gliff, sir.'

'Just getting a breather before turning in, Bill.'

'Your company went early.'

'Yes; yes, they did the night. It's nippy, isn't it? We'll soon have winter on us.'

'Aye, we will that, sir. I like winter meself, I'm partial to it: me feet on the fender, me pipe, and a book. I can never settle down like that in the summer somehow.'

'No; no, I can see that. There's things to be said for all seasons, I suppose.'

Bill was walking by his side now towards the open iron gates where, poised high on top of each of the two stone pillars, glowed an electric lamp, topped by a wrought-iron shade that sent the light spraying far into the middle of the road. They both stopped within the line of the gates, and there was silence between them until Bill, in a voice scarcely above a whisper, said, 'I had to drive up Dale Street the day, sir.'

Daniel remained motionless for a moment; then

23

slowly he turned his head and looked at the face now confronting his, and asked quietly, 'Do you often drive up Dale Street, Bill?'

'Twice before; but I never twigged then.'

'When was this? I mean, when you drove up before?'

'Last week, twice.'

'Is this just something new? You ... you haven't been ordered anywhere else?'

'Something new, sir, although I've been questioned.'

Daniel gazed across the road towards the open farmland that the gate-lights just touched on, and he thought, Will she ever let up? And what a situation for this man at his side having to obey the mistress's whims while bearing allegiance to the master. His voice was thick as he muttered, 'Thanks, Bill.'

'Any time, sir.'

It was as he was about to turn and go back up the drive that a car made itself heard by its approaching rattle.' He knew the sound of that car, and as it slowed opposite the gates he walked towards it, and when it stopped with a jerk he bent down and said, 'Why are you out at this time of the night, Father?'

'Oh, business, as usual. Had company?' He pointed towards the lights.

'Yes, they've all gone. Care to come in for a drink?'

'Now since you've asked me, I think I would. A few minutes ago, all I wanted was me bed. So hop in!'

Daniel turned now and shouted to Bill, 'Don't wait up, Bill. I'll see to the lights. Good-night.'

As the man called, 'Good-night, sir,' Daniel got into the car and asked of the priest, 'Where've you been to at this time of night?'

'Oh, at Tommy Kilbride's.'

'Not again! He's a hypochondriac, that fellow.'

'He was, but not this time. He doesn't know it, but he's for the hop, skip, and jump all right, and within the next couple of days or so. And you can believe me there'll not be a more surprised man when he finds himself dead. I bet he says, "Look, it's all a mistake; it's all in me mind. It's a fact; they've been sayin' it to me for years. Let me go back." And you know something? Life's funny in the tricks it plays on a man: he's imagined he's had every disease under the sun except the one that's crept on him unawares. I'm sorry for him, I am that, but he's brought it on himself; I mean the surprise he's going to get.'

'Oh, Father.' Daniel was laughing now. 'I bet you are wishing you could be there to see his face when he arrives. And by the way, it'll be yourself that'll be arriving and very shortly if you don't get rid of this old boneshaker.'

'I've no intention of gettin' rid of Rosie, so please don't insult her; she's a friend. Would you propose gettin' rid of all those elderly ladies with ageing bones who creak in every joint? Anyway, you've had a party or some such tonight; how did it go?'

'Oh, as usual.'

'You'll be glad when Saturday comes and is gone.'

'You've never said a truer word, Father. I certainly will that. And look, don't take ... Rosie right to the door, else you'll have windows popping

25

up and enquiries as to what's causing the rattle.'

A few minutes later they were both ensconced in the library. Daniel had put the bellows to the fire and it was blazing brightly, and on a table between the chairs was a decanter of whisky and a bottle of brandy, two glasses and a jug of water.

Pointing to the bottle, Daniel said, 'I thought you might like to try this. I know brandy isn't your drink but this is something special. I had it given to me by an old customer. It's all of forty or fifty years old; it's like elixir on the tongue. I've never tasted anything to equal it before.' He now poured a good measure into the glass and handed it to the priest. And he, sipping at it, rolled it round his mouth, swallowed, then, arching his eyebrows, he said, 'Yes. My! as you say, elixir on the tongue. But still, I think I'll stick to me whisky because I wouldn't like to get a taste for this kind of thing; you might have me robbin' the poor box ...' He lay back into the deep chair, saying quietly, 'Ah! This is nice. It's a beautiful house, you know, this. I remember coming into it first during the week that I arrived in Fellburn. The Blackburns were wooden Catholics, so to speak, and as such were never free with the bottle. A cup of tea, or a cup of coffee, and that watery, that's what you were offered. Of course they were living from hand to mouth at the time: it takes a lot of money to keep up appearances, you know, especially when you like horses.'

'You're telling me, Father, even without the horses.'

'Oh, aye.' The priest put his hand out and pushed Daniel's shoulder. 'I'm tellin' you. Anyway, how's life? Your life.'

26

'As bad as it could be, Father.'

'As bad as that? Well, open up.'

'Oh, you don't want a confession here the night; at least, not after being with old Tommy. And you must have listened to many the day.'

'I'm always open to confessions. But it needn't be a confession, just a quiet crack. What's bothering you, apart from all the other things I know of? Anyway, you haven't been to confession for some weeks, have you?'

Daniel took up his usual stance when troubled, his body bent, his elbows on his knees, his hands gripped together, and he stared into the fire as he quietly said, 'I've taken up with a woman.'

'Oh God in heaven! man, tell me something I don't know.'

Daniel now turned towards the priest, saying, 'Not that kind.'

'What other kind is there that you can take up with?'

'There are some good women, Father.'

'Are you aiming, Daniel, to teach a sixty-four-year-old priest the facts of life? What you seem to forget, and many more like you, is that we are men and that some of us weren't always priests. Meself, for instance, I never came into the racket until I was twenty-five.'

'Then why did you—' and a small smile appeared on Daniel's face now as he added, 'if you knew so much?'

'Because He wouldn't let me alone.' Father Ramshaw's eyes almost disappeared under the upper lids as he looked towards the ceiling. 'I nearly got married when I was twenty, but He put His spoke in there. The girl's father wanted to

27

knock me brains out and her brother threatened to break me legs if I ran away. But run I did. And, candidly, I've been doing that inside me head ever since. Well, perhaps not so much these latter years. Yet at one time, and that's not so long ago, here was somebody frightened to go to confession to the Bishop because I was brought up to believe that you sin by thought as much as by deed. But of course you don't get as much satisfaction out of the former as you do out of the latter.'

As Daniel now threw himself back into the chair, his body shaking with laughter, he said, ' Father, I don't believe a word you say.'

'That's the trouble, nobody does. They always think I'm joking; but you know the saying, There's many a true word spoken in jest. And all my jokes have a broad streak of truth in them. You can take it from me what I've just imparted to you is God's honest truth. Anyway, who's this decent woman that you're worrying about? Do I know her?'

A few seconds passed before Daniel said, ''Tis Maggie.'

'*Oh no! not Maggie.*'

'Yes, Father. Now you see what I mean.'

'Ah well, it had to come.'

'What do you mean?' Daniel now shifted round on the couch and looked at the priest who was staring towards the fire.

'Just that. She's been for you all these years. Why do you think she's stuck here? and stuck Winifred? Because, let me tell you, it's bad enough for a man to have to put up with a woman, but for a woman to have to put up with a woman is, I should imagine, much worse, and with such a woman as Winifred. God Himself doesn't demand

28

such devotion. And devotion of this kind is a sort of sickness, and there's a number around these quarters that's got the smit. Now, between you and me, and as if you didn't know it, Annette's mother is another one. As for her father, he's bordering on religious mania. There's moderation in all things. And you know Daniel, we've got a lot of faults, we Catholics. Oh dear God! we have that. And the main one, as I've always seen it, is to imagine that we are the sole chosen of the Almighty. Now if we could only get that out of our heads we'd be the perfect religion. But there, I could be excommunicated for voicing such an opinion, because on the other hand there's not a more lenient or tolerant sect. Which other lot would give you leave to get drunk on your Friday night's pay, batter the wife, then arrive at confession on the Saturday night, then take Communion on the Sunday morning, before making for the club for a skinful? I tell you, we are the most tolerant of God's creatures and so we don't go in for extremes.'

'It's a pity then, Father, you couldn't have put over that point of view to Winnie some years ago.'

'Oh, me boy! I did. And I keep at it to this day, and with others of her kin. But do they take any notice? No. They would rather listen to Father Cody spouting his hellfire. Oh, believe me, Daniel, there's more thorns in the flesh than women. Why on earth did they send that young man to me? Now why am I asking the road I know? Things want tightening up around Fellburn. That's what was said in high quarters. People were forgetting there was a hell, at least that old fool Father Ramshaw had forgotten. Instead of folks being sat

29

on hot gridirons minus their pants, that old fool was proposing a sort of nice waiting-room where the patients could just wait and think and ponder on their past life and be sorry for their misdeeds, sins, if you like; the worst, which I've always stated in plain language from the pulpit, as you know, being unkindness to one another ... But to get back to Maggie: how did this come about after all this long time?'

Daniel again brought his body forward, and his voice low now, he said, 'It was quite simple; it seemed to be all set up. It was her day off. I gave her a lift into town. Strange, but it was the first time she'd ever been in the car with me; I mean, alone. Years ago, when she used to take Stephen out on her day off, I would drop them at her cousin's. And there we were this day, and she invited me to go in with them. Outside this house she seemed different, and as she talked I looked at her and saw this smart woman that had lived in my house for twenty years, and the kindness emanating from her, and I knew then what I'd known for a long time deep within me that I not only wanted her, but I loved her too. And that was that. Apparently, as you said, she had the same feeling for me, even though it was well hidden. What am I going to do, Father?'

'Now what can you do? If I say to you, cut her out of your life, you'll say, how can you, living in the same house? If I say to you, if your wife gets wind of this there'll be hell to pay and no mistake, what'll you say?'

'I want to leave Winnie, Father. Once Don's married and out of her clutches'—he jerked his head towards the ceiling—'I mean to go. And I'll

30

take Stephen with me, Maggie an' all. I've thought about it, and seriously.'

'You can't do that, man, you can't do that; she'll never leave you alone. You know what happened the last time, and the time before that. And she would do it again, just to weigh on your conscience for the rest of your life, because once she's lost Don she won't have much to live for. I'll never know how she has allowed his wedding to come as close as it has.'

'Well, I can tell you that, Father; I've seen to it.'

'You have? I must have known all along you had a hand in it, for she would never let go of the reins on her own. I can recall her going to watch him play football on a Saturday and waiting to drive him home, hail, rain or snow.'

'Yes, in case he spoke to some girl or other. And what do you think of the latest, Father? What do you think she asked me to do tonight?'

'I couldn't give a guess, Daniel. Tell me.'

'She didn't only ask, she demanded that I go and find out whether or not he was a virgin!'

'No. Oh dear God! No.' The priest chuckled.

'You can laugh, Father, but oh dear God! yes.'

'What possessed her?'

'What's always possessed her? The mania that is in her to hold him tight to her for the rest of his life. Pure and unsullied, that's how she thinks of him. You know, since he was born and she saw that he was normal, you could say in all truth that she's hardly looked at Stephen or Joe; in fact, she dislikes them both, although for different reasons.'

Father Ramshaw now shook his head before slowly saying, 'But even if you were to leave her you couldn't be divorced. You know that.'

31

'That wouldn't matter to me so long as there was space between us, more space, because as you know I haven't had her bed for years; she even shrinks from my hand.'

The old priest sighed as he said, "Tis a sad state of affairs. But perhaps God has a strange way of working: after Saturday, when she knows she's lost Don, she might turn to you.'

'Oh, never, Father.' Daniel now reached firmly out and replenished the glasses with whisky and, again handing one to the priest, he said, 'I couldn't stand that. I really couldn't. Not after all this long time. Oh, no, there'll be no reconciliation like that, I can tell you.'

'What about Joe, should you carry out your plan?'

'Oh, Joe's a man in his own right; he'll order his life the way he wants it. He's in a good position now, being a full-blown accountant. And anyway, he's got his own little establishment in the cottage. There's days on end when he doesn't come into the main house here, not even for his meals. Oh, I don't worry about Joe; he'll get along on his own.'

'Aye. Joe's a fine fellow, but nobody gets along on their own, Daniel. And that reminds me, I'll have to be after him; he's been neglecting his duties of late; I haven't seen him at Mass for a couple of Sundays. But then he could have been at Father Cody's. I could have enquired about that, but I didn't. The less that devil-chaser and me have to say to each other the better!' He gulped at the whisky now, then laughed and ended, 'I'm a wicked man, you know. But there's only you and God know that, so keep it to yourself. That's a fine whisky an' all, Daniel, but it must be me last if I

32

don't want to drive home singing, because then, believe it or not, Father Cody would have me on me knees, he would that, and thumping me on the back, saying, "Repeat after me: Drink is the divil. Drink is the divil. Drink is the divil."'

They both laughed, and the priest went on, 'And I bet he would say that an' all, because he puts me in mind of Sister Catherine. They could be mother and son, you know, the way they deal with those who lapse, because that's what she used to do to the young lads. I caught her at it once, thumping a hapless little divil on the head for some misdemeanour and with each thump crying, "Say: God is love. God is love. God is love."'

'Oh! Father.' Daniel wiped his eyes with a handkerchief. 'I hope you'll attend my deathbed, because I'd like to die laughing.'

'Ah, that's nice, that's a very nice thing to say. But seeing how the two of us are set in years it could be the other way round. Now, give me a hand up. Let me see if me legs are steady. How many whiskies have I had?'

'Three, and the brandy.'

'It's the brandy, whisky never goes to me legs like this.' He put out a leg and shook it, saying, 'It's got the tremors. Come on, let me out quietly, and then get yourself away to your bed. I'll see you on Thursday at the rehearsal, then pray God Saturday will be here and it will all be over. We must talk again, Daniel. Do you hear? Promise me you won't do anything until we talk again.'

'All right, Father, I promise.'

And on that, Daniel led the way out of the house and saw this dear old fellow, as he thought of him, into his car, saying, 'I'll see you to the gates; I

33

promised Bill I'd put out the lights...'

Back in the house, he looked across the hall to the green-baize door. She was still in the kitchen—he had seen the light from the drive—but he didn't make towards it. Instead, he slowly went up the stairs.

CHAPTER THREE

It was a beautiful day; it could have been mid-July, for it was quite warm and there wasn't a breath of wind. Everyone said you would think it had been ordered.

The marquee had been erected on the lawn beyond the drive. A number of men were going quietly about their business unloading tables and chairs from a lorry; from a van outside the main door, a woman and a man were carrying baskets of flowers into the house, and another was taking armfuls of blooms towards the marquee; and on the drive, men were stringing rows of electric bulbs between the larches. There was no fuss, and everything appeared orderly, as it did within the house.

It was half-past nine. Winifred had breakfasted in bed; Daniel had been up for some time; Joe and Don had just left the dining-room, both dressed in light pullovers and grey flannels. They were crossing the hall towards the stairs when Maggie came down and, confronting them from the bottom step, she said, 'He's in a tizzy, he won't get up. You'd better go and see what you can do.'

'Well, if you haven't succeeded in rousing him,

there's little chance for us.'

Maggie looked at Joe as she said, 'We don't want any ructions today, do we? Cajole, invite, or threaten, but get him out of that bed.'

Don, passing her now to go up the stairs, said, 'I would have thought it was the best place for him, seeing he's not allowed to come to the service. Anyway, he'd have been all right; he can hold himself if he likes.'

Maggie said nothing but stepped down into the hall and walked away. And Joe, taking the stairs two at a time, was quickly abreast of Don and said in an undertone, 'You know as well as I do, Don, what excitement does to him. And there's nobody would like him there more than I would.'

'He never gets a treat of any kind.'

'Oh, you know that isn't right. Look what Maggie does for him. And I take him out at least once a week.'

'I didn't mean that kind of a treat. This, well ... well, I would have thought today was special and she could have stretched a point, even taking the risk of anything happening.'

As they mounted the next flight of stairs in a single file Joe, looking at the back of this younger man whom he couldn't have loved more had he been his own kin by birth, thought ruefully, he said, *she*, not Mam, or Mother as she more often demanded as her title. It was as well he was going, for although as yet there had been no open rift between them, he had long seen one opening. And although he had his own feelings concerning the woman whom he addressed as Mam, he had no wish to see her broken openly by the desertion of the one being she loved. And not only loved; there

35

was another name for such a feeling; but there was not a word in his vocabulary that would fit the need she had for her offspring.

'What's all this? What's all this?' Don was the first to reach the bed where Stephen was curled up in a position such as a child might have taken, his knees almost up to his chin, his arms folded across his face. 'Now look here, you, Steve. Are you out to spoil my day?'

The long arms and legs seemed to move simultaneously and the body lifted itself up against the wooden back of the bed, and the lips trembled as they muttered, 'No, Don, no. But I want to come to the wedding. Don't I, Joe? Can I, Don? Oh, can I?'

Sitting down on the side of the bed, Don now said quietly, 'I want you to come. We all want you to come, but you know what happened at the rehearsal, now don't you? And anyway, the wedding will be over like that.' He snapped his fingers. 'Then you'll see Annette in her pretty dress, and the first thing she'll do when she comes into the house will be to cry out, "Where's Steve? Where's Steve?" She always does, doesn't she?'

'I ... I wouldn't misbehave, honest, Don. Look, I haven't in the night. Look!' And with a quick movement he thrust the bedclothes back. 'It's all dry.'

Joe had turned away from the bed and now stood as though looking out of the window. It made his heart ache to see this big man reduced to a child. But no, not reduced, just acting his mental age. What would happen to the lad ... man when Don was gone and he himself was gone from this house, for he couldn't stand the atmosphere much

36

longer. Of course, there was always Maggie and his dad. But his dad was at the business all day, and out and about his own business most nights. As for Maggie, she was still a youngish woman. And he had just an inkling, too, of what might have kept her in this establishment all these years, and that it wasn't just Steve. But it was only an inkling. Altogether it was an unhappy house. He had been aware of this for a long time. Even so, in a way he was grateful that he had been brought up in it, otherwise he wouldn't be in the position he was today. Yet, should he be grateful for the ache that was racking his body at this minute? Two years ago he had imagined this day could have been his, but two factors had intervened in the shapes of his dad and Annette herself. But mostly his dad.

As he looked down on to the drive he became aware that the flower van was moving away and in its place was what he recognised as a Bentley. He was keen on cars, but the family tended towards Rovers and he couldn't recall one of their friends who had a Bentley. Then his mouth fell into a slight gape as he saw a man whom he imagined to be a chauffeur get out and then open the door to allow a woman to alight. Then his face spread into a smile as he exclaimed, 'Aunt Flo!' But she was early. She wasn't expected to arrive until later. Then again his mouth fell into a gape, but a bigger one this time, and he called quickly, 'Don! Don! Come here a minute.'

When Don reached his side, Joe pointed down on to the drive where a very smartly dressed woman was talking to the man he had imagined to be a chauffeur, and he said, 'Look at that! What do you make of that?' And when the man now slipped

37

his arm into the woman's and began to walk her towards the door, they both looked at each other, their faces stretched into expressions portraying glee.

Pressing the side of his head with his hand, Don groaned. 'Oh my God! We only needed this. Mam will go berserk.'

As though of like mind, they were turning together as Joe said, 'Get yourself down to her and warn her; I'll go and meet them.' But at the door he turned again and stabbed his finger towards Stephen, saying, 'Now you be a good lad: go and have a bath; make yourself smell nice; and put on your good suit. And then, yes ... yes, you may come downstairs. Do you hear?'

'Yes, Joe. Yes.'

'That's it. Be a good lad.'

'Yes, Joe.'

Joe now turned and hurried towards the stairway. On the first floor he paused for, standing at a bedroom door, Don was holding his mother by the shoulders and saying, 'Now stop it! Stop it! There could be an explanation.'

'Explanation!' Her voice was loud. *'He's black.'*

Don cast a worried glance at Joe as he almost ran past them towards the stairs; then pressing his mother back into the room and closing the door, he said, 'Now listen, Mother. If you make a scene you're going to spoil everything. Come. Come on.' And he pulled her towards the chaise-longue at the foot of the bed, saying, 'Sit down.'

'No, no; leave me alone. Oh! what am I saying? what am I saying?'—she held out her hand in a supplicating gesture—'Saying to you, of all people, leave me alone, when this day you are leaving me.

38

And ... and she ... she's done this on purpose. Yes, yes, she has.' Her whole fat body was shaking in confirmation of her statement. 'She has always tried to rile me one way or another. Now she's come here today with ... with, of all things, a black man.'

'But you invited her. And why? because she said she was engaged to a barrister. Now own up.'

'He can't be a barrister; he's black.'

'Mother! Mother! Don't be silly.'

She turned from him now and began to pace the room. 'This is your father's doing. Oh, yes, yes it is. They were supposed to bump into each other in London, and I hadn't heard a word from her for years, not since Harry died, and that's five or more years ago. And he came back with the tale that she was doing splendidly, doing something big in an office and was working for a barrister. He must have known the barrister was black. He's done this on purpose. Your father's a wicked, wicked man.'

'Be quiet, Mother.'

'I won't! I won't! And what's more, I'm going to tell you something. Yes, I am. It's he who's brought on this day.'

'What do you mean, brought on this day?'

'Just what I say: he was determined to part us, and he's brought it about. You know he has. You know he has.'

Yes, yes, he knew he had. He knew his father had brought about his wedding day, and he thanked God for it. But he had to lie, saying loudly, 'That's utterly ridiculous.' But having lied he now inadvertently spoke the truth, adding, 'I love Annette. I have done for years. Why, I went through agonies when I thought she fancied Joe.

And you thought she fancied Joe, didn't you?'

'Nothing of the sort. Girls are flighty; they don't know their own minds. And ... and I ask you now, Don—' Her voice had sunk low, her lids were blinking, the tears were pressing out of the corners of her eyes as she stammered, 'Do ... do you know what you are doing to me? Do you? You're breaking my heart. You are leaving me alone. When you go I'll have no-one, no-one in the wide world.'

'*Oh, Mother, please.*'

'Don. Don.' With a cry she had her arms about him, pressing him to her, her flesh seeming to swim around him, her lips covering his eyes, his brow, his cheeks.

It was with an effort he pushed her from him, then stood rigid, wide-eyed, looking at her body quivering from head to foot beneath her light dressing-gown. He watched her turn from him and fling herself on to the couch muttering brokenly, 'You don't love me. You don't love me.'

He made no response to this for a full minute, and then he had to force the words through his lips, saying, 'I do love you, Mother. But this is my wedding day. And what is more significant at the moment is that Aunt Flo is downstairs with her fiancé. Now how are you going to greet him? That's what you've got to think about. How are you going to greet him? Because you know Aunt Flo: she'll stand no nonsense. If you make a fuss ... well, she'll make a bigger one. So, please, put on a dress, anything, and come downstairs and see her.'

'I won't. And I don't want that man in my house.'

40

'He is in the house, and Father will welcome him. I say again about knowing people, and you know Father.'

'Yes. Yes'—her voice was almost a scream now—'I know Father. God in heaven! yes, I know Father. I've known him for thirty tortured years.'

After drawing in a long breath he turned away and walked towards the door. But there she checked him. Her voice was low now as she said placatingly, 'I ... I can't go down yet. You can see that, Don.'

'Will I send her up?'

She didn't answer: instead she turned her head away, which he took as an assent, so he left the room.

Pausing at the top of the stairs, he put his hands across his eyes for a moment as if to shut out something, and then went quickly down the stairs and towards the drawing-room from where came the sound of voices.

His father was standing with his back to the flower-decked fireplace; and there, too, by the end of the couch on which Flo was sitting, stood the man. On this closer acquaintance, his colour seemed not to be as dark as when first seen, but more a deep chocolate-brown. He was perhaps a half-caste, a very handsome half-caste, over six feet tall and well-built with it: not heavy and not slim, but more like an athlete.

His father greeted him with an over-loud voice, saying, 'Oh, there you are, the man of the day,' and almost before the words were out his Aunt Flo rose from the couch and, coming swiftly towards him with outstretched hands, cried, 'Hello there! My! My! I hardly recognise you.'

41

Don took her hands, then bent towards her and kissed her on the cheek, saying, 'Nor me you, Aunt Flo.'

And this, he told himself, was true, because her voice had become a little a-lah, as he termed it, and her rig-out, which was a mauve velvet suit with a matching coat, he noted was lying over the back of the chair, and was indeed something. From what he remembered of his Aunt Flo, she had been a bit slovenly; cheery and nice, oh yes, but not at all the classy piece who was now saying, 'Come and meet Harvey.'

She turned and led him by the hand towards the dark man, saying, 'This is my fiancé, Mr Harvey Clement Lincoln Rochester.' She emphasised each word as she smiled broadly up at her intended. And the man, now holding out his hand, said, 'How do you do? And let me explain right away that the Rochester doesn't mean I'm any relation to Jack Benny's stooge; and the Lincoln has no connection with a past president either; nor Clement with an English prime minister, nor Harvey with an imaginary rabbit that you might have seen in the film.'

They were all laughing, Joe loudest of all, and Don, looking at them, could not help but pick up the approval he saw in their eyes and allow it to register in his own. He liked this fellow. But by God! if he knew anything, he was going to throw a spanner into the works today because she would go mad. If the man had been a Protestant or an atheist even, he might have got by, but a black man who was likely to become her brother-in-law! Oh my, my, his being a barrister wouldn't make much difference in this case. But now, out of politeness,

42

he asked of the visitor, 'Being a barrister, sir, what kind of cases do you handle?'

'Rogues; mostly rich ones.'

'Oh, Harvey, you don't! not all the time. You take on poor people too.' She was smacking at the big hand which rested on the head of the couch, and he, looking down at her, said, 'Woman, they are still rogues, all of them.'

Joe stared at the man. He could imagine him in court: he would be powerful; even his presence would show strength. And that voice ... that was the second time in the last few minutes he had called Flo 'woman'. But the way he split up the word, it came out like a caress, woo ... man, as another man might say, dar ... ling. When he heard Don saying, to Flo, 'Mother would like you to go up and see her. She's in the middle of dressing, and you know how long that takes,' he thought, Yes, it would be a long time before Mam came down those stairs to meet this visitor.

'Oh well,' said Flo, rising from her seat, 'here's the mountain going to Mahommed.' Then she cast a sidelong glance at her fiancé, saying, 'Do you think you'll be able to cope until I return?' And Harvey's reply: 'You know how I am without you, so don't be long,' must have perplexed the assembled company, thought Flo, as she made her way upstairs, not only because of his choice of words, but also by his tone.

The nearer Flo got to the door of Winifred's room, the straighter her back became. When her knock received no response, she gently pushed open the door, and there, across the room, and seated near the window, was her sister.

Flo closed the door behind her, and had walked

43

halfway towards Winifred before she spoke. 'Hello, there!' she said. And when Winifred's lips tightened, it occurred to her that the bombshell must have already dropped. Of course, Don would have told her; he would likely have seen them arrive.

'How are you?'

At this, Winifred swung round and through tight jaws said, 'How dare you?'

'How dare I what?'

'You know what I mean; don't act the innocent: bringing a black man here!'

'Oh, that!' Flo shrugged her shoulders before going on, 'He's no black man; he's a half-caste, as if it makes any difference; a good-looking, handsome, half-caste. He's a barrister, a gentleman, and well respected.'

'Shut up! Well respected. They don't even let them into working men's clubs in this town. And you've done this on purpose, haven't you, you and him between you?'

'What do you mean, me and him? He knows nothing about you.'

'I mean Daniel.'

'*Daniel?* What *are* you talking about?'

'I was given to understand that you had bumped into each other in London and that you had told him you were a secretary to a barrister and engaged to him.'

'Yes, yes, that's what I told Daniel. But he never met the barrister, though I see now that's why I got an invite to the wedding: you thought I'd gone up in the world and you thought it would be one up for you to claim that your sister was engaged to a barrister. My God! you haven't changed a bit, have you, Winnie?'

'Well, that makes two of us, for first time around you had to go and marry a cheap insurance agent, a drunk.'

'Harry was no drunk, not in that sense; he was an alcoholic, and he was a decent enough fellow. But in your opinion he was somebody to be ashamed of. Just like Father. Remember Father?'

'Yes. Oh yes, I remember Father.'

'Well, that surprises me, when you wouldn't go to see him even when he was dying. You hadn't even the decency to go and see Mam. No, you were out for prize money and you hooked on to it through Daniel. It really wasn't him you wanted but what he could provide you with. Which has been proved, hasn't it?'

Her nose wrinkling, Winifred said scornfully, 'You ... you know nothing about it. You'll always be cheap and common. When you came into this room a moment ago you had an accent that any ignoramus could detect was assumed, but now you are yourself again, aren't you? Well, as yourself, you can go down and take your coloured man out of my house. You can give the excuse that this is just a flying visit. You understand?'

Flo slowly drew herself up to her full height, so dwarfing the standing, fat figure before her, and remained silent for a moment; then she said, 'I came up for Don's wedding and to Don's wedding I and my fiancé will go. And we'll attend the reception afterwards. And only then, perhaps, will we think of leaving. Mr Rochester is a gentleman, an educated gentleman, far above your husband or your sons in education, and if you don't treat him at least with civility, then you can prepare for

45

squalls, because you know me, Winnie: when I get going I've got a loud voice and I can put things over, especially home truths, in a very jocular way, and so make people laugh while they ponder. I have that knack, haven't I? Well, I can assure you I'll do my piece. If you are not downstairs within half an hour I'll promise you one of the best performances of my life, solely for your guests, one hundred and thirty of them I understand. Think on it, Winnie. Think on it.' And on this she turned slowly about and left the room: and her step was steady as she went down the stairs.

As she entered the drawing-room her fiancé was saying, 'My grandparents came over at the end of the last century. They were from California, and they went into service in a gentleman's family just outside of London. They had a son who grew up in the same establishment and became a sort of factotum; and just after the last war he married one of the housemaids. And they had a son, and about the same time the daughter of the house and her husband, who lived with her parents, had their third son. The young half-caste'—he now pointed his forefinger towards himself—'and the three boys grew up together. They were sent to boarding school, I was sent to the local school, from where I got to the grammar school. The only coloured boy there. I stood out, I can tell you.' His smile was broad now. 'And from there it was just a natural step to university. I didn't stand out so much there, for there were other dark faces to be seen. Well, I read law, and there you are.'

Flo came quietly into the room at this point, saying, 'And one of the sons of that house is a solicitor and he brings him cases. But there's not

46

much left of the younger one, for he was blown up during the war. But we go and see him every month. And those three sons are his closest friends.'

It was evident to Daniel, Joe and Don that, as they had expected, Flo had had a hard time upstairs, for her eyes were bright and her lips were trembling slightly.

It was also evident to Harvey, and when he addressed her, 'Woo ... man, come here,' and she complied, he took her hand, and gazing into her eyes, he said, 'Would you like to go home?'

Before she had time to reply, Daniel's voice broke in loud and harsh: 'Home? She's just come.' And he went quickly to her, took her by the shoulders and pressed her down on the couch, saying, 'You've come for the wedding,' then glanced up at the scowling face and added, 'You've both come for the wedding and for the wedding you will stay. You're my guests, and'—he looked across at his two sons—'Don's and Joe's guests. Am I right?'

And together they said, 'Yes, certainly.'

Flo put out her hand towards Daniel, saying, 'It's all right; I'm all right. Winnie's dressing; she'll be down shortly.'

'Oh, well; in the meantime we'll have some coffee, it's too early for the hard stuff, at least for me. What about you?' He looked towards Harvey who, smiling, replied, 'Me too. Coffee will be fine.'

'Well, excuse me for a minute; I'll go and tell Maggie. You haven't seen her yet, have you?'

'No; nor Stephen.'

'Oh well, we'll have to do a tour. There's plenty of time before the big show starts, although I think,

47

Don, you'd better get outside and see how things are going in the marquee.'

And so it was that Joe was left alone with them and, after a moment, looking at the man who was still standing at the head of the couch, he said, 'Come and sit down; you look too big even for me.'

With a slight nod Harvey took his seat on the couch beside Flo and immediately put his arm around her shoulders, drawing her tightly towards him, and as if he knew he had a friend in Joe, he said to her, 'A bad time up there?'

And lying with a smile, she answered, 'No, no, not really. But you know, as I told you, we've never agreed, not since I first lisped her name and called her Win instead of Winifred. I was three and she ten when she first boxed my ears. But I was six and she thirteen when I first hit her with the coal shovel. Since then our war has just been verbal.'

'What a pity'—Joe, sitting opposite to them was laughing now—'because, believe it or not, Aunt Flo ...' he now leant towards her and, his voice a whisper, he said, 'you're not the only one who would like to use a coal shovel at times.' Then straightening up and in a more sombre tone, he asked, 'I can tell you seriously, at least, I should say, I can't tell you what life is going to be like once her favourite lad walks back down the aisle today because, as you only too well know, Aunt Flo, he's all she's lived for for years.'

'Yes, I'm aware of that. But what puzzles me is how she came to approve of the marriage in the first place.'

'Well, to be truthful'—Joe's voice sank—'Dad manoeuvred it.'

48

'And she let him?'

'Well, it was a case of between the devil and the deep sea. You know Dad's got a cousin in America. Well, he's succeeded in much the same business as Dad's, only in a much bigger way, and two years or so ago Dad asked him to find a place for Don. At the same time ...' He hesitated now and glanced towards the flowers in the hearth, then passed one lip over the other before turning back to them again and saying, 'Well, in some way he found out that Annette was sweet on Don...'

'But she must have been still a schoolgirl, still at the convent.'

'Yes, she was a schoolgirl of nearly eighteen, Aunt Flo. She could have gone on to college—I think she wanted to be a teacher—but apparently she wanted Don more, and so Mam had to decide whether she would have her son in America or ten miles away in Hazel Cottage in Northumberland. So, with bad grace she plumped for the latter.'

'Ten miles away! And she still can't drive. I wonder she allowed that.'

'Oh, she has Bill to take her all over the place. Still, it's not on the doorstep exactly. Again, it was Dad's doing.'

As Joe pulled a face, Flo said, 'No wonder she's on a high key...'

'And my appearance hasn't, I'm sure, helped matters,' said Harvey.

'Oh, I don't know so much.' Joe grinned at Harvey now, saying, 'You've acted as a diversion.'

'Like a red light depicting a road up, in this case black. Never mind.' He squeezed Flo to him. 'What I'll do is imagine I'm in court and she is the prosecuting counsel and I'm defending a lone

49

woman'—he again pressed Flo to him—'who is not only beautiful, but kind and understanding. But her main attraction for me is she is the best secretary in the business.'

They were laughing when Maggie brought the coffee in. She showed no reaction. They were again laughing when Stephen came into the room, and he, seeing the visitor, exclaimed, 'Oh! you *are* a big black man.' And Harvey, knowing all about Stephen's condition, replied, 'And aren't *you* a big white man, and a fine looking one into the bargain.'

They were still laughing when, in a group, they inspected the marquee with its pink cord carpet and its garlands of flowers looped from stanchion to stanchion ... But their laughter and chatter dwindled away when Winifred appeared in the doorway, looking like a very overblown flower herself.

It should happen that Harvey was nearest to her, six steps from her, and when nobody moved or spoke he covered the distance and, standing in front of her, he held out his hand, and in a cultured tone, the like of which she had never heard in all her years in Fellburn, said, 'I must apologise, Mrs Coulson, for intruding on this your special day.' Then, his deep voice dropping to a level that only she could hear, he added, 'If you find my presence embarrassing I will take my leave, because I do not wish that you be upset, especially today.'

Her lids were blinking rapidly. To the side, she took in Flo, her face straight, her eyes bearing a threat that she could not ignore. And yet, even if there had been no threat she would have found it

50

difficult to order this unusual creature to leave. Such was her make-up that she was asking herself: how had their Flo come to be taken up by a man such as this, even if he was black, because there was something about him, not only the size of him and his looks, and that voice of his, there was just something. And she wasn't surprised when she heard herself say, 'I ... I am not in the least embarrassed. Why should I be?'

When her hand was taken and firmly but gently shaken, she could not put a name to this new feeling that she had for her sister, for she had never been jealous of her in her whole life...

Following the visit to the marquee a feeling of gaiety seemed to pervade the whole house.

It was just turned twelve o'clock when Don, fully dressed for the fray except for his grey topper, ran out of the side door and around the end of the house towards Joe's cottage. It was as he passed one of the small windows, which were original to the cottage, that he stepped back and his head drooped to the side, for there, kneeling by a chair, and obviously praying, was Joe.

Either Joe became aware of a shadow at the window or he sensed someone's presence, for he raised his head quickly, and they stared at each other for a moment.

On entering the room Don said quietly, 'You worried about something, Joe?'

'No, no.'

'But you were ... well...'

'Yes, praying. Don't you ever pray?'

'Never in the middle of the day. You're sure there's nothing wrong? Anyway, you haven't been to church lately. You'll have the sleuths after you;

51

or at least Father Cody.'

'Well, if you want to know, young 'un, I was just asking that ... well, that you'd both be happy.'

'Oh, Joe.' There was a break in Don's voice and impulsively he put his arms around his brother, for he thought of him as his brother in all ways, and Joe held him too before pushing him off and saying, 'What do you want in this neck of the woods, anyway?'

'I ... I just want to phone Annette, have a word with her, see how she feels, and I couldn't do it from the house, could I?'

'Go ahead.' Joe thumbed towards the adjoining room, which he used as an office, and he waited until Don had entered it before he himself turned about and went into his bedroom. And there he stood with his back to the door, while his head drooped on to his chest.

In the office Don was saying, 'Oh, Sarah? It's me. Could you get Miss Annette to the phone for a minute?'

'Oh, Mr Don'—the voice came at him in a whisper—'she's getting dressed. Oh, and here's Mrs Allison.'

'Hello! Who is it? Oh, Don, what on earth do you want? You know it's unlucky to have contact in any way before your wedding.'

'I thought it was only if we came face to face. Come on, Mother-in-law to be, just let me have a word.'

'You're not thinking of jilting her, are you?'

He held the phone away from his face, grinning widely now. Fancy Ma Allison making a joke. His laugh was high as he said, 'That's what I want to tell her. Come on, let me have a word with her.'

'It isn't right; it's unlucky.'

'Nothing's unlucky today.'

There was a pause. He heard the murmur of distant voices, then there she was.

'Oh, Don, anything wrong?'

'Not a thing in the world, darling. I ... I just wanted to know how you felt?'

'Oh, terrified, shaking, longing. Oh, Don, I can't believe we're nearly there.' Her voice was low now.

'Another hour and I'll see you coming down the aisle.'

'I love you. I love you very much.'

'I don't only love you, I adore you.'

'Eeh! You'll have to go to confession.' There was a tinkle of laughter at the other end. 'False idols.'

'Oh, yes, false idols, but an adorable idol. All right, all right, I'll let you go. Goodbye, my love. No, not goodbye; *au revoir.*'

He put the phone down and stood for a moment staring ahead. The next hour was going to be the longest in his life. It would be the longest in both their lives.

CHAPTER FOUR

The Nuptial Mass was over. They were married. They were one. The hour that had seemed to have been an eternity was finally at an end. They had taken Communion. They had listened to Father Ramshaw's kindly words. The choir had burst its lungs in song; the young boy soprano had trilled so sweetly he had brought tears to many eyes. And

53

they had just signed their names in the register: Annette Allison had become Annette Coulson. They had looked at each other and the relief on their faces could have been painful to a keen observer. But everything was bustle.

The organ was soaring as they left the vestry and walked towards the two front rows of pews. Annette's mother was crying openly, but Winifred Coulson's eyes were dry and her plump face was pasty white, and it appeared that Daniel had to press her forward into and up the aisle and then to mingle with the crowding guests outside the church.

The photographer soon seemed to take control, endeavouring to line up the bride and bridegroom, with the close relations on either side; the best man Joe, and the two bridesmaids, Annette's school friends Jessica Bowbent and Irene Shilton, both hanging on to Joe's arms while they giggled and each hoping secretly that one day she would be standing there with Joe as today Annette was standing with Don.

The usual groupings had then been assembled and photographed when Daniel, who had been standing with Harvey, surprised everyone by crying out. 'One more! come on, let's have our men now. What do you say, Harvey?' And to the further surprise of everyone he arranged himself and Joe on either side of Harvey, so, in his mind, pre-empting the guests from making assumptions, or perhaps making them wonder all the more who or what this black man was.

And they *did* wonder about him, but they were not to know who he really was until almost an hour later when the toasts were being drunk and Daniel,

54

with the devil in him, raised his glass to toast the happy couple and ended by saying, 'I know they'll be the first ones to say they hope that the next wedding from this house will be that of my sister-in-law and her fiancé.' And with this he indicated Harvey, who was sitting three chairs away from him on the top table. Then leaning forward, he looked along the row in the other direction to where sat Father Ramshaw, and he said, 'Would you marry them, Father?' And the priest came back jovially, 'Marry them? Of course, I'll marry them. I'd marry a Hallelujah to a Jew if it meant I could get them into the church.'

A great roar of laughter arose. But Winifred did not join in; nor did Joe, because he was thinking: that wasn't very kind of you, Dad. She's suffering and you know it. But then, perhaps it was Daniel's way of being kind, a way of staunching the bleeding from the knife-thrust that was piercing her.

It was his turn to stand now, and what he said was to the point: he didn't aim to be funny. He said frankly that everyone in the room knew there was no blood-bond between Don and himself, but had they been born Siamese twins they could not have been closer. And while he was on the subject he would like to thank the man he called Father, and the woman he called Mother, for their care of him over the past twenty-five years. Lastly, he turned towards the bride and groom and, raising his glass, said, 'To the two people I love most in the world.'

It had been an unusual speech for a best man, with nothing amusing about it, not even one joke. There was applause but it was sober applause,

55

accompanied by some shaking of heads here and there.

He was a strange fellow, really, was Joe Coulson, the sort of man you couldn't get to the bottom of. An excellent accountant; and always courteous and kindly, yet at the same time deep. Yes, that was the word for him: deep. But of course this often happened with adopted children and it was understandable, for you never knew from where they sprang...

*   *   *

The bride and bridegroom were getting changed: in separate rooms, of course. They were leaving at five o'clock to catch a train from Newcastle, which would begin the journey for their honeymoon in Italy and three whole weeks together.

When Don emerged from his room he wasn't surprised to see his mother standing at her bedroom door, talking to one of the guests. Others were milling about on the landing and the stairs, and the house was filled with laughter and chatter. They must have overflowed from the marquee. On the sight of him, Winifred said to the guest, 'Excuse me,' and, holding her hand out towards her son, she said, 'Just a moment, dear.' Her voice was high, bright, like that of an ordinary mother wanting to say a last farewell to her son in private. But once she had drawn him into the room and closed the door she stood away from him, her hands, gripping each other, pressed into the moulds of flesh at her breast. 'You would have gone without a word to me, a private word.'

'No, no, I wouldn't, Mother. I meant to come.'

'No, you didn't. No, you didn't. Do you know this is the end?'

'*Oh, please. Please.* Don't spoil this day,' Don said, closing his eyes for a moment. But when he opened them she was standing close to him, her breath like a hot moist wind on his face as she said, 'I mightn't be here when you come back. I don't think I'll be able to stand it. I could be dead.'

'For God's sake! Mother.' His tone was sharp; and when her head began to bob in agitation, he ground out, 'Don't start. For God's sake! Mother, don't start that!'

'Oh! Oh! You've never used that tone to me before. It's happening already. Why do I have to go through all this? What have I done to deserve it ...? Oh! Don. Don.'

Again he found himself in her embrace. But he couldn't bring himself to put his arms about her; he was repulsed by her nearness, and this was a new feeling. Putting his hands on her shoulders, he pressed her almost roughly from him, saying, 'Look, you must try to be sensible about this: I am married now; I'm starting a new life of my own. Can't you understand?'

'Yes, yes, I understand. I've lost you already.'

'You haven't lost me yet, but you're going the right way about it. I love you. You're my mother.'

'You love me?' Her voice was soft. 'You really do love me, Don?'

'Yes. Yes.' He moved his hands on her shoulders as if to shake her, but her body didn't respond.

She stared into his face, whimpering now. 'Promise you'll love me always? You'll keep some love for me? Promise?'

He had the desire to turn about and flee from her, from the house and everyone in it. Except for Annette. In his mind he had Annette by the hand running. But he heard himself say quietly, 'I promise. Now I must go.'

'Kiss me.'

Slowly he leant towards her to put his lips on her cheek, only again to be enveloped in her embrace. But now her open mouth was covering his, his slim body pressed into her flesh.

A moment later he managed to stagger from the room; although he didn't go straight downstairs but into the bathroom, and there, locking the door, he bent over the basin and sluiced his face with cold water. His whole body was shaking. She was mad. She must be. He sluiced his mouth with a handful of water and rubbed his lips; then he dried his face, wiped the drops of water from the front of his suit, and in an effort to compose himself he drew in a number of deep breaths before leaving the bathroom.

At the head of the stairs there stood his father.

'I was coming for you. Where have you been? Annette's downstairs waiting. What's wrong?'

'Nothing. Nothing.'

Daniel looked along the corridor, then said quietly, 'Your last goodbye?'

Don drew in a long slow breath before he said, 'Yes, Dad, my last goodbye.'

'Well, lad, it's over; the cord's severed. And keep it like that. You understand?'

'Yes, yes, I understand.' They looked at each other as might have two men of similar age and experience. 'Come on then.' Daniel took him by the elbow and led him down the stairs and into the

58

crowded hall, where everyone was talking at once; and then they all spilled out on to the drive.

And now Annette was being hugged by her mother; then her father who, seeming to find difficulty in unbending his stiff body, kissed her first on one cheek then on the other, then characteristically said, 'God go with you, child.'

That there were two people missing from the crowd wasn't noticed in the excitement: the bridegroom's mother and Don's brother, Stephen. Stephen had had another accident, which would not have been generally known; in any case he was now waving from the upper window, and quite happily, because his father had promised him he could come down and watch the dancing on the lawn later on that night. Perhaps only Daniel, Joe, Flo and Don himself were aware of Winifred's absence.

Don and Annette were in the car now. Daniel and Joe were at one window, Flo at the other, all talking together: 'Mind how you go.'

'Make it a good life, lad.' This was from Daniel.

'I'll have the house well warmed for you,' from Joe.

'Thanks,' they both said together, then turned their heads to the other window where Flo, her hand extended, gripped Annette's as she said softly, 'Love each other.'

They were both too full to make any remark on this; and now, as Don turned the ignition key and the car throbbed into life, Daniel's and Joe's heads disappeared from the window and their place was taken by Father Ramshaw's, crying now above the noise of the engine, 'Being me, I'll have to have the last word. God bless you both.' And with a mock serious expression on his face he now cried, 'If you should drop in on the Pope, give him me kind regards. And look, will you tell him on the quiet that I have a curate that would suit him down to the ground as a first secretary. I'll send him off any time; he's just got to say the word.'

They both laughed loudly and Annette said, 'I'll do that, Father, with pleasure.'

'Goodbye. Goodbye.'

'Goodbye. Goodbye.'

The voices sent the car spurting forward, and with the sound and feeling of a thump on the back of it Don said, 'I bet they've hung something on there. Anyway, we'll stop along the road and see.'

Annette now turned and looked through the back window, saying, 'They're running down the drive.'

'They can run, darling, they can all run, but they'll never catch us.' He glanced at her, his eyes full of love. 'We're free. Do you realise that, sweetheart? We're free.'

'Oh, yes, yes, and in so many ways. Oh, darling, no more worry, no more fear of what might happen if and when...'

He lifted one hand from the wheel and, gripping hers, he pulled it swiftly to his lips.

They were nearing the gates that led into the narrow side road as Annette once more turned and looked through the back window, crying now, 'There's Joe and your Dad. They're running side by side.'

And these were the last words she remembered speaking. She saw the pantechnicon. It was like a tower falling on top of them, yet not falling but lifting them in the air, and their screams sounded

60

to her ears like those of people on the high-flyer just before the car went over and into the dip, and she knew they were going into the dip, because the car had become a great horse, a flying horse. It mounted the railings bordering the fields, then hurtled into the sky, straight into it.

And all was quiet.

CHAPTER FIVE

It was half-past twelve, early on the Sunday morning. At the hospital, Daniel and Joe were seated at one side of a small table, Flo at the other. At another table sat Janet and James Allison, she leaning forward, her elbows on the table, but he sitting bolt upright, yet with his eyes closed. He could have been dozing, except that every now and again he would look with annoyance towards Winifred, who was pacing the room in the clear area in front of the doorway, sixteen steps each way.

No-one could have said when she had first started pacing, though all could have recounted how she had screamed at Daniel when he attempted to lead her by the arm to a chair, and then almost knocked Flo to the ground with that sharp flick of her forearm, with which she was adept; and again when Joe had said, 'Please, Mother, you're not going to help yourself like this,' that she actually bared her teeth at him.

The only one who hadn't approached her as yet was Harvey. It was he who now entered the room with a tray of tea, which he placed on a table, t handed a cup to each person. And when there were two cups left on the tray he picked one up, turned and, walking slowly towards Winifred, he blocked her pacing by standing in front of her and holding the cup towards her. For a moment he thought she was going to dash it from his hand. Then surprisingly she not only took the cup from him, but sat down in the nearest chair as if a crisis had been passed.

The tension seemed to seep from the room. But only for a moment, for they had barely started to drink their tea when the door opened and a night nurse appeared and, looking towards Mr and Mrs Allison and mentioning them by name, she said, 'Would you like to come and see your daughter now? She has come round. But you may stay only a moment or so.'

They both sprang from their chairs as if activated by the same wires, and as the nurse held open the door for them, Winifred caught at her arm, saying, 'My son?' And to this the nurse replied, 'He is still in the theatre, Mrs Coulson. The doctor will see you as soon as the operation is over. Don't worry.'

After the door had closed on the nurse, Winifred's pacing began again. But now she was muttering, 'Don't worry. Don't worry. Stupid individuals! Don't worry. Don't worry.' The words were emerging through closed teeth, and as her voice rose Daniel got swiftly up from the seat and, confronting her, gripped her by the shoulders and hissed at her, 'That's enough, woman! Stop it! And try to forget for a moment that you're the only one concerned.' And with a none too gentle push ~ thrust her down into a chair, stood over her, his

62

face almost touching hers, and growled, 'You start any of your tantrums here and by God! I'll slap your face until you can't see. Do you hear me?'

This was the second time within a week that he had threatened to slap her face, and as she glared back into his eyes, so deep was her hatred of him he could almost smell it and he straightened up and gasped as if he had just been throttled, then turned to where Joe and Harvey were standing side by side as if they had been ready to intervene and prevent him from doing her an injury.

After a moment they all sat down again and Flo, looking from one to the other, said quietly, 'Here, drink your tea. It's getting cold.' And like obedient children, the men took up their cups and drank from them.

Ten minutes or so later, the door opened and two men entered the room and introduced themselves as Mr Richardson, the surgeon, and Doctor Walters. Both men looked exhausted, particularly the surgeon, a man with a natural tan which, at that moment, looked as if it had faded.

Winifred sprang from her seat and ran towards them, and he patted her arm, saying, 'It's all right. It's all right.'

'How is he? My son, how is he?'

'Sit down. Sit down.'

She shook her head impatiently and remained standing, and Mr Richardson looked from her to the other woman and the three men and, his eyes resting on Daniel, he said quietly, 'It's been rather a long job.'

'Will ... will he be all right?'

'I have to say that remains to be seen; he's badly injured.'

'Will he live?' It was a demand from Winifred.

And now looking her straight in the face, he said, 'That too remains to be seen, Mrs Coulson.' His voice was terse now. 'One thing I must make clear'—he was again looking at Daniel—'he has lost the use of his legs. The spine is injured in the lumbar region. But that might not have been so serious except that one lung was crushed and his liver damaged. The latter, I'm afraid, could have serious consequences. However, it is very early days yet. Now, I would advise you all to go home and rest. There'll be time enough later on to ...'

'I'm not going home. I must see him. I will sit with him.'

'I'm afraid you won't, not tonight, Mrs Coulson.' The surgeon's tone was definite. 'This is a very crucial time. Come back in the morning and we'll take it from there. But at the moment it's imperative that he is not disturbed in any way.'

It appeared as if Winifred's body was about to expand to bursting point: her breasts heaved and her cheeks swelled as if she was holding her breath.

It was Flo's voice that seemed to prick the balloon, as she asked, 'How is Annette ... his wife?'

It was Doctor Walters who answered Flo. 'Oh, she's been very, very lucky,' he said; 'a broken arm, bruised ribs and slight concussion. It's amazing how she escaped so lightly. She'll be all right. Of course she too needs rest and quiet. So, as Mr Richardson has said, it would be wise if you all went home and got a little rest yourselves. As for us,' he inclined his head towards his colleague, 'we'll be glad to get to bed too. I'm sure you understand that.'

'Yes, yes of course.' It was Joe speaking. 'We'll ... we'll do as you suggest, Doctor. And ... and thank you very much.'

'Oh, yes, yes.' It was as if Joe's words had reminded Daniel of the courtesy expected of him, and his voice was hesitant as he went on. 'I ... we're all a little dazed. It ... it was so sudden. The wedding. They had just left the house. It seems impossible.'

Mr Richardson nodded before coming out with the platitude: 'These things happen. We don't know why. But there's always hope. I'll say good-night now.' He inclined his head to Daniel, then went out, followed by Doctor Walters.

With the exception of Winifred, they all made ready to go; she remained standing, stiffly staring straight ahead. After glancing at her, Daniel walked past her and out of the room. Flo too glanced at her; she even paused in front of her before walking on.

It was Joe who stopped and said quietly, 'Come on, Mother; I'll drive you back first thing in the morning.' For a moment it looked as if she was determined to remain standing where she was, but when she glanced behind her at the black man standing a few feet from her and seemingly not intending to move until she did, she thrust her body forward, at the same time throwing off Joe's hand from her elbow.

Joe exchanged a glance with Harvey; then together, they followed her out of the room.

     ★   ★   ★

It was two o'clock in the morning when they

65

reached home, and Winifred, still without speaking a word, made straight for her room. And a stunned feeling seemed to have descended upon the others too as they sipped at the hot drinks supplied by Maggie who, without complaint at the late hour, had set about preparing rooms for Flo and Harvey.

★   ★   ★

With the exception of Stephen, everyone was astir before eight o'clock that morning. Stephen had been heavily sedated the night before. Apparently he had witnessed the accident from his attic room and he had screamed and wailed and had become so obstreperous that the doctor had to be called to attend to him.

Maggie had been up since six o'clock. She had cooked a breakfast which no-one wanted. She was now in her sitting-room facing Daniel. Her eyes were red and swollen, her voice broken, as she said, 'He didn't escape after all, did he?'

Daniel swallowed deeply before he replied, 'No, he didn't escape.'

'But if he's as bad as you say, she could lose him yet. We could all lose him, but I think I'd rather see him dead than helpless, because then he'd be back to square one, or even beyond that.'

'Oh no! by God, he won't. They've got their own house, and, as I understand it, Annette hasn't been injured much, and she'll look after him. And there's always nurses. No, by God! Maggie, that's one thing I'll see to: in some way they've got to be on their own. She might never be off their doorstep but at least they'll be in their own home. And he'll have a wife.'

She stared at him before turning away and going to the chest of drawers, from which she took out a clean apron. Putting it on, she said, 'Will you all be back for lunch?'

'I doubt it,' he answered.

'Will Flo and Mr Rochester be staying on?'

'I don't know ... What do you think of him? Were you surprised to see who she had become engaged to?'

'Perhaps at first, but later, no. I should imagine there's many a woman would be glad to link up with a fellow like that, an educated one an' all, and he so good looking. But then aren't they all? I've never seen an ugly black man. Have you?'

'Come to think of it, no, not really. Anyway, we're both of the same mind: I think she's done well for herself, no matter what his colour is. Now, I must be off.' He stood for a moment gazing at her; then, taking a step forward, he thrust his arms about her, and hers went around him, and they held each other close; and with his head buried in her shoulder, he muttered, 'Oh, Maggie, I'm heart-broken, not only for meself but for him. I dread to think what's in the future.'

Pressing him from her, she rubbed the tears from her cheeks with the side of her finger before saying, 'You can do nothing about that. Yesterday should prove that. Man proposes but God disposes. Go on now; and phone me from the hospital, will you?'

He nodded at her but said nothing more and went out.

In the hall Flo and Harvey were already standing waiting with Joe, and on seeing him, Flo walked quickly towards him, saying, 'I've tried to speak to

67

her but she won't open her mouth.'

'Where is she?'

'In the breakfast-room drinking a cup of tea; she hasn't eaten a thing.'

'Well, that won't hurt her.' His voice was grim. 'She's got plenty of fat to live on. Go and fetch her. Tell her we're ready and waiting.'

'She's been ready and waiting for the past hour or more.' Flo sounded somewhat upset at Daniel's attitude, but did his bidding.

Tension seemed to be rising, and so Joe turned to Harvey and asked, 'Will you be going back today?'

'It isn't at all necessary. We're both on a week's holiday; we could stay on if we could be of any help.' He now looked at Daniel, and Daniel replied simply, 'You're welcome to stay, at any time. I'll leave it to you.'

Flo now emerged from the corridor, followed by Winifred, who passed them all as if they were invisible and walked out of the house and took her seat in the car waiting in the drive; and as she settled herself she tucked the skirt of her coat under her calf as if preventing it from coming in contact with her husband's leg.

Daniel averted his eyes from the broken railings as they went through the gate into the road, and he did not utter a word until they were nearing the hospital. Then, as if he were whispering to someone, he said, 'Don't you give us a show of hysterics in here this morning, because if you do I'll go one better: there's a simple cure for hysterics, you know.'

She gave him no immediate answer; in fact, not until he had pulled into a line of cars in the hospital forecourt did she speak, and then, her hand on the door, she said grimly, 'I'll see my day with you. *Oh yes, I will.*' To which, he replied, 'We'll see our day with each other, and pray God it will be soon.'

As she marched towards the hospital door, he turned to where the others were getting out of their car, and together they entered the reception area to hear Winifred proclaiming in no small voice: 'I want to see Doctor Richardson,' and the receptionist answering, 'I'm sorry, but Mr Richardson's operating at the moment, but if you take a seat in the waiting-room, I'll ask another doctor to attend to you.'

Daniel was standing at the desk now, and he cut in on what his wife was about to say by asking, 'Can you tell us which ward my son is in? You wouldn't have been here earlier; he was operated on. Coulson is the name.'

'Yes, yes'—the receptionist nodded at him—'I know, but as I've said, if you would take a seat in the waiting-room, I'll get someone to attend to you.'

'Thank you.'

He turned away, followed by Joe, Flo and Harvey, although Winifred remained standing at the desk for a full minute before following them.

The waiting-room was busier than when they had left it earlier that morning; there were now at least a dozen people present, so that only three seats were vacant. What was more, two small children were scampering after each other around the tables.

After one glance, Winifred went back into the corridor and, after a quick exchange of glances

69

between Daniel and Joe, the latter followed her.

Harvey now led Flo to a seat and sat down beside her, while Daniel stood near the door, and they each became aware of the silence that had fallen on the room. A white woman with a black man. And what a black man! And both dressed up to the nines, not like those mixed couples you might find in Bog's End who had to brave the community, these two were brazen. In some such way did the atmosphere emanate from the adults who, with the exception of a youth and a man, were all women.

But they had hardly been seated a few minutes when the door was pushed open and Joe said, 'Dad,' then beckoned towards Flo and Harvey. And there they were, all in the corridor again, standing before a young doctor who was saying, 'Mr Richardson would like to see you. He'll be free in about half an hour. In the meantime you may see the patient, but only for a moment or so. In any case, Mr Coulson has not yet recovered consciousness. It will be some time before he does. If you will come this way. And ... and just two at a time, please.'

He led them along a corridor, then another, and into a passageway leading to a ward where there was a great deal of activity and the clatter of dishes on a food trolley being wheeled from the ward. The young doctor stopped outside a door. Then nodding first to Daniel, then to Winifred, he gently pushed the door open and they went inside.

Slowly Daniel walked up by one side of the bed and looked down on his son, who might have already been dead, so drained was he of colour. There was a tube inserted into one nostril, there

70

were tubes in his arms, there was a cradle over his legs.

Daniel closed his eyes for a moment: his throat was constricted as his mind was yelling, 'His legs! His legs!' He opened his eyes to a sound of a gasp and he looked across the bed at his wife. Her face was screwed up in anguish, the tears dripping from her chin. He heard her moan.

A nurse whom he hadn't noticed seemed to appear from nowhere and, touching Winifred gently on the arm, said, 'Come. Come, please.'

Winifred jerked the hand aside, muttering now, 'I want to stay. I can sit by him.'

'Doctor says . . .'

'I'm his mother!' She almost hissed the words into the nurse's face, and the nurse glanced across the bed towards Daniel as if in appeal. In answer to it he moved down by the side of the bed and Winifred stepped quickly away. She made for the door, muttering, 'I want to see the specialist.'

Not the doctor, not the surgeon, but the specialist.

Daniel made a small motion of his head, then asked quietly of the nurse, 'When . . . when do you think he'll come round?'

To this she answered, 'I don't know . . . there's no knowing.'

He now asked, 'Which ward is his wife in? Mrs Coulson?'

'Oh, I think she's upstairs on the next floor.'

'Thank you.'

A few minutes later when he was ushered into a side ward, there, to his surprise, he saw Annette propped up in bed. Her eyes were open and as he neared her he could see that one of her arms was in

71

plaster and that the right side of her face was discoloured, as if she had been punched.

Her voice was small as she said, 'Dad.'

'Oh, hinny. Oh my dear, my dear.' He lifted her other hand from the counterpane and stroked it. And now she said, 'Don?' then again, 'Don? Is he very ... very bad? They ... they won't ... tell me.'

He swallowed some saliva before he lied, saying, 'He'll ... he'll be all right. I ... I understand his legs were hurt. He's not quite round yet, but he'll be all right. You'll see.'

The nurse who had followed him into the ward pushed a chair towards him, and he nodded his thanks to her and sat down. Still holding the limp hand, he said, 'Oh, don't, my dear. Don't cry.'

'We ... we were...'

'Yes, dear?'

'Esca ... ping.'

'Oh, yes, yes, you were escaping. And you will again, dear. You will again. Never you worry.'

'Why Dad? Oh, why?' The last word, dragged out on a higher note, acted as a signal to the nurse, for she motioned Daniel to his feet, saying to Annette: 'There now. There now. You need to sleep again. I'll bring you a drink and then you'll rest. You'll feel better later.'

Daniel walked backwards from the bed. Just a few hours ago she had been a bride, a beautiful bride, and now she looked like someone who had inadvertently stepped into a boxing ring and got the worst of it.

He waited in the corridor until the nurse came out of the ward, then he asked quietly, 'How bad is she, nurse?'

'Surprisingly, she's got off very lightly. She's

bruised all over, naturally, but the only bone broken is in her arm. She's had a miraculous escape, whereas her husband, I understand, is in a pretty bad way. You are ... her father?'

'Her father-in-law.'

'Oh, then he is your son?'

'Yes, yes, he is my ...' But he found he couldn't complete the sentence, and when the nurse said, 'It's a tragedy, isn't it? Just married for a matter of hours, and just starting their honeymoon. It's incredible the things that happen.'

When later he emerged from the toilet his eyes were red but he looked more composed. And it was as he was making his way back to the waiting-room that he almost bumped into the surgeon.

'Oh, there you are, Mr Coulson. I was wanting a word with you.'

'Good morning, Mr Richardson. I've just been to see my daughter-in-law.'

'Oh yes, yes. Now, she's been lucky. It's amazing how lightly she got off. Would you like to come into my office for a moment?'

They were in the small room now and the surgeon, pointing to a chair, said, 'Sit down a moment.' Then, taking his seat behind a long desk, he joined his hands on top of a clean blotting pad and, leaning slightly over them, he said, 'I'm afraid, Mr Coulson, I'll have to ask you to speak firmly to your wife with regard to her visits to her son, at least for the next few days until we can ascertain fully the extent of the damage. You know, as I pointed out to you, that he is unlikely to walk again, and that his liver has been damaged too. Quite candidly he's lucky to be alive, if one

73

can put it that way. Anyway, together with the liver problem he's likely to be incontinent. And added to this, we had to take away part of his lung.'

Now he paused and, putting his hand out, he tapped the edge of the blotter, as if it were in sympathetic contact with Daniel, saying, 'I know that sounds terrible enough, but there could be more. These are physical problems which, in one way or another, can be treated, but until he is fully conscious, to put it candidly, we won't know what has happened in here.' He now tapped his forehead. 'The point is, you have to ask yourself if you would rather see him dead and out of all the coming misery, or would you have him live, if only to be nursed for the rest of his life. And how long that will be ... well, I am not God and I can't put a time to it. We don't know if there is damage to the brain, although we do know his skull was slightly cracked. And the same question will apply to him, you know, when he knows about his condition: will he want to go on living? The will is a mighty force both ways, but we must just wait for time to answer that question. And, as I pointed out, the next few days will be crucial: so I must insist that he be put under no undue strain, for I hold the theory that many a patient who is apparently unconscious can imbibe the emotions of those around him. And your wife ... well, you'll know her better than anyone else, but she does seem to be a very highly strung lady. Am I right?'

Daniel stared at the surgeon for a moment before he said, 'Yes, you're right, only too right. The fact is, he's all she's lived for for years. And to put it plainly, she was already in a state yesterday, feeling she had lost him through marriage. But now, if anything was to happen to him ... Oh—' he waved his hand in front of his face as if he were flicking off a fly—'it's all too complicated. But I will see that her visits are kept short.'

Mr Richardson rose from his seat, saying, 'Thank you. I shall leave word that only you and she are to be admitted to see him during the next day or so, and then for a matter of minutes only. But'—he shrugged his shoulders—'she seems determined that she's going to sit with him. You *will* impress upon her that this would not be for his good at the moment, won't you?'

'I'll do that.' But even as he spoke he had a mental picture of the scene being enacted as he told her she was to carry out the surgeon's orders, or else. It was the 'or else' part that made him visibly shudder, for he doubted that, were she to act up again, he'd be able to keep his hands off her.

In a kindly tone, Mr Richardson now said, 'And you, Mr Coulson, I won't tell you not to worry, because that would be pointless, but you can rest assured we'll do everything in our power to bring him round; and when, or if, that is accomplished, to help him to accept the life ahead.'

'Thank you. Thank you very much indeed.'

They parted in the corridor; but there was no need for Daniel to go into the waiting-room to collect Winifred, for there she was standing at the reception desk. And what she had to say was drawing the attention not only of those behind the desk but also of other people in the hall.

'I will take this matter further. I shall write to the Medical Board. Other people can sit with patients, with their family. *Who is he*, anyway?'

Daniel's voice was scarcely above a whisper but

75

the words came out of his mouth like iron filings as he said, 'Only the man who saved your beloved son. Your son. Nobody else's. And nobody else is feeling pain or worry, only you. Have you been to see Annette? No. No. Now look! Get yourself outside.'

After casting a ferocious glance at the staring faces, she stamped out of the building. And as she went towards the car she turned her head to look at him, hissing 'You! to show me up.'

'Nobody can show you up, woman, because you're an expert at showing yourself up. Always have been. Now get into the car.'

He had taken his seat and started the engine, and she still stood there, until the sound of his engaging the gears drove her to drag open the door and to drop like a heavy sack on to the seat.

Again no word was exchanged during the journey, but he had hardly drawn the car to a stop before she thrust open the door and swung herself out. And again he was surprised that with her weight she could still be so light on her feet, especially so now when she ran across the drive as a young woman might.

Joe had already arrived, and he walked quickly towards Daniel's car and, bending down he said, 'Go easy on her, else ... well.'

'Or else what?'

As Daniel got out of the car Joe replied, 'I would call the doctor if I were you. She can't go on like this or something will snap.'

'It snapped a long time ago, Joe.' Daniel's voice sounded weary.

'Yes, in one way, but this is different. She's never had to tackle anything like this before.'

76

'None of us have had to tackle anything like this before.'

'No; you're right, you're right there. But will I do it? Will I phone the doctor?'

'Yes, phone him. Not that it'll do any good.'

Daniel knew it was too early in the morning to drink but he also knew he must have a stiff whisky before he went up and confronted her with the news that she could not baby-sit her son in the hospital.

He had just thrown off a double whisky when the door opened and a quiet voice said, 'Dad.'

He turned to see Stephen standing there hesitantly.

Daniel went towards him, saying, 'You're down early,' but stopped himself adding, 'Why, and all by yourself?' Instead, he asked, 'Where's everybody?'

'Maggie's in the kitchen, Dad. Lily's gone to church with Bill, and I think'—he paused as he put his head on one side—'Peggie is doing the bathroom. Not mine; I've been good. I have, Dad; I've been good.'

'That's a clever fellow.' Daniel put his hand on his son's shoulder, saying, 'Well, what are you going to do now?'

'I ... I want to see Joe. I ... I want to ask him about Don and Annette.'

It had been evident to Daniel for a long time that it was Joe whom the lad sought whenever he wanted help with anything, not him, his father. He said, 'Well now, I think Joe will be busy, as we've all only just come back from the hospital, so you should...'

He was cut off by Stephen, who quickly said,

77

'Don't ... don't send me back upstairs yet, Dad. Don't; please don't send me back upstairs. I'm ... I'm sad. I'm sad all over. I ... I would like to go and see Don. I ... I saw it happen yesterday. I...'

'Yes, I know you did,' Daniel sharply interrupted, 'and you are upset, but now I want you to keep quiet and be a good fellow. And I promise you this: as soon as Don and Annette are a little better, I'll take you myself to see them in hospital. What about that?'

'You will?'

'Yes, I will. I promise. Just as soon as they are a little better. But you will have to be good. You know what I mean?'

The man-cum-boy hung his head and in an almost childish whimper he said, 'Yes, Dad. Yes, I know what you mean. And I will; I will be good.'

'Well now, you go back into the kitchen and stay with Maggie while I pop upstairs, and then I'll come down again and we'll have a crack, eh? Or a game of billiards.'

'You will, Dad? Billiards with me?'

'Yes; yes, I will. Go on now.'

Stephen grinned with pleasure, then turned and at a shambling run made his way towards the kitchen. And Daniel, glancing back towards the decanter on the sideboard, hesitated for a moment before going out and up the stairs.

Rather than tap on his wife's door he called out, 'Are you there?'

He waited, and when there was no answer, he opened the door and went in. She had taken off her outdoor things and was sitting at the dressing-table. He had often wondered why she sat so long at the dressing-table, but assumed she was admiring her unlined skin and the lack of grey in her hair. And this had made him wonder too why she didn't concentrate more on getting rid of her surplus fat, because without it she would have been a very presentable woman. Her eating problems, so the doctor had said, came from inward anxieties. And he could say that again—inward anxieties—anxieties with which she had affected the whole family over the years.

He moved no further towards her than the foot of the bed, and there, his hand on a post, he said, 'I must have a word with you.'

She made no reply, but simply stared at him through the mirror, as she was wont to do whenever she was seated at the dressing-table.

'It's about the hospital visiting,' he said. 'Mr Richardson thinks it would be advisable if we make our visits very short for the next few days, just for a minute or two. It'll give Don a better chance...'

'A better chance?' As her body moved slowly around on the seat her flesh seemed to flow and ripple. He saw the muscles of her arms undulating under the tight sleeves of her dress. He watched her large breasts sway. On anyone else these motions could have suggested a certain seductiveness, but with Winifred, as he only too well recognised, they were but the signals of a rising rage.

Her words, like her movements, came slow at first. 'A better chance?' she said. 'A better chance? You're agreeable to giving him a chance? Is your conscience pricking you? You arranged his life: you arranged his marriage; you would have gone to any lengths to take him from me. But getting him married was a sort of legitimate cover-up for your

79

own actions, wasn't it?' Her voice had risen but was not yet at screaming point. 'You couldn't bear the thought that I kept him pure, that I saw to it that he didn't follow in your footsteps with your filthy woman.'

'Shut up! Shut your mouth!'

The movement that she made now was a spring. She was on her feet and standing at the foot of the bed gripping the other post as if she would twist it and wrench it from its support.

'Don't you ever tell me to shut up! But you listen to me now. If my son dies I'll kill you. Do you hear that? I'll kill you.' Her voice had risen to a scream. 'You were longing for last night, weren't you, when he'd be defiled, made into a man, like yourself with your dirty whoring.'

The blow caught her fully across the mouth; yet she didn't even stagger. Instead, her hands flashed out, and she was tearing at his face and screaming words that he realised were obscene, yet he could hardly believe his ears.

Gripping her throat now, he struggled with her; and as his rising hatred matched hers he would not have known what he might have done next, but for the hands pulling at him, and through a blur of blood he saw the black face close to his own and Joe with his arms tight around Winifred as she lay half-sprawled on the chaise longue at the foot of the bed.

When Peggie's shocked face appeared in the doorway Joe cried out, 'Fetch Maggie!' And it would seem that Maggie was already on the scene, for the next instant she was in the room, although she stopped and stared for a moment at the sight of Daniel, his face streaming with blood from the

80

torn flesh of each cheek.

Turning swiftly to Peggie, she cried, 'Get Mrs Jackson; she's in the garden with Stephen. Then phone the doctor.' And to Harvey she said quietly, 'Take him out. Get him out,' and Daniel allowed himself to be guided from the room. But on the landing they both stopped, surprised by the sight of the priest on the stairhead.

Father Cody was a man in his early thirties. He had the countenance of an ascetic, his tone was clipped, and his voice had no recognisable accent: 'I heard the commotion,' he said. 'I just popped over between Masses to see how the young couple were faring. Dear God! I see you have been fighting. This is not a time for recrimination, I would have thought. You wife has been suffering of late. Don't you know that? What she needs is comfort. And especially at a time like this. Those two poor innocents yesterday. But you know'—he raised a hand—'they do say the sins of the fathers will be visited on the children, even to the third and fourth generation. Everything in life has to be paid for. God sees to that. Yes, He...'

'*Get out!*' Daniel had pulled himself from Harvey's grasp.

'You wouldn't! You wouldn't dare!' The priest held up both hands. 'Don't take that attitude with me, Daniel Coulson. I am your wife's confessor and at this moment I'm sure she needs my help.'

'Look! If you don't want me to help you on your way with my toe in your arse you'll turn about and get out. And I don't want to see you again, not in my house.'

Father Cody now cast a glance at Harvey, expecting him to remonstrate with this perturbed

81

individual; but all the black man said, and in a deep voice, was, 'I would do what you are told, man, and quick, if I were you.'

'You can't intimidate me.' Father Cody looked from Harvey to Daniel. But when Daniel, with fists doubled, took a quick step towards him, the priest thought better of his stand and turned abruptly, saying, 'God has strange ways of working: He protects His own, you'll see.'

'*You go to hell*, and as far beyond.'

The two men remained at the top of the stairs watching the black-coated figure cross the hall and out of the house. And Harvey, now taking Daniel by the arm, said, 'Come on. We'll get you cleaned up.' Then in an aside that at another time would have raised a laugh, he added, 'There's no fear of him going to hell. Did you see him cross himself at the bottom of the stairs?'

*   *   *

The doctor gave Winifred a sedative almost without her realising it, for her rage was still blazing. And when he saw Daniel's face he said, 'A tiger might have gone a bit deeper but not much; I'd better give you an injection.' Then, later, as he was about to leave, he said, 'One of these days she's going to need help, special help. You understand that?'

Daniel understood it only too well and prayed that it would be soon...

It was around two o'clock when Father Ramshaw came. The house was quiet, unusually so. He let himself into the hall, then made straight for the kitchen, asking Maggie, 'Where's everybody?'

'I think you'll find himself in the study, Father,' she said; 'the others are in their rooms.'

'Well, it's himself I want to see. Have you any tea going?'

'No; but I could have it going any time, Father.'

'When you're ready I'll be glad.'

He went out, crossed the hall to the far end where the door led into the study and, after tapping on it, he called, 'It's me.'

Daniel swung his feet from the leather couch and sat up, although he didn't rise to his feet; and the priest stopped in his stride, his mouth dropping into a gape before he said, 'Oh, my goodness! no. What brought this about? But need I ask.' He sat down on the edge of the couch and, shaking his head, muttered, 'Something will have to be done. But what, God only knows. There's always a climax to these things, and your face, I should imagine, could be it. But will it? You're feeling rotten?'

'Not very good, Father. But have you come about your assistant?'

'Oh, yes. Yes.' And adopting a severe expression, the priest said, 'You've insulted my curate, do you know that? In fact, as far as I can gather you sent him to hell; you actually voiced it.' He turned his head to the side, saying, 'Oh, the times I've wished I was brave enough to say that.' Then he went on quickly, 'Don't try to smile; it'll hurt, I can see that.' And they looked at each other for a moment in silence before the priest, his tone serious now, murmured, 'She must have gone clean mad. What brought it on anyway?'

'She had made a scene in the hospital because

83

she wasn't allowed to sit with Don, and the doctor took me aside and asked me if I would impress upon her that, for the next few days, her visits had to cover minutes not hours, or days and nights as they would if she had her way. And I went in and put it to her quietly. But then'—he sighed now—'she's holding me responsible for the accident. If I hadn't inveigled them into marriage and they hadn't been going away in that car at that special time, none of this would have happened. It's all at my door.'

'Well, Daniel, look at it this way: she's right, you know, because on your own saying you brought them together; and you got them married yesterday. Strange, but in a way she's right. Your intentions were good. Oh aye, they were good. You wanted to save the boy from being swallowed whole by her. If ever there was an Oedipus complex in reverse this is it. It's probably the worst case I've known. And I've known a few. It isn't all that rare. Oh no; but a lot of it's hidden. How many women treat their daughters-in-law like dirt? Cause trouble? in fact, separate the couple? I know one who arranged a divorce. Yes, she did; and they were Catholics an' all. She had them separated, hating each other. Then the couple happened to meet by themselves on a street, and in his own words as he told me, he said to his wife, "I must have been mad to listen to her and put her before you. If you'll only come back I'll tell her where she stands." And you know, he did, and they had ten years of happy marriage. But it had a strange ending, for the young fellow up and dies and, would you believe it, the two women lived together quite amicably for years afterwards. Can you believe that now? There's nothing so odd as human nature. I see quite a bit of it you know, from the inside, you could say.' He paused, rubbing a hand tightly over his clean-shaven cheeks, then said quietly, 'One of these days, I fear, she'll have to be put away. You know that? At least for a time. She needs special attention. It'll be for her own good.'

Daniel stared at the priest. He was surprised to hear put into words the very thought that had been in his mind for a long time. In his mind, yes, but then he had told himself that you couldn't class anyone to be in need of mental attention just because they had an unnatural passion for their son. Yet, couldn't you? Hadn't it in a way turned her mind?

'I hear Don's in a bad state. By the sound of it I think it would be better if the Lord took him...'

'How do you make that out, Father? The surgeon, Mr Richardson, he didn't give up. What I mean is...'

'I know what you mean: where there's life there's hope. But I happen to know Freddie Richardson. I've known the family since I was a lad. I got on to him. I didn't know whether or not it was he who would be seeing to Don, but I sensed he would know about the case, and he said the lad's in a bad way. And I think, Daniel, you've got to face up to that. You'll be able to, I know, but I doubt if she will. You said to me a little while ago that you thought about walking out again and I was for putting you off, and I did put you off. But looking at you now, I wonder if I was giving you the best advice. Sometimes I wish I was nearer to God, then I would know what to do under such

85

circumstances.'

Daniel got slowly to his feet, and as he did so he said, 'I think you're near enough, Father, as near as anybody can get.'

'Oh, come off it. I wasn't implying sainthood or anything like that. I was pointing out my fallibility.'

'I know what you were aiming to do, Father, and I'll tell you something now. Perhaps I'm saying this because I don't know if I'm waking or sleeping, but you are the best friend I've got: you know all about me, the bad and the good; and I don't think, whatever I told you, you would turn against me, even if I told you I wanted to finish her off this morning.'

'Well, under the circumstances, that was a natural reaction, I'm sure, but you know we must curb such reactions. Yes, don't I know meself that one must curb such reactions.' He smiled wryly, then said, 'Thank you, Daniel, for calling me your friend. Thank you. Well, now I must be off, but'—and here he wagged his finger at Daniel—'but before I go I must admonish you for insulting my curate and sending him to hell. This has got to stop, you know; I'm the only one who can indulge in that privilege.'

A sound that could have been a laugh issued from Daniel and he said, 'Well, Father, you keep it up, and keep him out of my hair, for I've never been able to stand him. And today was the last straw.'

The priest leant towards him now and, his voice low and a grin on his face, he said, 'What annoyed him most was the black fellow daring to tell him to get out. I like that chap, you know. And what a voice! Lovely to hear. And he's too good-looking

86

for his own good. You know that? He caused a stir yesterday, in a nice way you know, surprisingly; yes, in a nice way. People were enquiring about him. As one old faggot said, he talked like a gentleman. Huh! Women! But what would we do without them? One thing I do know, me confessional box would be empty or near so. Well, I'm away. I don't expect to see you at Benediction tonight. My advice to you is to take two double whiskies hot and go to bed and pray—and it'll have to be hard—that face of yours will look a little different in the morning, because what excuse you're going to give for it I don't know. I'll leave you to think that one up. Goodbye, Daniel.'

'Goodbye, Father.'

He sat down on the couch again. Yes, yes, he'd have to think one up, wouldn't he? But who would he hoodwink? Nobody, not those in the works, or out of it.

PART TWO

CHAPTER ONE

Don lay with his eyes fixed on the door, longing for it to open to see one face, dreading for it to open to see another. How long had he been here? Years and years; six years it must be, not just six weeks. But it was just six weeks since the world had exploded.

He lifted one arm slowly from the counterpane and looked at it, then he lifted the other one. He still had his arms, he still had his head, and he could think. He still had his sight and his hearing, and he could talk. He had all these faculties, but of what use were they to him? His body had gone. Well, not quite; but he had to breathe heavily at times to know that he still had lungs. And dear God, he knew that he had a bladder and bowels. Oh, that was shame-making. If only, if only. But he had no legs. Yes, he had. Oh, yes, he had; his legs were there, he could see his toes sticking up. But what use were they? Why didn't they take them off? They had taken so much else from him. Hurry up, Annette. Hurry up. Dear God, don't let Mother come today. I'd like to see Dad and Joe. Yes, Joe was comforting. He had said yesterday he was going to try and bring Stephen in just to have a peep.

Just to have a peep. That's what people did. They came in and peeped and they were gone again. He wished some of them would stay longer. He wished Annette would stay all day and all night. She did yesterday, at least nearly all day, and the day before. No, not the day before. His mother had sat there—he looked to the side of the bed—and she had stroked him and patted him and whispered to him. That worried him. He was too weak to cope with his mother. They should keep her out. He would talk to his dad about it. Dad understood. So did Joe. And, of course, Annette understood. Oh, yes, yes, Annette understood. He didn't like her people. He had just discovered he didn't like her people. Her father was pompous and in a way her mother was stricken with God as much as his was. That was a funny thought: stricken with God. Odd that he could think amusing things, like a short while ago when of a sudden his mind cleared of the fuzz that would constantly float across it and he thought, I'll get up and get dressed. Yes, he had thought that, I'll get up and get dressed. He would never get up and get dressed again, he knew that. *Never*.

He closed his eyes tightly; then appealed to God: don't let me cry. Please! Jesus, don't let me cry. Holy Mary Mother of God, don't let me cry.

'Don. Don.'

'Oh! Annette. Oh! darling, I didn't know you were there.'

He moved his hand in hers, his fingers clutching weakly at the softness of it. 'Oh! my love, I've been longing to see you.'

'I've only been gone an hour; I've been down to the surgery. Look they've taken the plaster off my arm. I have to have massage and therapy, but it will soon be all right.'

'Only an hour?' He blinked at her.

'Yes, darling, only an hour.'

'I'm very muddled, Annette; my mind goes round in circles. Sometimes I can think quite clearly then it is as if a mist blots things out.'

'It will pass. You've improved marvellously in the last week. Why, everybody's amazed at the improvement in you.'

'Are they?'

'Yes, yes, darling.'

'Will I ever get home?'

'Of course you will, sweetheart.'

'I mean, to our home?'

'Yes, to our home. It's all ready.'

He turned his gaze from her and looked around the white ward, at the flowers banked up on one table, at the mass of cards arranged on another, and he said, quietly, 'I'll never be able to walk again, Annette.'

'Oh, yes you will. There's ways and means.'

'There's not, Annette. I heard them, Mr Richardson and the others. I heard them. I couldn't make out any words, but I could still hear. He was talking to the students about the operation, the lumbar section. I heard him say, "And what happens when that is smashed?"'

'Darling, listen. Don't dwell on it. You're going to get well, really well. I'm going to see to it. And remember what we've got to look forward to. Remember?'

He turned his head and gazed at her. Then, his face stretching into a smile, he said, 'Oh, yes, yes; I remember. Yes, Annette, I remember.' And his voice changing, he said, 'And you've only got a broken arm? I mean, that's what you said, just bruises and a broken arm?'

'Yes, that's all, darling, bruises and a broken arm.'

'That's wonderful, wonderful.' He turned his

head on the pillow again and looked upwards and repeated, 'Wonderful, wonderful. It had to be like that, hadn't it?' And she said tearfully, 'Perhaps, darling, perhaps.'

She bent over him and laid her lips on his, and he put his arms around her and held her. Then she twisted her body so that her head rested on the pillow facing his and softly she said, 'I love you.' And he said, 'I adore you. Always have, and always will, as long as I live ... as long as I live.'

When the tears dropped from the corner of his eyes she said, 'Oh, my dearest, you are going to live, you are going to get better. Listen ...' But her words were cut off by the door's opening; and there stood his mother.

For a moment their heads remained stationary: then Annette, twisting herself back into a sitting position, stared back at the woman who was glaring at her now, and she said quietly, 'Hello, Mother-in-law.'

Winifred made no reply, but went round to the other side of the bed and looked down on her son for a moment; then, bending over, she kissed him slowly on the lips before drawing a chair forward and sitting down.

'How are you, my dear?'

'All right, Mother ... much better.'

'I've brought you an apple tart that Maggie made; your favourite kind.' She motioned to a parcel she had placed on the side-table. 'And I've told them out there'—she nodded towards the door—'which ice cream you prefer.'

He closed his eyes for a moment, then said, 'Mother, they know what I should eat. They are very kind.'

'Yes, kind, but ignorant half of them. It is hospital food. Although you are now in a private room, it's still hospital food they dish out.' She looked across the bed at Annette, saying, 'Oh, you have the plaster off then?'

'Yes.' Annette flexed her arm. 'It wasn't such a bad break. I've been lucky.'

'Yes, indeed you were lucky.'

There was silence between them, but when presently beads of perspiration gathered on Don's brow and Annette went to wipe them away with her handkerchief, Winifred rose from the chair, saying, 'That's no good,' and going to the wash basin in the corner of the room, she wetted a face flannel, then returned to the bed and began to sponge her son's face, and all the while he kept his eyes closed. But when she started to wipe a hand, he jerked it away from her, saying, 'Mother! Mother! I've been washed. Please, don't; I've been washed.'

'Don't excite yourself. Lie still.'

Now looking across the bed at Annette, she asked, 'How long are you staying?' And when she was given the answer firmly and briefly, 'All day,' she said, 'Oh.' Then added, 'There's no need for two of us to be here. And I thought you were seeing about the house being put in order.'

'That's already been done. And this is my place.'

They were both startled as Don cried, 'Nurse! Nurse!' at the same time lifting his hand and ringing the bell.

When the door opened immediately and the nurse entered, he said, 'Nurse, I am tired.'

The nurse now looked from the elderly woman to the younger and said, 'Would you, please?' And

95

as they both made slowly for the door, Don's voice checked them, saying, 'Annette. Annette.'

And she, almost running back to the bed, bent over him. 'Yes, dear? Don't worry. I'll be back in a minute or so. Don't worry.'

In the corridor they faced each other. Before Annette had time to speak Winifred said, 'Two are one too many in the room.'

'Yes, I agree with you. And I have first place, I am his wife. Please remember that.'

'How dare you!'

'I dare, and shall go on daring.' With this Annette walked away towards a door marked 'Sister Bell'. And knocking and being bidden to enter, she went in and put her case to the sister in a few words, ending, 'Who has first right to be with her husband, sister? The mother or the wife?'

'The wife, of course. And don't worry, Mrs Coulson, I understand the position and I'll see Mr Richardson with regard to the visits his mother can make in the future. You've had a very trying time.' She came round the desk and, putting her hand on Annette's shoulder, she said, 'There, there, now. You've been very brave. Don't cry. Leave it to me, I'll deal with her. Is she still in the corridor?'

'She was.'

'Then you stay there until I come back.'

A few seconds later Annette heard her mother-in-law's voice finishing on the words she had become accustomed to over the past weeks: 'He is my son. I will see into this.'

There followed a silence, but the sister did not return immediately. When she did, her smile seemed somewhat forced as she said, 'The coast is clear now; you can go in to your husband.'

'Thank you. Thank you very much, sister. By the way, sister'—she paused—'could you give me any idea when I shall be able to take him home?'

'Oh.' The sister raised her eyebrows before she said, 'I'm afraid that will be some time, some weeks. You see, he's due for another operation later this week; and also, once you get him home, there'll be continuous nursing for a time. You know that?'

'Yes. Yes, I understand that.'

'But one day at a time. Take it one day at a time. He's progressing much more quickly than we had thought he would, and he always seems better when you're with him.'

Annette could give no answer to this, but she went out and into Don's room again. He was lying with his eyes closed and didn't realise who it was until she took his hand. And then he said, 'Oh, Annette. What ... what am I going to do about her?'

'Don't worry, don't worry; sister's seeing to everything.'

'She upsets me, dear. I can't help it, she upsets me. I dread her coming in now. What am I going to do?'

'You are going to lie quiet and have a little doze. And just think, in a few weeks I'll have you home. I mean to have you home.' She squeezed his hand between both hers. 'That's all I'm living for, to have you home as soon as possible.'

'But how will you manage?'

'Oh'—she laughed down on him—'if that's all that's worrying you, put it out of your head this moment. How will I manage? I'll have plenty of help. And I could manage you on my own. I'll let you see what I can do.'

'But ... but for how long, dear?'

She stared at him. Yes, for how long. There were two meanings to that remark, but she didn't know to which one he was alluding. So she evaded it by saying, 'As long as ever it takes. Close your eyes, darling, and go to sleep. You don't want them to throw me out too, do you?'

He made no answer but turned his head to the side and lay gazing at her. And with his hand held between her breasts she gazed back at him.

CHAPTER TWO

'Look, my dear.' Daniel put his arm around Annette's shoulder as they walked from the hospital to the car. 'There's nobody wants him to go straight to the cottage more than I do. Believe that, dear. But the only way the doctor's going to let him out is if we can promise him that Don will have adequate nursing. Oh, I know you can get a night and day nurse, but one nurse will not be enough. He's got to be lifted and turned. As you know he's incontinent and always will be. Then, with the damage to his liver and his chest, he hasn't got the strength to pull himself up and down. The only reason Mr Richardson has agreed to letting him leave is because he is getting depressed, mainly because he can't see enough of you. And remember: it isn't that long since they took the plaster off your arm. You couldn't possibly help a nurse with lifting, whereas at home there will always be Joe and me. And we couldn't be on hand if you were in the cottage, you know. So this is what we have thought up. It was really Joe's idea. You know the games-room next to the billiard-room? It's large and airy, with those two long windows looking on to the garden. Then there is that other room that at one time used to store all the paraphernalia for the conservatory before it was turned into the sun-room. As Joe said, the games-room could be fixed up as a fine bedroom. He's even picked a bed from upstairs, and also pointed out that with a couple of mattresses it will bring it up almost to the hospital height for a bed; you know, to make it easy for lifting the patient. Then the other room can be turned into a sitting-room. And you know how handy he is with wires in rigging up things—he should have been an electrician—well, he said he can fix up an intercom from your room to his along the corridor and another to my room upstairs, so that we'll always be on hand if needed. But only if needed.'

She stopped in her walk and with a touch of bitterness in her voice, she said, 'And what of ... Mother-in-law? She'll never be out of his room. There won't be any nurses or doctors or sisters to take my side. It's her house.'

'*It's my house.*'

'Don't split hairs, Dad. I ... I won't be able to stand it. And there's enough warring as it is. And you know how Don feels about her.'

'I know. I know, dear. But I promise you I'll lay down laws and that they will be obeyed. One threat will be that if she doesn't keep her place then you can move him to the cottage. Come on, love, try it for a while. It's for Don's benefit. Just

99

think of it that way.'

'No. I can't think of it that way, Dad, because most of his nervous trouble is through her. You've got to admit it.'

'Oh, I admit it. Oh, yes, I do, lass. But at the present moment I can't see any other way out. He's either got to stay where he is or come back to his old home; as I said, at least for a time. Later on, we may be able to get him into a wheelchair. Now, think of that.' He put his arm around her shoulder again and said, 'Come on. Come on. You've been so brave all along and I want bucking up. I'm very low meself at the moment.'

'Oh, I'm sorry, Dad.'

'By the way, how are you finding things at home?'

'Oh, as usual, Mother's fussing, trying to find the answer to why it all happened. Father's just the same, although he just looks on.'

He brought her round squarely to face him now, asking quietly, 'Are they kind and understanding?'

And she answered as quietly, 'Kind in a way, but not understanding. They never have been and they never will now.' They stared at each other for a moment before he said brightly, 'Oh, well, come on. I'll land you at your door.'

'I thought you were going into Newcastle on business?'

'I am, but I can still land you at your door and turn round and come back.'

'I can get a taxi.'

'You'll do no such thing. Come on.'

Five minutes later he dropped her at the gates leading to her home, saying, 'I'll call in at the hospital about eight to pick you up. Will that be all

100

right?'

'Yes, Dad. And thanks.'

He waved to her, turned the car around and drove back into Newcastle and straight to 42 Bowick Road.

Maggie opened the front door for him as if she had been standing behind it waiting, which in a way, she had. Once it was closed they put their arms about each other and kissed long and hard. Then in a matter of fact way she said, 'You look frozen. I've got some hot soup ready.' And to this he answered, 'We could have snow for Christmas, it's cold enough.'

'Here, give me your coat.' She took his outdoor things, went into the passage and hung them on an expanding hat rack. When she returned to the room it was to be enfolded in his arms again. But now they just held each other closely for a moment until she said, 'Sit yourself down,' and pointed to a two-seater sofa set at an angle to the open fireplace, in which a coal fire was blazing. And he sat down and stretched out his legs, then looked at the fire, and when his body slumped he leant his head on the back of the couch and his escaping breath took on the form of a long sigh. Presently, without moving, he called, 'What time did you leave?'

And her voice came from the kitchen, saying, 'Near twelve.'

'What!' He brought his head up. 'You were ready first thing before I went to the yard.'

'Yes, I know, but there was a bit to do with Stephen. You know what he's like on my day off, or at any time when he knows I'm going out. Well, he came down in his dressing-gown. I was in my

101

room when he entered the kitchen, but I heard him. You know how his voice cracks high when he's going to have a tantrum. When I went in it was the usual: he wanted to come with me or go and see Don. They should never have promised to take him to see Don; he remembers these things. It was decided long ago you know, not to promise him things he couldn't have or do. Well, who should give us a surprise visit at that time but herself, and at this he started one of his tantrums. He just wouldn't stop, throwing himself about, you know, in this three-year-old fashion. And so she slapped him.'

'She what!'

'She slapped him. And she was right. Oh yes, on this occasion she was right. And it stopped him in his tracks. But he started to howl, so I took him upstairs, told him to have his bath then get dressed. And I went down again and saw her.'

Her voice stopped, and he pulled himself up to the end of the couch, calling, 'Well, what happened next?'

She came into the room now carrying a tray on which were two plates of soup and, laying them on a small cloth-covered table set against the wall opposite the fire, she said, 'I went to her room. She was looking out of the window, with her hair hanging down. I'd never seen her with her hair hanging down, you know. She turned and looked at me. She had been crying, Daniel. She had been crying.'

He rose to his feet and walked towards her, saying, 'Well, she had been crying. She's got a good right to cry; it would be because she was sorry for herself, knowing she can't have all her

102

own way and her son to herself.'

Maggie looked away from him, then continued, 'When I asked if she would mind if I took him out for a little run, she said, "It's your day off." And I said, "I know that, but it doesn't matter, I've nothing special to do." And you know what she said?' Maggie was looking at him now, and in a low voice she went on, 'She said, "This used to be a happy house at one time, didn't it, Maggie?"'

'Happy house be damned! It was never a happy house; never from the beginning. She wanted it to show off, and it was a large enough place to push Stephen out of sight.'

'I know. I know. But I think she was making comparisons with then and now. And when next she said, "Life isn't fair, is it?" I answered her truthfully, "No, ma'am, it isn't fair." And when she said to me, "Are you happy?" what could I say? But I answered truthfully, "Only at odd times, ma'am, at very odd times." Daniel, for the first time in my life I felt sorry for her. In a way she has a side, she can't help feeling as she does about Don no more than I can help feeling as I do about you or you about me.' She put her hands upon his shoulders now, saying, 'Be civil to her, Daniel. You know, Lily tells me she hates to go in and serve the meals. You speak to Joe or she speaks to Joe; Joe speaks to you, or Joe speaks to her. She said that the other day the conversation was so stilted it was just like a puppet show. And it's better when you don't go in at all, because then Joe talks to her freely. It's not so bad when Annette's there, either, but better still when Mrs Jackson and Mr Rochester happen to pop down; he even makes her laugh at times.'

He took her hands from his shoulders and pressed them together, saying, 'It's odd that you should say you're sorry for her.'

'Well, I am, and feeling guilty an' all.'

'Oh my God! don't do that, Maggie. Don't be a hypocrite.'

She withdrew her hands from his, saying, 'I'm no hypocrite and you know that, but I'm in the house with her all day. I'm a looker-on, as it were, and I generally see most of the game. I don't like her, I never have, and not only because I've loved you; I don't like her as a woman. She's an upstart, she's selfish. She's all those things, but at the same time, because she's got this love; no, not love, but passion or mania for her son, I can understand in a way because, dear God, how many times have I wished I had a son that I could go mad over? Your son.'

'Oh! Maggie. Maggie.' His arms went about her again and he rested her head on his shoulder. But it was there for only a moment before she sniffed and said, 'This soup'll be clay cold. Come on, sit down, you must be starved.'

'Yes, I am Maggie, I am starved, but not for food.'

'Well—' she smiled at him, then patted him on the shoulder gently as she said, 'we'll have to see about that, won't we? But first things first. Sit yourself down.'

*　　*　　*

At about six o'clock he was ready to leave and, standing at the unopened door, he said, 'Maggie, not being the allocator of time, just like everybody else, I don't know how long I've got, but I can say this to you: I'd gamble away the rest of my life for just a few weeks in this house with you.' Then on a smile he added, 'Well, perhaps not exactly in this one, because I couldn't deal with Helen too. Give her my love, will you?'

'I'll do no such thing; I'll give her your kind regards. Good-night, my dear. Mind how you go; it's freezing, the roads will be slippery.'

He had hardly entered the house when Joe approached him from across the hall. It was as if he, like Maggie, had been waiting for him.

'May I have a word, Dad?'

'Yes, yes, what is it? Come into the study.'

Once in the room Joe said, 'Annette came here this afternoon. She went and had a talk with Mam. I don't know what transpired, not really, except that she made it plain that if she allowed Don to be brought here they would have to have a certain amount of privacy. There would be a day nurse but no night nurse, as she could call upon either you or me, and between us we'd see to him first thing in the morning and last thing at night. In the meantime what needed to be done the nurse herself could see to.

'She didn't say how Mam took that, only that it was settled. But since then, you wouldn't believe it, there's been so much bustle. Mam's had Lily and Peggie scrubbing away, and she even brought Stephen down to help me move furniture. I suggested that it would be better to wait until you came in, but no, Stephen would do, he was strong, she said. He is, you know, and he can do things when he likes. And of course he was delighted.'

'Well! well! things are moving.'

105

'Dad.' Joe put his hand out towards Daniel, saying, 'She seemed happy, changed, like her old self ... well'—he shrugged his shoulders—'as happy as her old self could be. Dad, try to go along with her, at least until...'

Daniel looked into the face of this man who could give him inches and whose whole body was filled with kindness, and he thought it odd that these two people for whom he had love and who were of no blood connection could be pleading for his wife's cause, pointing out that she had a side. Quietly he answered him, saying, 'I'll do my best; I was never a disturber of the peace. But what do you think is going to happen when the bubble bursts, as, knowing her, burst it will? I'm amazed it hasn't been pricked before now. It just needs a prick, you'll see. But all right ... all right, I'll go along, and I promise I'll not be the one to use the pin.'

CHAPTER THREE

The bubble burst just five days after Don had been brought home. And it was evident from the start that Winifred intended never to speak to her husband and to ignore Annette.

There had first been a little contretemps over the placing of another single bed in what was to be Don's bedroom, a bed that would have a double purpose: it would not only be a place for Annette to sleep near her husband, but be useful in being some place on which to lay him when his bed was being made. But on the evening before Don was due to arrive, the bed had been taken out and placed in the adjoining sitting-room. Apparently John and Bill had been called in from outside to remove it. But it wasn't Daniel who ordered it to be put back, because as yet he hadn't seen the move, but Joe who, with the assistance of Stephen, himself in a high state of excitement about Don's return, had taken the bed to pieces and then reassembled it where it had been originally. And as soon as Winifred knew of this her temper became evident, for she naturally imagined it had been at her husband's behest.

But when she knew it had been Joe's doing, she had upbraided him with, 'How dare you!' but what else she intended to say was cut off by his speaking to her in a fashion that stilled her tongue. 'You can do nothing about it, Mam,' he had said; 'they are married; she's his wife and her place is by his side. You'll feel better if you admit that to yourself. In fact, things will be better all round.'

She had certainly been, if not amazed, then greatly surprised because of all the members in the house it was he who always spoke civilly to her, and often in a placating tone.

She marched out and the bed remained where it was.

But each morning since, before the nurse came on duty, she had contrived to meet her in the hall and give her unnecessary instructions.

Nurse Pringle was a middle-aged woman. She had been in private nursing for years. She had met Winifred's type before, and so she would smile and say, 'Yes, Mrs Coulson,' the while determined to do things in her own way.

Following the issuing of instructions to the

nurse, Winifred would eat her breakfast. No calamity seemed to stop her eating: in fact, the more she was troubled the more she ate. And when the meal was over, and only then, she would visit her son's room. She had to suppress the temptation to go down in her dressing-gown as soon as she awoke, for she couldn't bear the thought of seeing that girl so near to him, even perhaps lying by his side.

During the past weeks she considered that Annette Allison had changed so much there was now no resemblance to the quiet, convent-bred girl who had been engaged to her son. It was as if, having married him, she had, at the same time, grown to maturity.

And there was something else she had to restrain herself from doing: to kiss her son and fondle him, for since his marriage he seemed to resent her nearness. She would not admit to herself that his stand against her proximity had begun a long time before his marriage.

She conceded to the arrangement whereby her husband and Joe saw to the changing of the bedding; but when she learned that the nurse would not be bathing Don, and she had told Annette that she would do it, the girl had answered, 'He won't allow me to wash him down, so he won't allow you.' There had been times during the past five days she had wanted to take her hand and slap that young, confident-looking face. She would not say 'beautiful', because she didn't think she was beautiful; to her she wasn't even pretty.

And so now, as usual, she was bracing herself as she crossed the hall on her way to pay her morning

108

visit, when her jaws stiffened at the sound of laughter coming from the direction of her son's bedroom. When she opened the door she saw the reason for it. Her eldest son—she couldn't bear to think of him as such, but nevertheless he was—was standing with his back towards the bed and laughing all over his face as he cried, 'Go on. Go on, Don, pat me on the back. Go on. Maggie always does when I've been a good boy. Go on, 'cos I've been a good boy. Ever since you came home I've been a good boy. Go on.'

Neither the nurse nor Annette turned at her entry. They too were laughing as they watched Don reach out and pat his brother on his back, saying, 'That's one extra for tonight.'

'Yes, Don. I'll be good tonight; you'll see, I'll be good. And you know, I'm goin' to help to lift you tomorrow. I asked Dad, 'cos he says, I'm strong as a bull. I helped Joe carry the other bed in. Yes, I did. I did...'

'*Stephen!*' The young fellow became quiet, and as he straightened up, his body became stiff and he said, 'Yes, Mam?'

'Go up to your room.'

'I've ... I've just come down, Mam. And ... and Don likes me to be here; I make him laugh.'

'Go on, go up to your room.'

Stephen looked down on Don, who nodded at him, saying, 'Go on now. Come down later. We'll have coffee together and chocolate biscuits, eh?'

'Oh yes, Don, chocolate biscuits, yes.' He backed away from the bed, moving in an arc around his mother as he made for the door.

And now Winifred, addressing the nurse, said, 'You must be firm with him: he cannot come and

109

go as he likes; he'll tire him.' She looked away from the nurse and back towards the bed, as though expecting no reply from the nurse; nor did the nurse answer, but Don said quietly, 'He doesn't tire me, Mother. I like to see him.'

She ignored this and said, 'How are you?' She had now moved to the head of the bed and was looking down on him.

'I've had a good night; not too bad at all, in fact, a hundred per cent better than I did in hospital. I'll soon be in that chair the nurse was talking about yesterday. What do you say, nurse?'

'Could be. It all depends. But like your brother, you'll have to be a good boy.' Then looking from her patient to Annette, she added, 'There now, you two, you can get on with your crossword. I'm going into the hall to do some phoning. There are some medicines I need and I want a word with Mr Richardson.'

'What do you want to say to Mr Richardson?'

Nurse Pringle looked at Winifred and she said quietly, 'I want to report on my patient.'

'You can tell me and I can do that.'

'I'm sorry, Mrs Coulson; this comes within the confines of my duty, and I'm obeying Mr Richardson's orders in doing so.'

'You're impudent.'

'I'm sorry if you find me so. If you have any complaints...'

'Nurse.' Annette was standing at the other side of the bed now; she had turned from arranging some flowers on a table near the window. 'Do what you think is right. And I don't consider you impudent. My husband is very grateful for your attention, aren't you, Don?'

110

Don's lower lip was jerking in and out and he muttered, 'Yes, yes, I'm very glad of nurse's attention. And ... and you must forgive Mother; she doesn't understand the routine.' He forced a watery smile to his face by saying, 'She's never been stuck in a hospital for weeks.'

The nurse went out leaving the three of them breathing the air that was thick with hostility.

'Something will have to be done; I'm no longer mistress in my own house,' Winifred said, and emphasised what she had said by drawing in her stomach.

'Mother! For God's sake, stop it, will you? If you start again I'll ask to be taken back to hospital. No, no, I won't'—he shook his head in much the same manner as Stephen would have when in a tantrum—'we'll go to the cottage. Yes. Yes, that's what we'll do.' He put his hand out and, gripping Annette's, he almost whimpered, 'I can't stand this arguing. We'll have a night and day nurse and someone like John, a handyman. Oh'—his voice rose—'a male nurse. Yes. Yes, a male nurse.'

'I'm sorry. Please, don't agitate yourself. I'm sorry. It ... it won't happen again,' said Winifred.

The words had cost his mother something, and both Don and Annette realised this. And it was Annette being placating now when she said, 'Please, Mother-in-law, try to accept things the way they are. It could all run smoothly. He ... he wants to see you. Don't you, dear?' She turned and looked at her husband, and when he nodded, she went on, 'You see if you'd only try to...'

The look on the woman's face checked any further words, and Annette watched her turn about and go hastily from the room.

111

'It won't work, Annette. It won't work.'

'Yes, it will, dear; she'll come round. I know she will. It will take time. In a way I know how she feels: I've stolen you from her. If someone tried to take you from me, I ... I would feel the same as she does.'

'Never!'

He was right, of course; she would never be able to feel the same way as that woman did. There was something about her that wasn't ... She couldn't find a word with which to translate her thoughts, but what she said was, 'You mustn't worry. That's the main thing, you mustn't worry. Because, as you've just said, we could go to the cottage. Any day, dear, we could go there. In fact, as you know, that's where I wanted to take you in the first place.'

'I wish you had stuck out, dear. Oh, I wish you had.'

So did she ... But they were here now, yet not for long, she knew, for the scene that had just been enacted was but a pin-prick to the one that was bound to come.

It came that evening at half-past nine.

*   *   *

Winifred's mind was in a turmoil: there was another person in her household that had been set against her: the nurse. Now, only the servants spoke civilly to her, and she didn't think it was because they were paid to be civil. Even Joe was totally on the side of that girl. But of course, he would be, wouldn't he?

She felt hungry. It was more than three hours since she had eaten. She must have something.

112

She went downstairs. The house was very still: there was only the throbbing of the boiler from the cellar penetrating the quiet. She went into the kitchen. It was empty. Maggie would, of course, be in her room. Lily would have been down at the lodge this last hour; she finished at eight every night. Peggie Danish would not yet have gone to bed; she must be upstairs seeing to Stephen, hoping no doubt that Joe would be up there too. She'd have to watch that girl; she was too fresh by half.

She went to the fridge, but found only a shop-bought veal pie and some cheese that could be eaten immediately.

She hesitated on the cheese; it generally kept her awake. So she cut herself a slice of the pie, put it on a plate, then stood for a moment with the plate in her hand; she never liked eating in the kitchen. She went out and walked towards the dining-room, but then changed her mind. There was a moon out; it would be nice in the sun-room. She would eat there. And then she would look in on the sick-room; just a peep.

The sun-room was softly lit by the moonlight. She sat down in a chair and munched on the pie. When she had finished she licked her finger ends and wiped them delicately on her handkerchief. Then she sat musing for a moment as she looked out on to the garden, so thickly lined with frost that it looked like a layer of snow.

Although she rarely felt the cold, she shivered and pulled her dressing-gown tightly about her before getting up and making for the door, only to stop before reaching it and to look to the far end of the conservatory to the door that led into what was

113

now Annette's sitting-room. Why shouldn't she go in that way? She did not add, and surprise them and see what they were up to; at least, what *she* was up to, for she wouldn't put it past her to be lying with him at night. That was why she had been against the night nurse. And in his condition. It was disgusting!

Swiftly, she walked to the other door. It opened quietly. She paused on the threshold. The only light in the room was that coming from under the door leading into the bedroom. But there was no obstacle in her way; the couch was to the side. She closed the door behind her; then, hand outstretched, she made her way towards the strip of light on the floor, sought the handle of the door and pushed it open. Then, at the sight of the tableau on the bed, she froze.

There was that girl, that hussy, that woman, stark naked! And there was her son, reaching out, his hand on her belly and her two hands covering it!

At the sound of the door opening, Annette swung round to grab at her dressing-gown, then Winifred heard her son cry, 'Don't! Don't! Stay as you are.' And the girl, the dressing-gown trailing from her hand, stayed as she was for a moment.

Winifred found it impossible to accept what she was seeing: it couldn't be! It couldn't be! her mind was screaming at her. The car accident had happened at the bottom of the drive; it would be impossible for them to have been ... The words were cut off in her mind by a dreadful thought that seemed to spiral up from some dark depth in her. And when it reached the top of her head it pierced her brain and sent thoughts splintering in all directions. She could read them but she could scarcely believe them. And so she screamed, 'You dirty slut, you! You filthy creature! You're pregnant and you're putting it on to my son. You low down...'

'Stop it!' Don's elbows were pressed into the bed, supporting his raised shoulders now as he cried at her, 'Shut up, woman!'

She took five steps into the room, and these brought her almost to the foot of the bed. And there she screamed back at him, 'Never! Never! I know you. I'm your Mother, remember? You were *good, clean, pure...*'

'Pure? Hell!'

'Don. Don. Lie down; I'll ... I'll deal with it.'

Annette had by now pulled the dressing-gown around her; but Don ignored her and dragging himself a little further up the bed, he yelled at his mother in a voice as loud as hers had been, 'Listen! woman. Listen! for once. The child is ours ... *mine*. We've been together for a year, a whole year. And what do I mean by being together? I mean, having it off under your nose. Having it off. You couldn't expect anything else, could you? her mother treating her like a vestal virgin and you trying to tie nappies on me. A full year we've been together. When this happened'—he jerked his head—'it was no mistake. I wanted it. I wanted an explosion. Yes, do you hear? an explosion *to blow you out of my life.*'

'Don! Don! Enough! Stop it! Lie down.'

'I've lain down long enough. It's got to be said, and I'll say it: it's been a wonderful year, a time I think of as a year of the virgins.'

Winifred's mind was refusing to recognise the

man in the bed as her son. This man was talking common, dirty, just like her husband, and her son wasn't like her husband. But there was one thing certain: he was so much enamoured of that creature that he would like just to save her face and name.

Now she screamed at him: 'I don't believe a word of it! You can't hoodwink me. You're just shielding her.'

There was the sound of a door banging in the distance. It must be the door at the far end of the corridor, the one that led into the cottage, she thought. Yes, that was it. Joe. And so she cried, 'It was him, wasn't it? Joe. It was Joe. He always wanted you. And he would drive you here and there, wouldn't he? Even when you two were supposed to be engaged he would drive you. It was Joe. Tell me, girl. Speak the truth. But there's no truth in you. You're a dirty, filthy slut. You're a . . .'

The opening of the door and Joe's appearance did not stem the flow of vituperation, but simply redirected it, and now she screamed at him. 'Getting my son to hide your filthy deeds, were you?'

Joe's face screwed up. He looked perplexed for a moment before asking of Don, 'What's this?'

But it was Winifred who interrupted her son as he was about to answer, yelling, 'Don't you ask "what's this?". Look at her stomach! But of course, you know all about that, don't you? Being a bastard yourself, you've given her one too!'

'Oh my God!' Don gasped and fell back on to his pillows the words, garbled, tumbling from his mouth. 'She's m . . . mad, clean mad. She . . . she

116

always has been. Get … get her out of here, Joe. Get her out…'

Joe didn't move towards his adoptive mother, but stood gazing at her, wishing to God that what she was saying were true. And then, through gritted teeth, he said to her, 'You were glad to take in a bastard baby at one time. But there's more ways of being a bastard than being born on the wrong side of the blanket. Think on that. Now I'd get yourself away to bed.'

For answer she swung round, grabbed the carafe of water from the table at the side of her and threw it at his head. It struck him on the ear and sent him reeling to the side, and as she came at him, her arms outstretched, her fingers clawed, the door opened and Daniel rushed in shouting, 'In the name of God! what's up now?'

It took both Joe and Daniel all their time to hold her and drag her from the room as she screamed abuse at them, using the same words she had previously yelled at Don.

In the hall, she brought Peggie Danish's eyes popping and her mouth agape, but the language made no impression on Maggie as she tried to avoid the kicking legs and helped the men get her up the stairs.

At one time Maggie thought the four of them would come tumbling down backwards, and as she clung to the banister with one hand, she shouted down at Peggie, 'Phone the doctor. Go on, girl, phone the doctor.'

Once on the landing, they propelled the wriggling, screaming woman to the bedroom; and there Daniel, kicking open the door, shouted at Joe, 'Let go!' Then he thrust her forward on to the

117

floor and, turning quickly, he pulled the key out from the inside lock of the door, pushed Joe and Maggie into the corridor again, then locked the door from the outside. And as the three of them stood panting, a high scream came from the room, followed a few seconds later by the sound of articles being thrown about. When something heavy hit the door they all stepped back, and Daniel, looking at Joe, said, 'What brought this on?'

Joe was still gasping but his voice snapped, 'She opened her eyes at last and actually looked at Annette. I came in at the tail-end. I don't know what had happened before.'

When something again hit the door, Maggie said, 'She'll wreck the room.'

'Let her.'

Daniel turned and went down the stairs, and they followed him into Don's room, to find his son white and shivering.

'What actually happened?' he asked Annette. 'How did the news break?'

She bent her head a moment before she said, 'I was undressed and she could see Don had a hand on my stomach. She must have been in the sun-room; she came in that way unexpectedly.'

'Well, she had to find out sometime, hadn't she?'

Annette looked up now and said, 'I'm moving him tomorrow, Dad.'

'There mightn't be any need, lass; when the doctor comes, he'll need to take a second opinion, but she's got to be put away. It's been coming for a long time.'

118

When, half an hour later the doctor, together with Maggie, cautiously entered Winifred's room, he stopped on the threshold and gazed around him in amazement. The only item seemingly to be in one piece was the four-poster bed, and sprawled across it was the woman whom he had attended for years and to whom he had doled out pills that he knew would do her no good whatever.

He moved towards the bed, and avoiding the side over which her legs were hanging, he went round to where her head lay. And cautiously he touched it, saying quietly, 'It's all right, Mrs Coulson, it's all right. Sit up, there's a good woman.'

She raised her head and stared at him. Her face was empty of expression, quiet; yet her voice belied this when, as if he knew all that had transpired, she said, 'I tell you he was a virgin. I watched over him. Except—' She turned her head to the side and screwed up her eyes as if trying to recall something and then, springing from the bed, she cried, '*He* did it! He was going to make him like father like son; he couldn't bear to see anything pure. No, no.' She shook her head wildly now and, putting her hand out and gripping his arm, she appealed to him: 'No; it was Joe. *You* see that he owns up. Joe gave it to her. Joe always wanted her.'

'There, there. Sit down. Come on, sit down.' He drew her gently down on to the side of the bed again; then glancing towards where Maggie stood, he motioned his head towards his bag, which he had dropped on to the floor, and she brought it to him and placed it on the bed. And when he opened

119

it and began to pick out one thing after another, Winifred jumped to her feet, saying, 'You're not putting me to sleep; I haven't finished yet. Oh, no, I haven't finished yet, not by a long chalk. I'll destroy them and everything in this house. It won't be fit to live in when I'm finished with it.'

'Well, we'll talk about that tomorrow. Come, sit down.'

As she backed away from him, he stood for a moment, looking at her helplessly; then, without turning his gaze towards Maggie, he said quietly, 'Fetch the men.'

As they were both outside the door it was only a matter of seconds before they were in the room, and when Winifred saw them she looked wildly about her, searching for something to throw. And when she made towards the dressing-table and the glass bottles and powder jars scattered around it on the floor, both Daniel and Joe rushed towards her and held her as best they could, trying to ignore the volume of obscenities once more pouring from her mouth, while the doctor inserted a needle, none too gently, into the thick flesh of her arm.

Winifred struggled for another few seconds before finally subsiding on to the floor.

As he stood looking down on the huddled form, Doctor Peters let out a long slow breath before saying to Daniel, 'She'll have to be admitted, of course. And before she comes round. I'll phone the hospital and arrange for an ambulance.'

'The County?' Joe's voice was small as he continued to stare at the crumpled heap of flesh, more animal than human.

'If not the County, then Hetherington. In her case I think the Hetherington would be preferable.

120

It will depend on which one has a vacancy, though, so I'd better find out,' Doctor Peters answered.

While this was going on, Daniel hadn't spoken a word, and he didn't break the silence that followed when left with Joe and Maggie.

They both watched him as he stared down at his wife, and he was unaware of Maggie's touching Joe on the arm and of their leaving the room, for he was searching deep into his mind, asking questions, giving himself answers. Was he to blame?

No, no. He couldn't say he was to blame because he would never have taken up with anyone else if she had behaved as a wife.

But had she ever been a wife, a willing wife? Wasn't it that she hadn't wanted a husband so much as security and position?

But when had the big rows started? the recriminations?

From the time she knew that Stephen was retarded.

Had she been a wife to him during the time she had played mother to the adopted boy, Joe?

Only under protest.

How many women had she caused him to use? Because he *had* just used them; there certainly had been no feeling of tenderness or love in his dealings.

Perhaps Father Ramshaw could answer that question better than he himself, for he had a good memory for confessions. Following each time he had gone off the rails, he had gone to confession.

Had it been just fear of the retribution of God that had driven him to confession? Or the fact that he had liked the priest and thought he would

121

understand? And he did understand, even about Maggie.

How was it that he loved Maggie? He must have loved her all the time, but had only become aware of it during recent years. Now, if she had given him some hint, he wouldn't have had to sully his soul as much as he had done, for he had never kept up a connection with any one person for long.

Looking at his life, it had been hellish. He had money, a thriving business, a fine house and, except by a few men, one being Annette's father, he was highly respected. Yet what did it all amount to? He could only repeat: hell. The only thing that mattered in life was love. It wasn't even essential to be able to write your own name; you could be deaf or blind, or just dim; but if you really loved that's what got you through.

He stretched his body now and looked away from his wife. Hadn't she loved? No; that wasn't love, that was a mania, a possessive mania; more than that, it was almost incest. Love was something else. What else?

He looked around the room as if searching for an answer and then said aloud, 'Kindliness. Aye, that's it.' To be kind, that was love. To give comfort, that was love. To like someone for themselves, forgetting their faults, yes, that was the best kind of love. And he would have never known anything about it except that Maggie had come into his life. Odd that. She had always been there, but she had just come into it.

He turned and, stooping, righted an upturned chair; then as he was about to pick up a broken picture from the floor, he straightened, saying to himself, there'll be plenty of time for that tomorrow, for the house will be at peace tomorrow, and for the next day, the next week, the next month, please God.

He turned again and looked at his wife. And now the knowledge that she would soon be gone, as well as the sight of her lying in that undignified heap, brought from him the urge to go and lift her on to the bed, to straighten her limbs, to bring back to her a little digniy, because this heap that now represented her had stripped her of all dignity. And he recalled that when she walked she had done so with dignity. Fat she may have been, fat she was, but she carried it well.

He could not, however, make the move towards her; for now an overwhelming feeling of revulsion was preventing him from touching her. When the ambulance men came they would see to her, or perhaps Joe, or the doctor, or anybody.

He scampered from the room, tripping over broken furniture as he went. Joe was waiting outside. It was as if he was always waiting, waiting to be of help, and it was natural for him to put his hand out towards him, saying, 'I'm going to be sick, lad.' And Joe, taking his arm, hurriedly led him across the landing, pushed open the bathroom door and guided him inside. And he continued to support his head while the retching continued, and even after the stomach had given up all it held. Then he sat him down on the bathroom chair and sponged his face with cold water. This done, he said, 'I would go to bed if I were you, Dad; I'll see to things.'

'No, no; I'll see it through.' Then he added, 'The doctor's been a long time on the phone.'

'He had to go and see Don; he was in a state. He
123

gave him a sleeping draught. He's with Annette now; and she's not much better.'

Daniel got to his feet and adjusted his clothes. Pulling his tie straight, he said, 'It's odd that Stephen should sleep through all this.'

'He hasn't slept through all this; he's downstairs in the kitchen with Maggie. He must have run down when we were all in the bedroom. He was stiff with fear.'

The sound of a commotion in the hall now brought them both out of the bathroom and down the stairs, there to see two ambulance men and the doctor in discussion. And the doctor, turning towards Daniel and taking in his blanched face, tentatively said, 'Do you think you'll be able to accompany us to the hospital? Someone must come along. Perhaps you would rather your son...'

'No, no; I'll come.'

'Very well.' The doctor and the two ambulance men, preceded by Joe, went up the stairs, while Daniel, standing in the middle of the hall, grappled with the fact that it wasn't all over yet; he'd still to see her into the place.

* * *

There was a weird stillness on the house, a kind of stillness that exaggerated the ticking of the tall grandfather clock, which now boomed three times, announcing that it was a quarter to twelve. Don was in a deep sleep which would take him through until the morning. Stephen too was asleep, as also was Peggie. Maggie was in her room, but she wasn't asleep. She wouldn't go to sleep until she

124

heard Daniel's car draw up in the drive. And Joe and Annette weren't asleep. They were in the drawing-room, sitting on the sofa opposite the log fire. They had been sitting there for some time, both wanting to speak but not knowing how to begin. It was Annette who first made the effort. Looking at Joe, who was sitting bent forward, his elbows on his knees, his hands hanging between them in his characteristic fashion, she said softly, 'I'm sorry that you are implicated, Joe. She ... she didn't know what she was saying. You understand that?'

Joe now slowly turned his head towards her and he gazed at her for a long moment, in which his thoughts were racing and shouting at him: if only there had been even a vestige of truth in the statement. But what he actually said was, 'I know that, dear. It was an utterly ridiculous suggestion to make. But as you say, she didn't know what she was saying. And ... and you've always been like a little sister to me.'

She smiled wanly now, saying, 'Oh, I didn't think of you at one time as a brother! Remember when I used to follow you about? I had a kind of pash on you when I was fourteen.'

He made himself smile, saying, 'And it would be a *kind* of pash.'

'Don't be silly, Joe; you always underestimate yourself. You always have done, and there's no need. There's Irene, Irene Shilton. You would only have to lift your little finger. And Jessica Bowbent's another.' Then, her voice dropping, she said slowly, 'You should marry, Joe, and get away from here. Yes—' She shook her head now and turned and looked into the fire, repeating, 'Get

125

away from here, from all of them ... from all of us, from Stephen, he's Dad's responsibility, and from Don; he's ... well he's my responsibility now, and from Dad himself, because if you don't, you'll find us all on your shoulders.'

When she turned her gaze on him again he wanted to put his arms out and pull her into them and say, 'I'd carry you on my shoulders at any time. I'd wait a lifetime if I thought there would be any chance of bearing you as a burden.'

She went on, 'They take advantage of you, Joe; you're too kind. You've always been kind. You think you owe them a debt because they took you in when you were a baby. To my mind you owe nobody a debt; you've paid it by filling a gap in their lives.'

'Maybe, but only for a short time.' He shook his head ruefully. 'From the moment Don arrived, the gap was closed. I faced up to that as a child, but it didn't make me think the less of Don. I loved him. I still do.'

'Joe. Oh, Joe.' She put her hand out to him, and he hesitated a moment before taking it; then he gripped it and said, 'Don't cry. Oh, please, please, Annette, don't cry. It'll all work out, you'll see. We'll get him better in the end.'

The tears now were raining down her cheeks; her lips were trembling and her words came through her chattering teeth as she said, 'Don't hoodwink yourself, Joe, or try to hoodwink me. He'll never be better. If it was just his legs there'd be some hope, but he's all smashed up inside. You know he is. He knows he is. We both know he'll never get better.'

'Annette. Annette. Oh, my dear.' Her head

126

came on to his shoulders and his arms went about her, and as he felt the nearness of her he made a great effort to disbelieve her words, because it was true what he had said: he loved the man he thought of as his brother, the brother who had usurped his place in her life.

He let his mouth drop into her hair as he said, 'He'll live a long time yet. Between us we'll see to it that he holds his child, and see it romp an' all.' And he was about to mutter more platitudes when she drew herself away from him; and after she had dried her eyes she put her hand out and gently touched his cheek, saying, 'You're the kindest man in the world, Joe. I could tell you anything and not feel ashamed. I didn't feel ashamed when I told you about the baby coming. And now I can tell you of my fears too. I'm afraid of going home tomorrow—I still think of my parents place as home—and giving them my news. Because you know what will happen, Joe? They'll disown me.'

'Never! Never!'

'Oh, yes, they will, Joe. In a way, my mother is akin to Mam; she's got religion bad. I never pray now, you know, Joe, I never pray to God for Don or for anything that I want because all my young life it was prayers morning, noon, and night, at the table and away from it; and religious books, The Lives of The Saints, the martyrdom of this one and that one; then life at the convent school: Mass and Communion every morning during Lent. I would feel faint with hunger but she would make sure I went to Communion. Even the nuns didn't expect me to have Communion every day; but they could see me as a potential saint, such a good little girl. And all the while I was getting to hate God.

Dreadful, terrible feelings inside. As for the Virgin Mary, I suffered agonies in what I thought about her. And I longed, longed for escape. And on our wedding day we both thought we had made it. But as Mother always says, God is not mocked, and after the accident I began to believe it was true, and that what had happened to us was retribution. But not any more. It's people who bring retribution, not God. And you know, Joe, it's people who turn us away from God; it's the talk and actions of others that turn us against Him. Anyway, you can see why I'm dreading tomorrow ... And ... and you know, Joe, I fear this house. There is something evil about it.' She raised her eyes and gazed round the room, saying, 'It looks lovely, but I'm afraid of it. I want to get away from it, or from her. She's just gone, Joe, but already I feel she'll soon be back. And then we couldn't possibly stay here; I'd have to take him away. You understand that?'

'Yes, my dear, yes, I understand. And don't worry. But in the meantime, you must take care of yourself and the baby ... and Don.'

'Yes; yes, of course. You know, we were going to ask you something before this last business happened. We had made up our minds to leave and we were going to ask you if you'd come to the cottage with us. Would you ... would you have?'

How much pain could one put up with without wincing? or even crying out? Here he could retreat to his rooms after doing what was expected of him morning and night and saying, 'Hello, how are you, old fellow?' and smiling, and talking small talk. But to live with both of them!

He stalled by saying, 'Now that won't come

128

about. The way things are, you'll have no need to take him to the cottage.'

'You wouldn't have come then?'

He took her hand again and, looking into her face, he said, 'I'd do anything you ask, Annette; anything to make you happy.' He qualified this by adding, 'And Don.'

CHAPTER FOUR

The Mass was nearing its end. The Missal was moved from one side of the altar to the other. The priest covered the chalice and genuflected before the tabernacle before being preceded from the altar by two small altar boys. It was eight o'clock Mass and there were no more than twelve people present and they were regulars, all except one.

After Father Ramshaw had taken off his surplice he didn't as usual go through the side door into the yard and across the lawn that led to the presbytery and his breakfast—he was always ready for his breakfast—but instead went back into the church, knowing there would be one of the congregation still seated.

At a pew near the back of the church he sat down beside Daniel, muttering, 'If you'd got any further, you'd have been out of the door. How are you? You look awful.'

'I feel awful, Father.'

'What's happened now?'

'Winifred went off her head last night, clean off her head. She found out ...' He paused.

'Well, what did she find out?'

129

'That Annette is pregnant.' He paused again, then said, 'She's going to have a baby.'

'Yes, I understand; there's no need to spell it out for me. Only one thing surprises me and that is she took so long to twig Annette's condition. What happened to her?'

Daniel looked towards the altar. 'She wouldn't accept it, that it was Don's. She pushed the blame on Joe and went for him. And when we got her upstairs screaming, we had to lock her in her room where she smashed up everything movable. She was taken to the County.'

'Oh dear God! The County. I'm heart sorry to hear that it's come to this. Although it's no surprise. But God help her when she comes to herself in that hell-hole. I'm telling you, I hate to visit there. It isn't the real mad ones I'm sorry for. Oh no. They're happy in a way being Churchill or Chiang Kai-Shek or merely one of today's television so-called stars. No; it's the ones that have snapped temporarily through breakdowns and the like, because they are conscious of what's happening to them. And she'll be in that category.'

Father Ramshaw now put his hand on to the back of the seat in front of him as if for support; then, narrowing his eyes, he asked of Daniel, 'Is it guilt that's brought you here this morning?'

'Why ... why should I feel guilty? You know what my life's been like. You...'

'Yes, yes, I know all right. But you're not free from blame. And ask yourself what's brought you to Mass this morning when, to my knowledge, you've never been to week-day Mass in your whole existence. Yes, Daniel, you've got to share the blame, it's not all hers. In a way we're all

130

accountable for another's sins. More so are we accountable for our thoughts, for they prompt our speech. And do we ever say anything, I ask you, that doesn't have a reaction on something or someone? All right, all right, we don't do it in all cases with the intention of bringing disaster in its train. But look at you, look at yourself, Daniel. You wanted to free your son from his mother's apron strings, and what happens? Yes, I know I'm laying it on thick, and at this time too when you feel you need sympathy. But I want you to realise that you are not free from blame.'

Daniel stared at the priest. He had come here to find comfort. He'd not returned home from the hospital until almost two this morning and he hadn't been able to sleep. He had glimpsed only one ward in that place but the sight and sounds were haunting him. He had said to the doctor, 'Isn't there any private place she could go?' And he had replied, 'Not in her present condition. And there's none such around here.' And now for his dear friend here to take this attitude! His voice was stiff as he said, 'You seem of a sudden to be siding with her, Father.'

'I'm on nobody's side, Daniel. As always, I'm on the touchline, running meself skinny, asking the referee to see fair play done. But I've got to catch His eye, as it were, for most of the time He's under the impression, like many another, that's it's up to me, so He doesn't look the side I'm on. I'm an ordinary man, Daniel. I'm not one of God's chosen and I've no aspiration to be, and I don't see the world divided into saints and sinners; there's always a lot of grey in the middle.'

Daniel remained silent. He had never known the

131

priest's parables to irritate him before. But now he was finding that this outlook of a middle man was anything but helpful, particularly this morning when he was feeling desperate.

'I won't keep you, Father,' he said; 'you'll be wanting your breakfast.'

As he made to rise the priest's hand pushed him none too gently back on to the seat while he said, 'Me breakfast can wait for once, and I wouldn't be able to stomach it if I knew you were going off in a huff. Look—' He leaned towards him and, his hand now on Daniel's shoulder, he said, 'I know what you've been through all these years. I've even condoned in me own mind your antidote against her, when I should have been condemning you for your rampaging with women. I've thought many a time, as I've listened to her ranting on about her son and God and goodness, that in your place I would have done the same. God forgive me. But Daniel, I'm sorry for any human being who has to shoulder the burden of an unnatural love like she has. She couldn't help it no more than those two youngsters could help giving in to nature. If you want to know, I'm on your side, but at the same time, as I said before, we're all accountable for another's sins. And you can't come into church here and make your confession, talking to God through me or anyone else and think, that's that, the slate's clean. It isn't. You know'—his tone lightened—'that's what Protestants think we do. They think you just have to go to confession, tell the priest you've committed murder and he says, "Oh, you've committed a murder? Well, it's all right. I'll have a crack with God about it, and he'll wipe your slate clean. Carry on." That's extreme, I
132

know, but it applies to drunkenness, whoring, and coming in here to Mass on a Sunday while refusing to speak to your neighbour or relative or some such. Anyway—' He now patted Daniel on the shoulder, saying, 'Everything in this life must be paid for in one way or another. But I'm with you, Daniel, all along the road. Just remember that. Now get yourself home and I would suggest that you have a bath, for you don't look your usual spruce self this morning. Eat a good breakfast, then get off to work. Yes, that's it; work, there's nothing like it.'

They were back on their old footing. And the priest took Daniel's outstretched hand, then he walked with him to the door, and there he shivered, saying, 'By! it's cold enough to freeze the bacon in the frying pan. We'll surely have snow for Christmas. I'll tell you something, I hate snow. Mind how you go; the roads are like glass.'

Odd, people were always saying that: mind how you go, the roads are like glass. It was like a warning against life.

'Goodbye, Father, and thank you.'

'Goodbye, Daniel.'

*   *   *

Lily and Peggie were clearing up the debris of the bedroom, and Peggie, holding the cut-glass powder bowl in her hands, said, 'My God! She did go at it.' And to this Lily said, 'Her brain must have completely turned. It was the shock of finding out.'

'Oh, to my mind her brain was turned a long time afore that. Anyway, she must have been blind

133

not to notice. And Miss Annette being sick an' all and lookin' like a sheet most of the time. But wait till it gets around; it'll set the church on fire.'

Standing in the greenhouse, John Dixon and Bill White were discussing the events.

'We hadn't gone to bed,' Bill said, 'when we heard her. I didn't like to go up because I thought it was an ordinary shindy they were havin'. But when the ambulance came, well, I ran up then, and I couldn't believe it. There she was on a stretcher. I thought they were taking her to hospital, but no, it was The County. My God! To end up there. But in a way I'm not surprised, for she's been a tartar both inside and outside the house for years. Oh, the airs she used to put on when she was in the car. D'you know what she suggested just a while ago? That I should wear a uniform. I put it to the boss and he said, "You don't want to wear a uniform, do you, Bill?" And I said, "No fear, boss." "Well, you're not going to then," he said. And that was that. By! he's had a life of it. I would have done her in afore now if I'd been him.'

'Oh, he's seen to it that he's had his compensations.'

'Who's to blame him? Not me. Anyway, things will be quiet now for a bit, I hope.'

'Quiet for a bit, you say. Wait till it gets round about the youngsters. My God! If it had happened only one day after the wedding they would have been in the clear. I wonder how her people will take it? Now, there's a pair for you. Have you ever seen a fellow like her father? He stands there, doesn't say a word, but just looks. Ah well, let's get on; there's wood to chop. We'd better get a stock in afore the snow comes, because I can smell it; it's in the air.'

★ ★ ★

Nurse Pringle had just left the room after saying, No, no; she wasn't surprised at what had happened last night. It took a lot to surprise her. And almost before the door had closed, Don said to Annette, 'She's a cool customer.'

'She has to be.'

'Are you all right? You look white.'

'Of course I'm all right. Don't you worry about me, please.'

'Who else have I to worry about?' He stroked the hand he was holding and, looking at it, he said, 'Strange, but that scene last night, it's just as if I'd had a nightmare, that it wasn't real. But then, it's not even like a nightmare, because I've had a good night's sleep. I should be feeling terribly sorry for her, but I can't; I'm just glad that I won't see her face coming in that door. It's dreadful, isn't it?' He looked up into Annette's face. 'It's unnatural in a way. Yet nothing about our association has been natural.' He let his head fall back on to the pillow, saying, 'Strange but it's the first morning I can remember that I haven't had any pain. I feel as if—' he smiled wryly, before adding, 'I could get up and walk.'

'That's good. That's a good sign.'

'How long do you think they'll keep her there?'

'Oh, I don't know. Dad will be going today. He'll find out more. I should think it will be some long time; she needs treatment.'

Oh yes, Annette thought, she hoped it would be

135

some long time. Enough time to let her baby be born and for her to be strong enough to insist that she take Don to their own home, because she knew that the case put forward both by Daniel and Joe that it was necessary for Don to stay here so that they would be on hand to help, was only part of their strategy; she knew it was also because they didn't want to lose touch with him. As long as he was here the family, as it were, was still together.

She felt knowledgeable about things and people now. Four months ago such thoughts would never have entered her head. Yet from the moment she woke up after the accident she had felt so much older, as if it had made her into a mature woman. But then, hadn't she been made into a woman months before that, as Don had yelled at his mother; a whole year before that? She recalled the time they had first come together. It was the day on which they had escaped her mother's vigilance, and had supposedly gone to the pictures. If only her mother had known that day what had happened, she too would have gone insane.

Oh dear me! She still had that journey before her and that inevitable scene.

She said now to Don, 'Look, dear, you know what I've got to do this morning.'

He screwed up his face for a moment, then said dolefully, 'Oh, yes, yes. It isn't fair that you've got to stand this on your own. I should be there. I should. I should...'

'Now don't get yourself agitated. If I know anything it'll be over before it's hardly begun. That'll be that. And it's not going to worry me.'

'You're sure? Because, after all, they're...'

'Don't say it: my parents. We've discussed this,

136

haven't we?' She bent over him and kissed him; then smiling down into his face, she said, 'Do you remember the day that I told you what I thought of my parents and you nearly choked yourself laughing? And I felt dreadful at saying the things I did. But the tears were running down your face, remember? And then you told me about your mother. I'd always known that she smothered you, more than mothered you, but at the time you made it sound so funny, and we clung to each other laughing. Remember?'

'Yes, yes.' He traced his fingers now around her face, and there was a break in his voice as he asked, 'Why had this to happen to us?'

She did not immediately answer him; but then she said, 'I've asked that every day for weeks.'

The muscles of his face tightening now, he asked the dreaded question: 'And you have told yourself, "He'll never be able to love me again".'

'No, no'—her voice was firm as she pulled herself upright—'because you do love me and I you ... even without that.'

'Oh, Annette'—again he put his hand out to her—'don't delude yourself. It's all part of the process.'

'Well, we've had a good share of the process, haven't we?' There was a break in her voice now. 'Just think of that. I'm carrying the results of the process, aren't I?' She patted her stomach and, forcing back the tears, she brought laughter into her voice as she said, 'And tonight I'm getting into that bed with you, so move over, Don Coulson.' Then giving his face a light slap, she turned swiftly away, saying, 'I'm going to get ready.'

Half an hour later she got into the car. It would

137

be less than a five-minute run to her old home, and she knew exactly where she'd find her parents when she reached there at about ten o'clock. Her father would be in his study, going over the previous day's reports from their shops: four grocery and three greengrocery establishments, as well as an antique shop in the upper quarter of the town, and a junk shop near the market. At half-past ten he would leave the house and do spot checks on the establishments, varying his time of arrival so as to catch out someone, as he saw it, not doing his duty. It was said that he had the quickest turnover of staff in the town: misdemeanours, however small, were not tolerated under his management.

Her mother would have already been in the kitchen and given Polly orders for the meals of the day. She would have examined the larder and the refrigerator. She would have checked the stores in the cupboard. And it being Thursday, and with the Catholic Ladies' Guild meeting being held in the afternoon in the drawing-room, she would likely have given Janie and Sarah their weekly admonishment as to their duties—she still insisted on their wearing frilly caps and aprons after lunch. She had often wondered how Janie had reigned so long in the house, because she hated wearing them. She had watched her snap one from her head and throw it on the kitchen floor, then pick it up and, laughing, say, 'You won't split, will you, miss, will you?' And she could hear Polly saying, 'She won't split, else she won't get a jam tart at eleven.' There had been no eating between meals in her home.

It was Sarah who opened the door to her. 'Oh,

hello, miss,' she said. 'But isn't it cold? Freeze the drops in your nose, this would. How are you?'

'I'm fine, Sarah. How are you?'

'Oh, you know, miss; you know me, waiting for that rich man to come along and sweep me off my feet.'

It was her usual remark, and Annette said, 'Well, if I meet him on the road back, I'll tell him to hurry up.' This was their usual banter. Sarah, Polly and Janie and their predecessors were the only light relief she had found in this house.

'Where's Mother?'

'Oh, in her rest-room, miss; you know.'

'Polly all right ... and Janie?'

'Yes, miss.' Sarah's voice was subdued now. 'Nice if you could pop in afore you go.'

'I'll try, but I doubt it will be this morning.'

'Oh.' Sarah's mouth was pursed ... which said a lot for her understanding of the situation in the house.

For such an imposing house it lacked a hall; in its place was a very broad and long corridor, at the end of which was a similar but shorter one. She turned into it and knocked on the first door. It was several seconds before a voice called, 'Come in.'

She entered the room that had always appeared to her to be partly a chapel, for in one corner stood a small altar, in the centre of which was a crucifix flanked on one side by the figure of Mary and on the other by the figure of Joseph, and to the right of it, attached to the wall, a glass holy water font. In front of the altar was a padded knee-stool from which she knew her mother had just risen.

'Hello, dear.'

'Hello, Mother.'

139

You're visiting early.'

'Yes, yes, I suppose I am.'

'How is Don?'

'Much the same ... Mother?'

'Yes, my dear?'

'I have something to tell you. Sit down.'

Mrs Allison stared at her daughter. She wasn't used to being told to sit down, at least not by this child of hers. She sat down, but noted that her daughter didn't. And now she said, 'Well, I'm sitting down, so what have you to tell me?'

'Mother-in-law was taken to the County asylum last night.'

'*What!*' Mrs Allison half rose from the chair, then subsided again, to sit breathing heavily for a while before saying, 'Well, it's really not surprising, Winifred has always been very highly strung. But what brought this about? Some kind of fracas?'

'Yes, you could say that.'

Her mother stared at her and her mouth opened and closed twice before she said, 'Concerning you?'

'Definitely concerning me ... You see, Mother, I'm pregnant. I'm going to have a baby. I'm surprised you haven't noticed. But then, of course, I've been wearing loose dresses and coats. And you've very rarely looked at me, have you, not properly?'

She watched her mother's hand move slowly across the lower part of her face; she saw the thumb press into one cheek and the fingers into the other, forcing colour into the pale skin around them.

'Oh, my God!' she cried, the words muffled by the palm of her hand. 'I ... I knew there was

140

something ... something that I should have seen, but not this. Oh! ... Oh! your father.' She now took her hand from her face and placed it on the top of her head as if pressing herself down into the seat and muttered, 'Dear God.'

For her mother to mention God's name twice, apart from in a prayer, was an indication of how the news was affecting her. Yet she had not raised her voice. And that was the difference between the two mothers: her mother-in-law had screamed her anger, whereas her own mother was able to contain herself. Appearances must be kept up.

Annette watched her mother press a bell on the wall, while she continued to stare at her daughter. She said nothing until the door opened and Sarah appeared; and she listened with amazement at her mother's composure, as in a perfectly calm voice she said, 'Ask Mr Allison if he can spare a moment; I would like to speak to him.'

'Yes, ma'am.'

When the door had closed the shock returned to Mrs Allison's voice as she said, 'This will have a terrible effect on your father and his standing in the church. Oh!' She closed her eyes for a moment. 'Do you realise what you have done, girl? You have ruined us. We won't be able to lift our heads up again. And that wedding! All those people at that wedding, and you in white ... purity. Oh!' She jerked herself up out of the chair and began to pace the room.

It was just as Annette was about to defend herself that the door opened and her father appeared. As usual, his presence seemed to fill the room and make it appear smaller: his height and breadth, and his sheer bulk ... the stiff, quiet bulk

141

of him which she could never recall being disturbed in any way. 'Good morning, Annette,' he said. His tone was level.

'Good morning, Father.'

'You're early. Is everything...?'

That his wife dared to cut him off in the middle of a sentence by saying, 'James, this is no time for niceties; she has something to tell you,' caused him to breathe deeply before he turned his enquiring gaze from his wife to his daughter, at whom he now stared for a full minute without speaking, and then he said simply, 'Yes?'

Her stomach had trembled all the way here; she had felt sick with it. But the fear was not new; she had always been afraid of this man. He was her father; yet, unlike other fathers, he had never put his arms about her. He had never held her head against that broad chest. When he had kissed her, it was on the brow, and that was rarely. More than once since she had conceived the child within her she had wondered how her own conception had come about: what had stirred his bulk to create, and how had her prim, composed mother responded? Had they both later been ashamed of the act? Yes, yes, she could imagine that. And ever since they must have prayed to expunge it, for she had never seen them kiss. She had never even seen them hold hands. They slept in separate beds. As far back as she could remember they had always had separate beds. Her mother, she knew, undressed in the dressing-room and under her nightie, and had taught her to do the same. Her mind now gave a jump back to the previous night, when she had stood naked with Don's hand on her stomach. Would that sight have broken down her

142

father's façade?

'I'm going to have a baby, Father.'

No muscle of his face moved, except that his eyelids seemed to droop slightly.

'You've heard what she said, James? You've heard what she said?' Her mother was clutching the front of her woollen dress with both hands as if she was suddenly very cold. 'You see, it must have happened...'

'Quiet!' The word itself was said quietly, but it was a command. 'You say you are going to have a child?'

'Yes, Father.'

'Conceived out of wedlock?'

'You could say so, Father.'

'I could say so? But what have *you* to say? You who were brought up in strict piety—have defiled yourself.'

'We'll have to move. I couldn't bear it,' her mother put in.

He cast a glance at his wife, but his attention was brought back swiftly to Annette for she was exclaiming, 'Oh yes, follow the Tolletts. They too couldn't stand the shame of Maria having a baby. She was another one who had been brought up in strict piety. You're hypocrites, both of you.' Now she did see a change in her father's face: she watched the purple hue take over and she saw that for a moment he was unable to speak, staggered apparently by the accusation and audacity of this child, as he thought her—at least, he had until a moment ago—for she went on, 'I've thought it for a long time and I'll say it now: it's all show; stained-glass window in the church; offering to pay for the new organ, but begrudging your shop staff

143

a shilling or so rise. It's all show. And look at you.' She flung her hand from one to the other. 'Have you ever been happy together? I was glad to be at school, just to get away from this house.'

Her father was now speaking through tight lips: 'Do you know what you have done, girl?' His voice was thin and sounded deadly, with a deep finality about it. 'You have severed yourself from me.'

Annette stood staring, her eyelids blinking, her throat full. She had thought she could get through this meeting without breaking down, but now the tears rained down her cheeks and she cried, 'My mother-in-law was taken to the asylum last night, not only because she came upon me standing naked before my husband, but also because, like you both, she has religious mania, and is an unnatural parent. And you needn't worry about severing me from the family. That certainly works both ways.'

If she had turned into the devil incarnate they could not have looked on her with more horror and distaste, and it appeared to Annette at this moment that her father was actually swelling, his whole appearance so frightening she felt she must get out of the house at once.

She turned and pushed her way from the room and along the corridor to where Sarah was waiting near the front door. And on the sight of her, Sarah exclaimed, 'Oh, miss. Oh! Oh, miss. Don't take on. It'll be all right. You just stick to your guns. We're all for you.'

Annette could say nothing in reply. She ran blindly across the drive to the car, but once she had seated herself, she would not allow herself to set off until her spasm of crying had stopped when,

144

having dried her eyes and face, she turned the car about and drove away from the home of her childhood, knowing that whether they stayed or went, her parents would never recognise her again.

CHAPTER FIVE

It was nearing the end of March. The sun was bright and the month had ceased to keep to pattern, for there was no high wind today. It was Saturday and visiting day at the County Mental Hospital. Daniel, Flo, and Harvey were standing in the hallway amid a gentle toing and froing of patients and visitors. The grounds outside were already dotted with people walking between the flower beds, and as Daniel glanced out through the open door, he said, in an undertone, 'If the inside was half as attractive as the outside of this place it would do.'

'Why do you think we have to wait?' asked Flo.

'Your guess is as good as mine and you know it, Flo: somebody's just mentioned my name to her and she's had a screaming fit.'

'She seemed much improved when we were last here.'

Daniel looked at Harvey. 'Yes,' he said; 'no offence meant, but she could even tolerate you, whereas I'm still the thorn in her flesh and always will be apparently. So it would seem there's not much chance of her improving unless I could be got rid of in some way.'

'Don't talk like that, Daniel,' Flo said sharply. 'Anyway, the impression I got is that they are very good to the patients.'

'You've only been here twice, Flo, so we have different opinions on that. From what I've seen, if you're not quite round the bend when you come in you'll certainly have travelled the distance before you're ready to go out; I'm sure they must imbibe one another's disorders. I hate the place.' Daniel turned quickly towards an approaching nurse who, smiling broadly, said to him, 'Matron would like to have a word with you, Mr Coulson.' She passed her smile over Harvey and Flo, then turned away; and Daniel followed her down a bare stone corridor and into an office where, behind a desk, sat a comparatively young woman and, to her side, a middle-aged man.

The man stood up and held out his hand to Daniel, saying, 'How are you, Mr Coulson?' to which Daniel replied, 'Quite well, doctor, thank you,' then inclined his head towards the matron.

When seated, he waited for one or the other of them to speak. And it was the doctor who said, 'Naturally you'll be wanting to know how your wife is faring. Over the last two or three weeks ... it is three weeks since you were here?' He now turned his head to the matron. 'That so, matron?' And, looking down on a ledger, matron said, 'Yes; yes, it is three weeks since Mr Coulson's last visit.'

Thinking they must be blaming him for his neglect, Daniel now put in, 'I've been under the weather myself; sort of 'flu.'

'Oh. Oh—' the doctor wagged his finger at him now—'we are not criticising you for your absence, don't believe that for a moment, but matron felt that you should be put in the picture as to your wife's progress and what might impede it...'

146

As he paused Daniel put in, 'And what is that?'

'Well'—it was the matron who now took up the conversation—'I'm afraid Mr Coulson, it is yourself; you know what happened the last time she saw you. Well now, it's any mention of your name or that of your son that puts her ... well, puts her back, we'll say. The only persons she seems to appreciate a visit from are her sister and her friend.' And the doctor, nodding in agreement, said, 'It's strange, isn't it? We had thought that in her condition she would be against all men, but it seems no, for the twice he has been here she has greeted him quite normally, and there has been no reaction. Otherwise she has progressed in that she no longer goes into tantrums; in fact, she has responded to treatment amazingly well. So, what we think Mr Coulson, is that it would be better if she doesn't see you for a while but that her sister could, if possible, visit her more frequently. Up till your last visit we had hopes that she would soon be well enough to go home, at least for a day or even a week-end. That won't be possible, I'm afraid. We are sorry about this.'

'Oh, you needn't be sorry; I quite understand. But tell me: if her attitude towards me and the mention of her family upsets her like this, how long do you imagine that it will go on?'

'Oh, that is hard to say in these cases,' the doctor answered. 'It's a time-taking business. We are hoping that she will respond to the electric treatment in that it will eventually tone down, if not obliterate, her animosity towards you.'

Daniel made no comment, but his thoughts were: only death would obliterate her hate of him. He rose to his feet now, saying, 'It will be better if I

147

don't come at all then?'

'For the time being.' The doctor moved towards him. 'But as I said, if her sister could come more frequently it might be helpful.'

'She lives in London. It would be impossible for her to come up every week.'

'Well, as often as she possibly can would be appreciated.'

'I'll ask her. Thank you.' And he nodded to one then the other and went out.

In the hall, Flo was standing at the window watching Harvey talking to a patient. She turned at Daniel's approach, saying, 'Isn't it sad? She's been talking to him, that woman out there, quite normally, as normal as you or I, more so I should say; then she asked him if he would like to go out and see the garden.'

Daniel's mind was not at the moment sensitive to such feelings, and he said abruptly, 'They don't want me to visit her again, but they're asking you to come more often. How about it?'

Flo paused for a moment; then shrugging her shoulders, she said, 'Yes, it's all right. We may not be able to manage it every week, but we'll try. Anything to help her. May I go to see her now?'

'Yes. Yes, I suppose so.'

She was turning away when she stopped and said, 'You shouldn't be surprised at her not wanting to see you, Daniel.'

'No, I shouldn't. I don't know why I come.'

'Because you feel it's your duty, I suppose.'

'Yes, I suppose so. But now, apparently, I'm relieved of it and the burden's been passed to you.'

'Oh, don't look at it that way. Anyway, we'll talk about it later.'

148

When she was gone he stared through the window, to see Harvey was now strolling with the woman; then presently he went out and joined them.

'Oh, there you are.' Harvey did not go on to ask why he wasn't visiting Winifred, but said, 'This is Mrs Deebar.'

The lady in question, who was in her early sixties, leaned forward towards Harvey and, smiling broadly, she said, 'You haven't got it right. It's De ... bar. It's not like the De in Debrett.'

'Oh, I'm sorry.' Harvey now turned to Daniel, saying, 'Mrs Debar is a novelist. She's had a book published called—' He paused and looked at the woman, and she, still smiling a very sweet smile, said, 'Manners and Decorum in The Victorian Era.'

Daniel made the required motion with his head now, saying, 'That sounds very interesting,' to which the lady replied, 'Well, one tries one's best. I've had a lot of help from Mr Disraeli.'

Daniel and Harvey exchanged glances. They said nothing, but continued to look at the lady. And she, turning to and giving all her attention to Harvey, said, 'Thank you for your company. It isn't often one has the opportunity to meet and converse with the uncivilised, but it is nevertheless very enlightening, even instructive. Now, if you'll excuse me, I'm expecting Mr Macmillan to tea. Good day, gentlemen.'

They each muttered something that was inaudible, then watched her walking, in fact, tripping between the flower beds and across the drive towards the main door. Not until she had disappeared did they look at one another; and then

149

it was Harvey whose voice held a chuckle as he muttered, 'I ... I should have guessed, I suppose. But she was talking as sanely as you or I.'

'God help her!'

'Oh, I don't think you need to be sorry for her. If it could be analysed I think she's happier in her world than we are in ours. You only had to look at her face; it was quite serene. And—' his voice taking on a sad note now he said, 'She must have been quite beautiful in her day. But that last bit'—he chuckled—' "uncivilised". Well, it's only what a great many still think, I suppose.'

As they both turned to go back inside, Harvey asked, 'What has happened?'

'Something that mightn't please you. Apparently the onus is going to be on Flo. They've worked it out that the sight of me only makes matters worse, and that the only one they think it advisable for her to see is Flo.'

'Well, I can see no obstacle to that. It's all right with me. I certainly don't mind coming; in fact, I'm glad to get away from London.'

'But you don't know how long it's going to last.'

'Well, we'll just have to wait and see, won't we? But if that's all you've got to worry about, Daniel, you can stop now. As you know, Flo and Winifred never got on, but since this happened, Flo has ... well, become sorry for her.'

'Most people have.'

'Yes, yes, I suppose so. It's like an assault case: the victim is often forgotten; the main objective is to get the perpetrator off. Anyway, don't worry about us; you have plenty of that to do back in the house. It's just on Annette's time, isn't it?'

'Well, no; she's a bit longer to go yet. And that's

150

another thing: how will she take the news of a grandson or daughter? I've little hope that it will revive some sort of interest in her. I can't see anything stirring that apathy of hers now, except the sight of me.'

But there Daniel was wrong. Winifred was sitting in the large room, Flo by her side. There were other people, seemingly family groups all about; some were talking together, others were just sitting still staring at the patient while the patient looked into space. In one group two small girls were laughing. It was a strange sound because it was ordinary laughter.

Flo, looking at her sister, felt pity rising from the depths of her. She had never liked Winnie: they had nothing in common, but she wouldn't have wished the devil in hell to find himself in a situation like this ... in a place like this. Winnie, she knew, had always been good to herself, had her fill, food-wise and comfort-wise, but had remained empty. She had needed love, oh yes, she had needed love, and to love. But she had centred this on the wrong one.

She now put her hand on Winifred's and said, 'Don sends his love.'

'Who?'

There was no insanity in the eyes that looked into hers; at least, the look in them was not that which she would have expected in the eyes of anyone insane. Whatever this new attitude was she felt it didn't stem from madness. And her voice was slightly sharp as she said, 'Now Winnie, don't act like that! Don is your son and you love...'

'I have no son.'

'You have three sons.'

151

'Huh! Three sons you say? Would I be mother to an idiot, a bastard, and a cripple?'

Inwardly Flo felt herself shrinking away from the hate showing on her sister's face as she hissed out the truth, for indeed, she was mother to an idiot, a bastard and a cripple. But put like that it sounded horrifying. She stared at Winifred now realising that her sister wasn't mad in that sense, she was just burned up with hate. Hate was a terrible emotion, a consuming fire that in Winifred's case could never be douched. That would mean she would remain here for ... Oh! She actually shook her head at the thought of her sister having to spend the rest of her life in this place, a place which gave her the creeps even to visit.

Thinking as she did, she was afterwards to ask herself what made her make such a remark, as 'Don't talk like that, Winnie; you could have so much to look forward to. There's a child coming; you will be a grandmother,' for her hand was thrust away so quickly that it hit the edge of the chair and she had to hold her wrist tightly to stop herself from crying out. And now she was gaping at Winifred, whose body was shaking as if with an ague, and through her trembling lips she was hissing: 'It's you who should be in here, daring to suggest I will be a grandmother to a child with a whore for its mother and fathered by the other bastard. My son was pure, do you hear? My son was pure...'

Flo was aware of the approach of a nurse who said nothing, but with a slight motion of her hand conveyed to Flo to take her leave; which she did hurriedly. Yet she was not quick enough to escape Winifred's voice yelling obscenities after her, and causing an uproar in the room.

Both Harvey and Daniel came towards her as she entered the hallway.

'What is it? You're as white as a sheet.' She looked at Daniel for a moment then, lowering her head she said, 'I was a fool. I brought up things I shouldn't. I thought to create ... to ... Oh dear!'

Harvey said nothing but, putting an arm around her shoulder, led her outside.

In the car, Daniel said bitterly, 'It will be better if nobody comes; let her stew in her own juice.'

'Oh, Daniel, don't be like that. One could go insane just being in that place and among those people.'

'Come; don't upset yourself; don't you cry.'

Harvey pulled her tightly to him. 'And don't be sorry for those people. Listen, I'll tell you what happened to me and Daniel.' And he went on to tell her about Mrs Debar.

But he failed to make her laugh, or even smile. Instead, she said, 'God help her. God help them all.'

★   ★   ★

They had just finished their evening meal. Throughout, the conversation at the table had been stilted; and now Daniel, looking at Annette, said, 'You all right, hinny? You look a bit peaky.'

'Yes, yes, I'm fine, Dad.'

'She's tired.' This came from Joe. 'She's been on her feet all day. Why do nurses insist on the week-end for their days off? Of course, yes, don't say it.' He closed his eyes and flapped his hand at them. 'That was a silly thing to say because we are

153

all on hand at the week-end.' And poking his head forward across the table towards Annette he said, 'We can manage you know, and when I say we I'm including Stephen, if you'll leave us alone.'

She smiled now as she said, 'I think you need supervision, both of you.'

Flo now said, 'It's amazing how that boy has changed, isn't it, seemingly in all ways.' She was looking at Daniel and she emphasised, 'Well, it is. We are not with him all the time so we notice it, don't we, Harvey?'

'Well, yes; we can see it: he's no longer the child, or shall I say childish.'

'You're right there.' Joe was nodding at him. 'The amazing thing to me is he's had a dry bed for weeks now. You could say it was from shortly after'—he paused, not quite sure of his choice of words which would have been, 'since Mam left,' so he substituted, 'since Don had to be seen to.'

'He loves being with Don,' Annette put in, 'and the nurse is wonderful with him. She calls him the superintendent. He glows at that. And Don likes him to be there. Imagine, a few weeks ago we couldn't have left them for this length of time. What is it?' She turned and looked at the clock. 'Over half an hour, which tells me I must return to duty.' But in a low voice, she added, 'But it's no duty.'

'Duty or no duty, you sit where you are and have a natter. I'm going along now, so do as you're told.' Joe stabbed his finger at her and repeated, 'Do as you're told for once, stay put.' Then turning to Flo, he said, 'And you see she does, woman.' Then his laughter joined Harvey's as Harvey cried, 'Be careful, you big fellow, I'm the
154

only one who has the right to call her woman, me being uncivilised.'

Joe left the room amid laughter that had its basis in an attempt to bring normality into the atmosphere, and as he entered the sick-room he was greeted with more laughter, the hiccupping kind, from Stephen, who cried at him, 'I've been tellin' Don about that time, you remember, Joe? when Mrs Osborne came. You remember? And I told her she could drink out of the saucer and blow on her tea if she liked.'

He was laughing again, and Don too was laughing, and Joe said, 'Oh, yes, I remember that day. You got your backside twanked, didn't you?'

As he spoke he was seeing Stephen not as he normally thought of him, as the lad or the boy, but as Harvey saw him now. He did indeed seem to have aged a little. And it was true, he hadn't wet his bed. And, now he thought of it, he hadn't had a crying fit for months, either. And then he could help lift Don as well as he himself or his dad did, and help to change him too, and with gentleness.

Looking at the tray on the side table, Joe remarked, 'You didn't get him to eat his dinner though, did you, clever clogs?'

'I wasn't hungry.' Don now put his hand out towards Stephen, saying, 'You know that game we used to play?'

'Tiddleywinks, Don?'

'No, no; the one you call bumps, you know with the checkers. It's up in your room. Do you think you could get it, because I would like a game?'

'Oh, yes, yes, Don. I'll go now. I'll go now.' And he was about to rush from the room when he turned and looked at Joe and said, 'All right?'

155

'Yes; yes, all right. Go ahead and get it.'

Once they were alone together Don, with the aid of his elbows, edged himself on to the pillows, saying, 'I ... I want to have a word with you before Annette comes in. We never seem to be alone, do we? I've been wanting to ... well say something to you for some time now, Joe. Sit down and listen, will you?'

Joe drew the chair up close to the bedhead and, looking tenderly down on the white face, he said, 'Fire ahead.'

'It's ... it's about Annette.'

'What about her? She's all right, she's doing fine. You won't have all that long to go before you see your ...'

Don's hand came on to his now and pressed it as he said, 'You've put your finger on it, I won't have that long to go.'

'Oh, now, now!' Joe pulled his hand roughly away. 'Stop that nonsense. Don't take me up wrong. You've been doing fine since you came home.'

Don now turned his head away and said slowly, 'Joe, please. If ... if I can't speak the truth to you, who can I speak it to? You know as well as I do time's running out.' He now tapped the counterpane in the direction of his stomach, before saying, 'They were thinking of taking me in again with that. But if they do, it'll be a quick end, so they suspect. That's why they're putting it off. But I don't suspect; I know. And my breathing's getting ... worse. Now, now!' He was looking at Joe again. 'Please, Joe. She'll likely be back at ... any minute, and it's about her I want to speak. And listen to me, don't say a word until I'm

156

finished. No matter what you think, don't ... don't say a word. And it's just this. By rights you should have married Annette ... Please!' His fingers went into a fist and when Joe was about to emphatically check his words, Don put in, 'If Dad hadn't manoeuvred and pushed me forward just because ... because he thought it was best, I know that, to get me out of ... Mam's clutches, she would have continued to admire you. She always did, you know ... from when she was a schoolgirl. But even when ... when she turned to me, I was afraid at first that it was only a flash in the pan and then there would be you again. I loved you, Joe, but I loved her too. So I—' He paused for breath, gasped for a moment, then almost in a rush he said, 'I deliberately made sure she would be mine. I was the one who made the first ... move, not her. And ... and once done, it went on. Then that didn't seem enough. I could have continued like that with no results, but ... but I made up my mind there *would* be a result; at least, I hoped there would and that would clinch it. And it did. But then I was scared, we were both scared, very scared. That's why I insisted on the wedding being brought forward ... "The best laid schemes o' mice an' men gang aft a-gley". God, there's never been a truer saying...'

'No more. No more. I know all about it.'

'You do?'

'Yes, yes, I do: Dad being supposedly with you all the time when you went out, but him going off too, leaving you two alone, and you went straight to the cottage.'

'How did you know that?'

'Intuition, partly, but I happened to go to the

157

cottage one day with the plans. You remember Annette wanted the kitchen extended, and before I turned up the farm track I happened to see the car outside. And that night both you and Dad talked as if you had been together all the time. So, what are you worrying about? Tell me something I don't know.'

'Yes, yes, I will. When ... when I'm gone I ... I want you to look after Annette and the child, to do what you've always wanted to do: marry her.'

Joe got slowly to his feet, saying now, his voice firm, 'You're alive, Don. You're going to be alive for a long time yet. What you haven't taken into account is that Annette looks upon me as a brother, a big brother. She loves you and always will.'

'Sit down, Joe, *please*. This business of ... of love and death, I've given them a lot of thought of late. Yes, Annette loved me during that year we were together. Funny, but when I went for Mam that time I called it "The Year of The Virgins"; and yes, we were both virgins. But love can still be love even if it changes. Annette still ... still loves me but in a ... a different way. She is my nurse, my companion, and yes, she even plays the mother, strangely while waiting to be a mother herself. And because she ... she is waiting for that I think she is somehow apart. I think if the accident hadn't happened I would have learned to understand that ... because she was carrying the child she had in a way grown apart, somehow self-reliant, taken up with what she is nourishing. All ... all women must feel that. And you know, lying here thinking, I don't believe that love can ever be the same once a woman has a child ... because ... because she's

158

housed it in her body and in some way the man has lost a piece of her. Strange thing.' He smiled wanly now. 'But along those lines I can even understand Mam, although, oh God! I don't want to see her again, ever, Joe.' He turned and groped for Joe's hand. 'That might s... sound awful of me, but I dread the thought that she'll ever come back here.'

'I don't think you need worry very much about that. By what Dad's said and by what Flo confirmed, the very thought of facing your Dad again would indeed send her mad.'

'Well, with treatment, she will likely get over it some time. But I hope I die before that time comes.'

'You're not going to die. Will you stop it?'

'No, I won't stop it, Joe, because, let me tell you, I'm ... I'm not afraid of dying. I was some months ago, but not any more. It's those who are so healthy and strong and ... and all people like you who are afraid of dying. But when you lose your body and you've only got your mind left it puts things in perspective. The only thing ... I want to live for is to see my child born. And then I'll be quite glad to go, because'—his voice ended on a break—'I'm in pain, Joe, deep pain. The pills don't erase it entirely. The injections do, but I don't want too many of those.'

Joe was unable to speak and it was with relief that he greeted Stephen when the door burst open to admit the young fellow who was carrying a narrow wooden box and saying, 'I had a job to find it. It was on top of the cupboard. You remember, Maggie put it up there because it made so much rattle when we played it.'

'That wasn't why she put it up there,' said Joe,

159

'it was because you cheated.'

'I didn't, Joe. Did I, Don?'

'No, you didn't Stephen, you never cheated.'

'You were just jokin', Joe, weren't you?'

'Yes, big boy, I was just joking.'

Joe ruffled the head that was on a level with his own and, in a quieter voice, he said, 'I don't think I would play the game with Don tonight; he's a bit tired.'

'You tired, Don?'

'Yes, I am a little, Stephen. We'll have a game tomorrow. Ah'—he looked towards the door—'here's the boss, and she wouldn't let us play on the clean counterpane, would she?'

'What's this about playing on the clean counterpane?'

'I ... I brought the checkers game.'

'Oh, that rattly thing.'

'There you are.' Joe nodded at Stephen now. 'I bet you don't reign long with that one.'

'Ah! you.' Stephen now punched Joe in the chest, saying, 'You would get me into trouble, wouldn't you?'

'Yes, if I could, but it's so difficult to catch you out in anything these days.'

He watched the big form wriggle as a younger boy might, then say, 'Oh! Joe; you're teasin' me, aren't you? Pulling my leg, you are, aren't you?'

'I've never touched your leg. I wouldn't touch your leg with a barge-pole.'

As Stephen laughed it came to Joe that legs were a tactless topic. But Don was smiling and saying, 'Go on, you two, get out. I never seem to get a minute alone with my wife; there's always one or the other of you here. All right. All right.' He

160

wagged his finger towards Stephen. 'I'll play you a game tomorrow.'

'Come on, big boy.' Joe marshalled Stephen from the room, and Annette, taking the chair that Joe had vacated, said to Don, 'Don't you think there's a change in Stephen; I mean, for the better?'

'Yes. Yes, I do. I thought I was imagining it, but since you mention it, yes.' He looked up at her now and paused a moment before asking her: 'How are you feeling, really? Tell me; don't just say, all right.'

'To tell the truth, darling, I don't know exactly how I'm feeling, never ever having had the privilege of being in this condition before.' She tweaked his nose now. 'I suppose it's natural to feel ... well ...' She screwed up her face now. 'Sometimes I think that he or she could come tomorrow; but I've got several weeks to go yet.'

'Do you feel ill? I mean, just a...'

'No, I don't feel ill. And stop worrying. Here, let me put your pillows straight.'

As she rose from the chair she asked herself, 'Do I feel ill?' And the answer she was given was, 'Yes, in a way more like feeling odd; so odd I should go and see the doctor on Monday.'

CHAPTER SIX

It was the last week in March 1961 and very cold. Some were saying they could smell the snow, while others countered with, Don't be ridiculous; all that's happening is we've had two nights of keen

161

frosts.

It was after seven o'clock and the house had dropped into its evening quiet when the front door bell rang. Maggie happened to be passing through the hall and, on opening the door, said, 'Oh, good evening, Father.'

'Good evening, Maggie. And what a snifter! I shouldn't be surprised if we have snow; I shouldn't at all.'

'Oh, the times I've heard that today. We're touching April, the daffodils are out. Anyway, are you better, Father? I hear you've had a nasty time of it.'

Maggie was helping him off with his coat now as he said, 'I'm the fellow who created the saying, "Swinging the lead". They say it was originally a timing device; don't you believe it. I've had them all run off their feet for the past two weeks or more and I've enjoyed every minute of it.' He coughed now, a deep rumbling cough, and Maggie nodded at him, saying, 'Yes, yes, I can believe that, Father. At the sound of that chest I can believe it.' She laughed now as she took his coat and placed it over the back of a chair. 'What I can believe, too, is that you're a very queer individual, Father.'

'I am that, Maggie, I am that. And anybody who says different I'll call him a liar. There's nobody queerer than me. That's another saying that sprang with me birth: "The Queer Fella". Where's everybody?'

'Oh, scattered around, Father.'

'Well, I'll find them, I suppose.' And he was on his way when he swung round, saying, 'Got a minute, Maggie?' And when she turned enquiringly and walked towards him, he said,

162

'Lent's nearly over and we're supposed either to give up something that's dear to our hearts or do something that could be dear to our hearts. And you know, Maggie, there's one thing I've always craved to do and that's make a convert. I've never knowingly made a convert, not in my whole career. Now wouldn't you like to please an old man and step over the wall?'

She pushed him as she gurgled with laughter, saying, 'Go on with you, Father. If anybody could have got me into your tribe it would have been you; but even you and all the tea in China wouldn't make me take that step.'

'You're a hard woman, Maggie. I've always known that you're a hard woman.' His smile denied his words. Then leaning towards her and lowering his voice, he said, 'When you produce the bottle, bring some hot water and sugar with it, eh?'

She was chuckling too as she said, 'Hot water and sugar it is, you queer fella. Hot water and sugar it is.'

As he turned, laughing, from Maggie, he saw Annette coming along the corridor and she greeted him with, 'Hello, Father. You're up?'

'Well, if I'm not, I must be walking in me sleep with all me clothes on. How are you, my dear?' He put his hand on her shoulder. 'The last I heard, you were ordered to bed for a time.'

'Yes, but I'm fine now.'

'Sure?'

'Nearly sure.'

'Like that is it?'

'Like that, Father.'

'Strain telling?'

'No, not really; it's just that ... well'—she

163

smiled now—'I'm not used to this business, you know.' She put her hand on her high abdomen, and he, serious now, said, 'No, no, you're not, child; but I'd go careful, it's a critical time. Obey the doctor's orders. I had a word with him the other day when he was trying to find out what was wrong with me, and he couldn't, so he said, "Get up on your pins because I'm not coming in any more." He then told me you were tired. And it's no wonder, so—' his voice serious again, his hand on her head, he said, 'Go careful; he would like to see his child. You know that, don't you?' He did not add, 'That's what he's hanging on for.' But she answered, 'Yes, yes, I know that, Father.'

'And you know there's a possibility he will have to go into hospital again?'

'Yes, yes, I know that also, Father.'

'Ah, well, we all know where we stand, don't we?' And his voice rising, he ended, 'Where's the head of the house?'

'The last time I saw him he was making for his study.'

'Well, I'll slip along and see him, then have a word with Don.'

'He'll be pleased to see you, Father. He's missed you these last few weeks.'

'Ah, that's nice to know. It's nice to be missed. I'll tell you something, though: there's one who didn't miss me. He's had the time of his life, I understand, in that pulpit. You know who.'

'Yes, I know, Father. The church has been very warm these last few Sundays.'

His laughter rang out as he said, 'Ha! ha! That's a good one. Opened up a few more furnaces, has he? Well, let me get back on to that stand and I'll

164

cool 'em down. You take me word for it.'

'I've no doubt of that, Father.'

They went their separate ways laughing, and the priest, knocking on the study door, called, 'It's me! May I come in?'

'Oh yes, yes, come in, Father,' Daniel called, and on the priest's entering the room, he said, 'I never expected to see you; I didn't know you were up.'

'Nobody seems to expect to see me except at me funeral. I've disappointed a lot of people, I can tell you. Anyway, I'm here and I've just given Maggie orders about the hot water and the sugar. Is that all right?'

Daniel made no answer to this but said, 'Sit down. Come up to the fire.'

The priest sat down and gazed at the flickering electric logs, saying, 'They give off a good heat; a little imagination and you feel you could stick a poker into them. I'm going to treat meself to one of those some day and put it in me bedroom, because, believe me, Iceland's nothing compared with that room. That's what's given me this.' He tapped his chest. 'Now the damage is done, they're going to put in central heating. The belief that freezing cold is good for the soul and dampens the emotions is poppycock; there's more people jump into bed together in cold rooms than there's ever been counted. Anyway, how are you?'

'Oh, I'm all right, Father. But how are you? How long have you been up and about?'

'Oh, for the last three or four days. By the way, if you don't mind me saying so, I don't like the look of Annette. She looks peaky, very tired. It's natural of course to be tired at this stage of her condition,

165

but she doesn't look right to me.'

'She's been worrying about Don, as we all are.'

The door opened and Maggie came in with a tray on which stood a decanter, a jug of hot water, two glasses and a bowl of brown sugar. And the priest greeted her with, 'Ah, here's the soul's solace. Thanks, Maggie, you're one in a thousand. You're still determined not to come in?'

When Daniel looked from one to the other in enquiry, the priest, with a solemn expression, said, 'I made her an offer to be my first convert, but she refused; threw it back in my face. She doesn't know what she's missing. You know, when I was a lad I believed, at least so me mother used to tell me, if you could make one convert in your life it was as good as the key to heaven, no matter what you did after, for it could never be taken from you. I worked hard at it as a lad, because I understood that once I had the key I could rampage about as much as I liked and me heavenly future was fixed: a house with a billiard table, the lot...'

'He's a dreadful man, isn't he?' Maggie was looking at Daniel now and he said, 'The worst I've come across. Thanks.' He nodded down at the tray.

Maggie now said, 'When you get through that lot, ring for refills.' And at this both men burst out laughing.

With the room to themselves again, the priest said, 'She's a good woman, that Maggie, and you're not a good man towards her. You know that, Daniel?'

'It all depends, Father, on what you term good. Good for what? Good for whom? Good for each other? Or not good for each other? I've had a

166

lifetime, as you know, of not being good for each other.'

As Daniel poured out the whisky the priest watched him, then took the glass from his hand and sniffed it appreciatively, before taking a long drink. Then he lay back in his chair, staring ahead for a moment as he said, 'I saw her this afternoon.'

'You did?'

'Yes, I was over there, and I looked in on her.'

'And how did you find her?'

The priest sighed. Then, placing his glass on the table, he said, 'I think it would take a miracle, a large one, to bring her back to normality. And yet she talks sensibly enough, at least until'—he flapped his hand—'this house is mentioned, or any person in it. Perhaps I shouldn't have brought it up, but I did. I pointed out that her beloved son was soon to be a father and she a grandmother, and wasn't that marvellous?'

'And she went wild.'

'No, no, she didn't. she just sat there and stared at me. But I couldn't bear to see the look on her face nor watch her body go rigid, so I called a nurse and left. On my way back I was set to thinking of the things we do in the name of morality, such as persuading people to stick to a recognised code, to follow a line of duty, and I thought if I hadn't persuaded you to stay, but let you do what you wanted and leave her that first time, things mightn't have reached this state today.'

'Oh, don't trouble your head with that, Father. They would have reached this state in any case, because don't forget, she had a son who—and I'm not blaspheming when I say this, Father—I'm sure

167

she had convinced herself she had come by the Immaculate Conception, or the Virgin Birth, or whatever. It wasn't only the fact of losing her son to another woman, but the fact that he had bespoiled himself—that is a favourite word of hers—with a woman before marriage, and that this filth, as she used to term it so often, had been going on for a year, practically under her nose. That's what finished her. Of course, I've known for a long time that she couldn't stand the sight of me, but at the same time she didn't want me to leave because she wouldn't then have been able to bear the thought of being the deserted wife, nor the covert satisfaction of all her friends in the church seeing her brought low. We both know, Father, that she wasn't liked even among her own kind, because right from the beginning she played the lady, and the veneer was so thin it could be seen through. Moreover, she was one of those women who wanted to rule, whether it was a Mother's Meeting, or the Children of Mary, or the Holiday Committee for Poor Children. Oh yes, she liked to be thought the good doer of good doers.'

'Don't sound so bitter, Daniel, because, God help her, she's paying for her vanities. And in a way, she knows it, and that is the worst of her troubles: she is not mad, only deranged with hate and bitterness and failure. It takes a strong man or woman to face up to failure and come out of that battle unscathed. Well, what I want to say is this: that as things stand, and from what I gathered from the matron in our chat later, she's going to be there for a long time, because were she to be sent home as she is now, she would be a danger to herself and to everybody else.'

168

'I can't say I'm sorry Father, I'd be a hypocrite otherwise, but once she entered this house again, I'd have to leave. And definitely Annette and Don would too.' He looked to the side, saying, 'But, as you know only too well, Father, Don could go at any time soon. So it would be better for us all if she was never let out.'

The priest made no comment on Don, but hypothesised further: 'Say she did come out and you left and Annette left, what about Joe and Stephen?'

'Stephen would come with me; he's my responsibility. And Maggie would come with me, Father.'

The priest did not take his eyes off Daniel's face and said, 'And Joe?'

'Oh, Joe wouldn't stay here on his own, nor would he come with us. Joe would start a life of his own, because, somehow, he's always lived a separate existence. He looks upon me as his father and I think of him as my son, but it's a game, really. He's one alone. You know something? We found out only recently that he had been looking for his parents; at least, trying to find out who his mother was. I just happened by chance to come across an old nurse who, for years, had been at the Catholic Home we took him from. She retired last year and she was well into her seventies, and she was very forthcoming and said what a fine fellow my adopted son had turned into. I didn't realise she knew him, and I said as much. Oh, she said, he had been to see the matron some time before, but had got no joy out of her. She said she could have told him what he wanted to know, but said he hadn't asked her. In any case, she said, they were

169

supposed to keep closed mouths. But she didn't agree with this; she thought they should know.'

'And did you ask her who his mother was?'

'Yes, I did.'

'And what answer did you get?'

'The correct one. She gave me the married name and last address she knew of.'

'And have you taken it further?'

'Yes, in a way. I went to the house, but the occupants were an Asian family and they had lived there for eleven years. The previous owner, they thought, had emigrated to Australia.'

'And you haven't told him?'

'No.'

'Do you think you should?'

'I'm in two minds. He could easily go off to Australia on a wild-goose chase. What would you do, Father?'

'I'd keep me mouth shut and mind me own business, because, let me tell you, it isn't anything unusual you're talking about. And I can also tell you its only one in ten who turn out to be glad they've made the search; most come away ashamed of their findings. It's a strange thing about illegitimates, you know, they've got to have something to cling on to bigger than themselves, because society has made them have a low opinion of themselves. So, who do they pick for a father? or a mother? but mostly, who do they pick for a father? It's never a docker or a bus driver or a window cleaner or a lavatory attendant. Oh, no, no, no. They usually start with doctors, climb the ladder to surgeons; or if it's in the teaching line, then they are likely to go for one that's been to Oxford or Cambridge. It's not unknown for them to imagine they are in line with a family connected with the Crown. Oh, you can raise your eyebrows, but a priest is a receptacle for lost ideals and idols. When a nice girl with a nice job in an office and with nice adoptive parents, has the urge to find out from where she sprang, it's usually a mother she's after, and then she finds out that her mother is from a large family, and a family who don't want her. Why? Because she's been on the streets for years. I'm not giving away confession confidences here by relating that, because it happened to my sister and brother-in-law, who adopted a child and doted on her. The girl was never the same afterwards. Did she stay with her adoptive parents? No; she broke their hearts as *her* heart had been broken. But then you might say a man like Joe would look at matters differently; he could take a blow like that and survive. Don't you believe it. Men are more critical of their mothers than any woman could be, because every man, at the bottom of it, wants to feel that his mother is a good woman. A wife could be a whore but never a mother, and knowing that he was conceived on the wrong side of the blanket, he carries a feeling of shame in him for the rest of his life. I've got proof of this; I'm not just talking through me hat. So my advice to you is to let sleeping dogs lie, in Australia or in Timbuktu, or wherever. Well, now—' His tone changed and he held one hand out towards the warmth of the artificial logs, saying, 'I'm so comfortable, I don't want to move. But I must go and have a word with Don. Would you like to lead the way?'

They both got to their feet. Then the priest, after a moment's pause, during which he looked up

171

towards the ceiling then down at his highly polished black boots, said, 'About the last rites for the boy. You'll let me know, won't you, if there's a sudden change? I don't want to administer them too soon, because although in ninety-nine cases out of a hundred it brings peace, I know it does, there is a chance in his case he might just let go. And we want him to hang on, don't we? So when you think his time has come, any time of night or day, just let me know.'

'I will, Father. But I don't think you need be worried about it precipitating his going, because he knows he's due to go, and soon. As I said, he's only hanging on to see his child.'

*   *   *

Later that night Daniel stood in the kitchen facing Maggie, saying, 'What difference does it make, here or at your place.'

'All the difference in the world to me, Dan. This is still her house. To tell you the truth her presence is thick in it. And you're askin' me to go upstairs to your bed. That's insensitive of you.'

'I don't see it that way. I've just told you what the priest said: she's not likely to come back for a long time, if ever, so are we only to be together once a week? Oh! Maggie'—he put his arms about her—'I need you. I need you, in all ways. There are even times in the day, in the thick of business in the yard, I want to break off and go to the phone just to hear your voice. When I come in at night I want to come straight to the kitchen and hold you. I just don't want you for one thing alone: you represent everything to me, companion, friend,

172

lover. And yes, and lover, very much that. At night up there'—he jerked his head—'I toss and turn knowing that you're just a staircase and a corridor away from me. Look, my dear, if you won't come upstairs, will you let me come to your room?'

Standing within the circle of his arms, she bowed her head until her brow rested on his shoulder and her voice was a mutter as she exclaimed, 'You don't want me any more than I want you, Dan, and in all ways, for I, too, lie down here thinking of you up there and I long to gallop up those stairs. Yes, I do, I do. But there's something in me that won't allow it. I have scruples about it.'

He released his hold on her and stood back, and there was a suspicion of a sad smile on his face as he said, 'There was Winifred who wouldn't let me in to her room for fear my body touched hers, and there is you who won't come into *my* room for the same reason.'

'Oh, that's unfair, Dan, and you know it. You're twisting things. I'll come into your room anywhere but here.'

'Well, don't come in up here, but let me come into yours down there. Look, Maggie, this state of affairs could go on for years; I mean, her being where she is and likely to stay there. What are we going to do? Live our separate lives, as you said? Being with each other once a week? Making ourselves love then as if to order, mustn't miss an opportunity? As much as I need you, I don't need you to order. As I said, I need you in so many different ways: to sit quiet with you, to lie peacefully with you, just to know you are there.'

As they stood looking at each other in silence for

173

a moment they heard the phone ring from the hall, and Daniel said, 'Who can it be at this time of night?'

'I'll go and see.'

He pressed her aside, saying, 'No, no; I'll see to it,' then hurried into the hall, picked up the receiver and said, 'Hello.'

'Daniel, this is Flo.'

'Flo! What's wrong?'

'Nothing's wrong at this end; everything's very right. At least, I've got some news for you: Harvey and I are to be married.'

He paused a moment before saying on a laugh, 'Well, I'm not surprised at that.'

'Well, you may not be, but it's going to be quick. It's to be next Saturday and I'd like you to come down.'

'Next Saturday! Why the rush? You're not ... ?'

'No, I'm not pregnant; but he's had a wonderful offer. And it's come at the right time, a time when things aren't busy here, at least for him. It's in Canada and naturally he wants to take it.'

'Oh, yes, of course. I'm pleased to hear that, Flo. But on the other hand we'll be losing you. Oh, I'll miss you and Harvey. I've taken to that fellow, you know.'

'So have I. Apparently he's known about it for some weeks; at least, about the impending offer, but he didn't tell me in case it fell through. And Daniel...'

'Yes, Flo?'

'You understand there won't be any more weekly visits to Winnie? You'll have to do something about that.'

'I can do nothing about it. Father Ramshaw was

in earlier this evening. He had seen her today and from what I gather, even my name sends her round the bend. But don't worry on that score; I've got to thank you for what you've done over the past weeks. Anyway, I'll be down on Saturday. If not me, it'll be Joe.'

'Couldn't both of you try to come? Oh, no; I suppose that's too much to ask. I understand. I'll be glad to see one of you. How's Annette?'

'Not very bright at the moment, I'm afraid. Doctor has ordered her to bed for a week. Well, she stayed there about twenty-four hours. Between you and me I'll be surprised if she goes her time, although I hope she does. By the way, how long do you mean to remain away? Are you going to make that your permanent home?'

'Yes, as far as I know. But of course we've got to go there first and see how we are received. You understand?'

'Yes. Yes, I understand. But once they get to know Harvey they'll accept him wholeheartedly, I'm sure.'

'I wish I could be as sure. He won't go to any of the main hotels. You know that, don't you? Or any clubs. And I've always thought him wise that way, because Gerry Morley—you know, the friend we've spoken of—he was turned away from a working men's club. You wouldn't believe that, would you? And he's not a bit like Harvey, who is contained and can take it. He caused a bit of a rumpus and it just missed getting into police hands. So with regard to Canada, we'll have to wait and see, won't we?'

'Well, I wish you both all the luck in the world, you know that. And I shall miss you both. We'll all

175

miss you both, because quite candidly, Flo, you and Harvey have brought a little lightness into this house over the past months. And that was badly needed.'

'Thanks, Daniel. Well, until Saturday. You'd better come down on the Friday night, because it'll be an early do on the Saturday morning.'

I'll do that, Flo. I'll do that. Good-night. God bless.'

Back in the kitchen Maggie, on being told the news, said, 'How wonderful for them. Yet I doubt if they'll have an easier time there than they have here. It's awful to think of, for they are two of the nicest people in the world. And I've never met a man like him before, with the manners that he has. He's a gentleman of gentlemen, but he has to be persecuted because of his colour. By! when you think of some of the swabs round about it makes you want to spit, and them in high places. And you don't have to look far, do you? Look at Annette's father. He's the only one who never spoke to Harvey. But then he's not speaking to his own daughter. Is it true that he's trying to get rid of his businesses?'

'No, no; that was just a rumour. They are too profitable for him to let go.'

'But it's true that they're moving, isn't it?'

'Yes, as far as I can gather, that's true enough.'

'Somewhere around Carlisle, somebody said.'

'Well, they can move to hell for all I care. But to get back to us, Maggie; what about it?'

She turned from him and went towards the fire and, bending, she pushed in the damper to the side of the boiler, then said quietly, 'I'll ... I'll have to think about it, Daniel. Leave it for the present, will

176

you?'

She turned and looked at him, and he, walking over to her, put his arms about her again, saying, 'Then make it a short "present" will you? Please, Maggie, make it a short present.'

CHAPTER SEVEN

It was half-past six on the Thursday morning that Annette took ill. She felt a sharp pain at the base of her abdomen, and for a moment she felt she was going to faint. Slowly she brought herself up to the edge of the bed and looked at the clock. Daniel and Joe didn't normally come into the room until seven o'clock and the nurse didn't arrive until eight. She got out of bed, looking towards where Don was still sleeping under the influence of the night pill and walked carefully past the foot of his bed and towards the door leading to the sitting-room. She just managed to reach the couch there before the pain gripped her again and she was brought double, her hands hugging her abdomen.

She looked at the bell pushes on the wall; then, making an effort, she took stumbling steps towards them and pressed one, and it seemed only a minute before she heard footsteps running along the corridor, and there was Joe, saying, 'What is it?'

'Joe.'

'Yes, dear? Take it easy. Take it easy.' He had guided her back to the couch, and now sat down beside her, his arm about her. 'You've got a pain?'

177

'I ... I think it's coming, Joe. You ... you had better get the doctor.'

'Are you sure?'

She gasped now before she said, 'Dreadful pain.'

He rose immediately and went to the phone that was placed on a side table.

Presently he came back to her. 'He's coming,' he said. 'He won't be long. Lie down.'

'I ... I can't, Joe. Oh dear!' She groaned out the words. And he was now holding her tightly to him, saying, 'There, there. It'll be all right. Look; just rest easy, I'll ring for Dad. He'll get you a hot drink. That might help.'

He stretched out his free arm and pressed the other button, and within a minute or so Daniel came hurrying into the room, only to hesitate for a moment before he approached her, saying, 'This is it then?'

'Dad ... Dad, it's too early.'

'I know. I know, love. But it's all right; these things often happen. You'll be all right, you'll see. The doctor?'

'I rang him; he's on his way.'

'Oh my! Oh dear!' Her face was screwed up in agony now, and they both held her twisted body while Daniel muttered, 'Why the hell doesn't he hurry up!'

'He was asleep. I woke him. He has to get dressed.'

'He's only a five-minute car-ride away.'

'Look; go and wake Maggie. But go carefully, we don't want Don to know about this; not yet, anyway.'

Maggie and the doctor arrived in the room almost simultaneously. Annette was lying back on

178

the couch now, her body heaving, and she put her hand out to the doctor and, gripping his, she said, 'Please! Please, do something.'

'We'll do something, dear, don't worry. How often have the pains been coming?'

'It ... it seems to be all the time ... all the time.'

He turned from her, looked around the room, then pushed past Daniel and went to the phone. Then after a moment, he said, 'The ambulance will be here in a few minutes.'

'The ambulance?' Annette went to pull herself up into a sitting position, and he said, 'Yes; the ambulance. And lie quiet, you're going into hospital.'

'I ... I thought...'

'Whatever you thought, you can think in hospital, my dear. That's the place for you, and you'll be all right in no time. There's nothing to worry about.' He turned to the men now, saying, 'I would get your clothes on; one of you had better go in with her.'

As they both made to go from the room Joe said to Daniel, 'You stay here, Dad, and see to Don. I'll take her in.' Strangely, Daniel made no objection, but just said, 'All right, lad. All right.' And each hurried to his room to dress, as both missions were equally urgent.

Before the ambulance arrived Annette, hanging on now to Maggie, had three more painful spasms. But when the men brought in the stretcher, she waved it to one side, saying, 'I ... I can walk. And ... and I want to look in on my husband.'

The doctor and Daniel between them helped her to her feet, then led her through to the bedroom. Thankfully the hustle and bustle had not

179

awakened Don, and she bent over him and kissed him on the cheek. But when he stirred and muttered something, the doctor turned her quickly from the bed. Once in the corridor, however, he said, 'Now you've walked far enough. Lie down on the stretcher and we'll tuck you up, then you can forget about everything but that you will have a fine baby. I'll be along to see you later. I've been in touch with Doctor Walters, so he'll be waiting for you.'

When, overcome by another spasm, she began to groan, the ambulance men stopped and she, gasping, looked up at Joe, saying, 'You'll stay with me ... Joe?'

'I'll stay with you. Never fear, I'll stay with you.'

*   *   *

Two hours later, Joe had had four cups of tea and had explained at least six times to three expectant fathers in the waiting-room that no, he wasn't the father, he was the brother-in-law. And when a young fellow asked, 'Where's the bloke, then? Scarpered?' he had answered good-humouredly, 'No; he's still in bed,' to which the reply, after a moment's hesitation, was, 'You don't say!'

'I do.'

'Drunk?'

And to this Joe had said, sadly, 'No, not drunk—I wish he were—he had an accident.'

'Oh.' The enquirer was obviously very sorry. 'Hard lines, that,' he said. 'It's every man's right to know what's going on, don't you think?' And when Joe had said, 'Yes. Yes, I suppose you're right,' the young fellow had pointed to the far end of the room to a pacing expectant parent and, in a low voice, had said, 'That bloke demanded to be in on the show. Can you believe it? He can't have gone through what I have else he'd bloody well want to steer clear of that. Eeh! some folks.'

Part of Joe was laughing; but only part of him; the other part was bitterly engaged in alternately begging God and demanding of Him that Annette would be all right; and if it should be either her or the child, to let the child go. This business of the child at any price was all hooey to him. The church was wrong there, and he would tell them so the very next time he saw Father Ramshaw; or, yes, Father Cody. He would be the one to throw it at. If they let anything happen to her to save the child, what light was left in his life would be extinguished.

He had had to wage a constant struggle to carry on, even behind the façade he had put up: for as he had watched her abdomen swell, so his own envy of Don had grown. Although he knew that never again would Don give her another life to carry, he was still, in a way, jealous because, he would keep reminding himself, it needn't have happened. He should have been strong, forceful, shown his hand before his Dad set to work developing his own ideas for his son's escape. If he had come into the open and declared his love, Don wouldn't be on his back now, nor would his own adoptive mother be in an asylum.

'Mr Coulson?' The nurse was tapping him on the arm. 'It's all right. It's all right, Mr Coulson. Don't look so worried; everything's fine.'

'She's . . .'

'Yes, she's all right, I tell you. She's asleep now.

181

We had to give her a caesarian. You have a little girl ... I mean'—she laughed—'you have a little niece.'

'A girl?'

'Well'—the nurse laughed again—'if she's a niece I suppose she's a girl; there're only two types.'

His relief and thankfulness showed as a deep exhalation of breath, enough to bring a number of heads turning in his direction, and as he followed the nurse out of the door, one of those heads turned to another, saying, 'Funny bloke, that. He's supposed to be the brother-in-law. Huh! He's been more stewed up than me.'

The brother-in-law was now gazing through a window to where a nurse was pointing to a cot in which he could just make out a small wrinkled face like that of an old woman.

When the nurse at his side said, 'She's beautiful; small, just over six pounds, but beautiful,' Joe smiled down on her, saying, 'Can I see her? I mean, Mrs Coulson,' and she said, 'It wouldn't be any use, she'll sleep for some time yet. If I were you I'd go home and give the father the news, then have a bath and a big breakfast, by which time she should have come round.'

'Thanks, nurse. I'll do that. But do you think I could have a word with the doctor before...'

'Oh—' she cut him short by saying on a laugh, 'you'll have a better chance when you come back, because he's still in the theatre bringing another one ... out of the depths.'

He laughed with her, nodded, then said, 'Thank you very much, nurse,' and walked away.

Out of the depths, she had said. Was she a
182

Catholic?

Out of the depths I have cried unto Thee,
O Lord: Lord, hear my voice.
Let Thine ear be attentive to the voice of my
  supplication.

How many times of late had he said that, and at
the same time wondered why he was saying it,
because he had his doubts, his grave doubts, about
anyone or anything being there to listen to the
voice. What was more to the point, he knew that if
anything had happened to her this morning, it
would undoubtedly have made him realise that for
years, like millions of others down the ages, he had
been talking to himself, and that would have been
the finish of 'I believe, help Thou my unbelief', for
never again would he have prayed for faith.

But she had survived.

He stepped out into the cold morning and took
in long breaths of icy air. He looked upwards. The
sky was high and blue but it was still cold enough
to be deep winter.

Having arrived in the ambulance, he took the
bus home, one that would leave him nearest the
house. The bus was full of people, all remarking on
the sudden cold, apart from one passenger, the
woman that was sitting next to him, for she turned
to him and in a low voice said, "Tisn't sudden at
all; it's been like this for two or three mornin's
now. I said last week we'll have snow, and we will:
end of March or no end of March, you'll see. I'm
gettin' off here.' He moved his knees to let her pass
and she said, 'Ta-ra.'

He answered likewise 'Ta-ra.' And he remarked

to himself that you missed a lot when you had a car: not only did you fly through the countryside without seeing anything, but also you missed people. 'Ta-ra,' she had said. Nobody had said 'Ta-ra' to him for a long time. The three fellows and the two girls in the office would say, 'Bye! Be seeing you.' The nearest they got to 'ta-ra' was, 'so long'. He sat now looking out of the window. That woman, she could have been his mother. He cast his glance backwards. Anyone of these women could have been his mother. But then, no; they all looked very working-class, and his mother had been ... What had she been? Oh! not again. He should stop deluding himself, because it wouldn't end there; once he found her he would want to find his father, wouldn't he? Anyway, to stop the nagging there was only one way to tackle it: he'd go back to the home and ask.

During his teens he had thought that, as he grew older the questioning would lessen, but it hadn't. It had grown in intensity. But what if he *did* find her and she turned out to be a disappointment? He'd have to risk that. But could he? He'd been rejected by his mother, he'd been rejected by his foster-mother. He had, in a way, been rejected by Annette. Could he risk another rejection or disappointment? But he had this great emptiness inside. He needed something ... someone to fill it, and no matter how soon dead men's shoes became vacant, he couldn't see himself jumping into them, no matter what Don wanted ... it wouldn't be decent. Anyway, there was Annette, to whom he was just a brother.

Oh, he wished he hadn't got on the bus. No, he didn't really, because he liked to be among people.

184

Yet that was a contradiction, wasn't it? Why had he asked to have his rooms in the cottage, separate from the family? Oh, he knew why, because he had to get away as much as he could from the rejection by her; and also from his dad breaking his neck to make up for the rejection which, in a way, was just as bad.

What about Jessica? Jessica Bowbent; or Irene Shilton ... yes, what about them? No, not Irene. So that left Jessica or, better still, Mary Carter. Yes, better still, Mary...

Maggie was waiting on the doorstep, with Daniel behind her, and Peggie and Lily behind them.

'Well?'

'She's fine. It's a little girl.'

Daniel closed his eyes and he, too, exhaled loudly; then his voice almost attacked Joe as he cried, 'Why the hell didn't you phone, then? We've been on tenterhooks.' But then he showed his surprise when Joe barked back at him in the same tone: 'There's a phone at this end; you could have phoned the hospital yourself, couldn't you?'

'All right, lad. All right. Calm down.' Daniel patted him on the shoulder. 'You've been there and I can understand you must have been worried. But quite candidly, I was afraid to phone. Come on. Come on. Have something to eat.'

'I will in a minute; I want to go along to Don.'

'Of course. Of course. He's been on hot bricks. He couldn't believe that she had gone and that he hadn't woken up.'

Joe went swiftly along to the sick-room, but before entering he braced himself, then thrusting the door open, he cried, 'Who's a papa then?'

185

The nurse turned from the bed, crying, 'She got it over?'

'Yes, she got it over.' He was standing now looking down on Don; but Don didn't speak, and so he cried at him, 'Well! say something, man!'

'How ... how is she? Is she all right?' Don's voice was thin, weak.

'She's fine.' Joe didn't know if this were true or not; but for the moment she had to be. 'You have a daughter,' he said.

'A girl?' The words were short, but Joe's voice was extra loud as he said, 'That's what a daughter means: yes, a girl. Anyway, that's what the nurse said to me.'

Don now pressed his head back on the pillow, looked up while his teeth drew on his upper lip, and the nurse asked, 'What did she weigh? Is she all right? I mean, not sick or anything?'

Joe, and still in a loud voice, said, 'Of course she's all right. I don't know what the baby weighs. Oh yes, I do. I think the nurse said just over six pounds. I was in a daze. I tell you, the room was packed with men all striding about waiting to be dadas.' His voice low now, almost at a whisper, he said, 'Oh, don't, man. Don't.' He looked down on Don's closed eyes and the tears running down his cheeks. 'It's wonderful news. Come on. Come on.'

'Well, why can't a man cry with joy? That's what he's doin'. Aren't you?' The nurse now wiped Don's face as if he were a child, saying, 'What you need now is a celebration. In fact, we all need one. What about it?' And she cast a cheeky glance up at Joe, and he, catching her mood, said, 'Yes. Yes, that's a good idea.' And he hurried from the room.

He had been surprised that Daniel hadn't

186

followed him along to Don's room and so, as he made his way to the dining-room and seeing his father coming down the stairs, he stopped and said, 'What's the matter? Why didn't you come in with me?'

Daniel now ran his hand through his hair as he said, 'I ... I somehow couldn't face him ... I felt I'd break down. I'll go along there now.'

'I'm going to get us a drink.'

'That's an idea.' Daniel smiled now, saying, 'And we'll have them all in. I'll shout Stephen down an' all. Peggie's up there with him.'

As Joe was about to turn away Daniel said, 'Just a minute. Look, could I ask you to do something?'

'Well, you don't have to ask, you know that. What is it?'

'Would you go up in my place on Saturday to Flo's wedding? It means leaving on Friday night. Would you do it?'

'Yes. Yes, like a shot; but I thought you wanted to be there.'

Daniel turned away for a moment and looked across the hall before he said, 'Yes ... I would like to be there, but I've got a weird feeling on me: I don't want to leave Don; I think he's failing fast, Joe. What do you think?'

It was some seconds before Joe said, 'He's fading, we know that, but not, I would say, fast. He could go on for some time yet and the birth of the baby will give him an incentive.'

'I don't think it's up to incentives. But there, perhaps you're right. I feel, though, I'd rather be on the spot. You understand?'

'Yes, yes. But I'll not stay up there; I'll come straight back after the wedding. I'll be back here on Saturday night. By the way, I think we should ring Flo and tell her about the baby.'

'Yes I suppose so. But what about letting him do that; Don himself? We'll bring the extension in from the other room.'

'Yes, that's an idea. Go and tell him, I'll get the drink and I'll call the others in.'

Ten minutes later they were all standing around the bed: Maggie, Lily, Peggie, the nurse, Daniel, Joe, and Stephen. And they had glasses in their hands, except for Joe, who had just dialled Flo's number, saying as he waited for a reply, 'She's bound to be somewhere in the office.' Then his chin went up and he said, 'May I speak to Mrs Jackson, please?'

'Mrs Jackson speaking. Who's that?'

'Well, don't you know by now? It's your secret admirer, Joseph Coulson.'

'Oh, Joe. Joe. What is it? Something wrong?'

'No, no. There's a gentleman wants to speak to you. Hang on.'

He now passed the phone to Don and he, pulling his shoulders up from the bed, said, 'Hello there, Flo.'

'That's Don!'

'Yes, it's Don. Who did you think it was? And ... and put a little respect in your tone, for you're speaking to the father of a daughter.'

'Oh my goodness! She's had her baby. Is she all right? And the baby?'

'One thing at a time, woo-man.' He said the word as he had heard Harvey say it, which caused laughter from those around the bed; then he went on, 'Yes, she's all right, and we have a baby daughter.'

'Oh, that's wonderful, wonderful. Oh, I'd love to come up now, Don, but I'll make it sometime next week.'

'Flo?'

'Yes, love?'

'We're going to call her Flo.'

As he spoke he looked at the surprised faces around him and he nodded as he spoke again into the phone, saying, 'Annette and I said if it was a boy we would call it Harvey, and if it was a girl she would be Flo; not Florence, just Flo.'

There was a pause on the line before Flo's voice came again, saying, 'Oh, that's wonderful. Oh, I'm so proud. And to think you would have called the boy Harvey. Oh, if only he had been here when you phoned. He's just gone into court, but he'll be over the moon. You know we're going to be married on Saturday?'

'Yes, yes, I know, and I hope you will always be happy. I know you will; he's a fine man, your Harvey.'

His breath began to get heavy and he said, 'I'll pass you back to the big fellow.' And of a sudden he dropped back on to his pillows.

Joe, speaking now, said, 'Isn't it wonderful news?'

'Oh, yes. And how is she really?'

He paused before he could say, 'Oh, she's fine. I've only just come back from the hospital and I'm going to have something to eat and then I'll call in again on my way to work.'

'Give her my love, won't you? And thank her and Don so much. I'll hear all the further news tomorrow night when Daniel comes.'

He did not say, 'I'm coming in Dad's place,' but

189

said, 'They are all straining at the bit here, Flo, all with glasses in their hands to toast young Flo. Bye-bye, dear.'

'Bye-bye, Joe. Bless you.'

He put the phone down, then picked up his glass and, holding it out towards the gasping figure of Don, together with the others, he said, 'To young Flo,' and he added, 'And her mother and father.'

They had hardly finished their drinks when Nurse Pringle took over, saying briskly, 'Well now, we've all got work to do, so I'd be obliged if you would let me get on with mine, with a little help from you, Mr Coulson, so you two big fellows can go and have your breakfast.'

Joe understood her urgency, for Don was now finding it difficult to breathe and so, guiding Stephen, he made his way quickly from the room. And Stephen did not protest. He was very quiet these days. He would remain for hours in the sick-room, making himself unobtrusive when the nurse was there, sitting in the corner just looking towards Don and smiling when their eyes met, but once the nurse left the room he would slip quickly to the side of the bed and hold Don's hand as long as he would let him. And, strangely, he didn't chatter.

The nurse now said to Daniel, 'Help me lift him, will you?' And when he did, she said, 'Hold him there while I get some more pillows.' And Daniel, holding his son and watching his heaving chest, suffered with him, but more with remorse than with physical pain, for more and more he was blaming himself for having brought his son to this pitch, this hard way of dying. The question now seemed to be: had he really wanted to free him from his mother or merely to get the better of her in the parental war?

Some minutes later, after swallowing two pills washed down with a thick brown liquid, Don's breathing eased, and he opened his eyes and looked at his father, saying on a weak smile, 'I would have to break the party up, wouldn't I?'

'Never mind about that. Pain gone?'

'Yes, nearly. Ain't science wonderful!' He drew in a long slow breath now, saying, 'I ... I shouldn't be making game of that because I often lie here thinking what it must have been like before there were such pills and potions; because, you know, Dad'—he looked up into Daniel's face—'there's only so much one can take, of everything; happiness too. Oh, yes, that's sure. Isn't it wonderful about the baby? When do you think they will be home?'

'I don't know, son. I'm going to slip along with Joe on his way to the office, but I won't stay long. I'll hurry back and give you the news of them both.'

Don pulled his chin into his chest and looked down the length of the bed to where his useless legs formed a valley in the counterpane, and for a moment he saw his toes as the tops of two mountains and the dip in the counterpane a gorge. It wasn't the first time his mind had played tricks with him like that. The other day he had watched a fly crawling on the ceiling. It was the first fly he had seen this year and he wondered where it had come from; and he realised that its view was limited, but then he realised also that it had more power than he had. He had a mind that could think about it, but he couldn't move. It was at the time the pills weren't having the desired effect; they had been slow to act that day because the nurse hadn't given him the brown liquid at the same time. He was only supposed to have so much of the brown liquid, whatever it was. He had never enquired, but it was on that day he realised the wonder of the fly, but more so of an ant or of a mosquito because, as he had pointed out to himself, in those minute frames there were digestive tracts. They could suck and evacuate. And strangely, he realised he had never thought like that before; not along those lines anyway. And the wonder of the construction of a workable system in a pinpoint of a body had in a strange way brought him near to God for a moment. And he had asked Him to take the pain away, and strangely it had gone; or perhaps he had just fallen asleep. He didn't seem to be responsible for his thinking these days and sometimes could not even restrain himself from expressing his thoughts, as now when he said, 'They must have taken Joe for the father, Dad.'

'*Oh no, no*. He told them who he was.'

'No. He said they were all walking up and down together, all those fathers waiting. He wouldn't have told them; they would have thought he was the father.' He turned his head fully now to the side, then looked up into Daniel's face as he said, 'And he should have been, shouldn't he, Dad?'

'Nonsense. Nonsense. What's put that into your head? There's only been you in Annette's life; Joe and she were like brother and sister. That was the relationship there. Now, now, don't you be silly. Anyway, I think you want to rest now. I'm going to leave you in nurse's hands; she'll make you toe the line.'

Why did one say such silly things. He flapped his hand now at his son, saying, 'I'll pop in again before I go to the hospital. Perhaps you would like to write her a note.'

'Yes. Yes, I'll do that, I'll do that...'

Twenty minutes later, as Daniel was about to leave the house, Maggie hurried towards him across the hall, saying, 'I've been thinking: if Flo won't be here on Saturday to go and see her, I think you'd better phone the hospital, for she'll likely be waiting for her coming, seeing that she happens to be the only one she ever wants to see.'

'Yes. Yes, I suppose they must be told.' He nodded at her. 'Do you think you could do it? I've got to be off now, but I'll pop back after I've been to the hospital, and then I've got a full day ahead of me.'

'Yes, I'll do it.' Then, after opening the door for him, she said, 'My goodness! It's starting to snow, and at this late date too! Take care.' And he smiled at her and said, 'For you I will.' They exchanged a long look, and he went out. And after she had closed the door she picked up the phone and got through to the hospital and asked if she could speak with the matron: she wished to enquire about a patient, a Mrs Coulson. When she was told the matron was in conference but that Nurse Pratt from Mrs Coulson's ward happened to be at the reception desk and would she like to speak to her, Maggie said, 'Yes, yes, of course.'

When she heard the nurse's voice she said, 'I just wanted to tell you that Mrs Jackson won't be calling on Saturday to see Mrs Coulson. The fact is, she's getting married.'

193

'Oh, that is nice. I'll tell Mrs Coulson. It'll be something of interest for her.'

'Would you also put it to her gently, please, the fact that she is now a grandmother? Her daughter-in-law had a little baby girl this morning.'

'Isn't that exciting!' said the voice on the other end of the phone. 'Oh yes, I'll tell her. And as you say I'll put it to her *gently*. Goodbye.'

'Goodbye.' Maggie stood looking down at the phone for a moment. Was that nurse being sarcastic when she repeated her own word 'gently'? No; she didn't think so; she sounded very nice.

She turned towards the kitchen again. It was one of those weeks; everything seemed to be happening at once. She was sorry that Flo and Harvey would soon be leaving the country. She'd miss their visits; they brought lightness to the house. That was an odd thought when he was a black man. She wished something would happen to bring lightness into *her* life. And yet it would be so easy to go up those stairs at night. But wouldn't it be just as easy to let him come down at night and into her room?

Yes, she supposed so, and she knew she wouldn't be able to hold out much longer. But it was their coming together in this house that was the trouble. Why she should feel like that she didn't know, for she had never had any liking for Winifred Coulson, not from the first day she had entered the house to look after Stephen. And she could say there were times when she had been a bitch of a mistress. And look how often she'd had to bite her tongue to prevent herself from telling the woman just what she thought of her. An upstart would barely be the beginning of it. So why was she standing out against Daniel? Was it

194

conscience?

She had become a little tired of that word over the years. This was a Catholic house—she was the only non-Catholic in it—and it seemed to be the privilege of Catholics to have a conscience. But she knew that her conscience was more alive than that of any member of this household. Yet no; Daniel had a lot on his conscience, but with reason. Yet she could never blame Daniel for anything he had done or would do. She had loved him for so long and so hopelessly that now their association should be filling her with delight, yet it wasn't. It was too furtive and she couldn't bear the thought of the others finding out about it. But that must come some day. Oh, yes, it must ... some day.

*   *   *

Daniel was sitting by the side of his son's bed. He was in his dressing-gown, as was Stephen, who was lying on the single bed reading a comic from which he would look up every now and again and smile across at his father or Don.

Daniel, having answered the smile, found himself again saying in an undertone, 'It's amazing the change in that fellow these last few months. Have you noticed it?

'Yes. Yes, I have. He seems to have grown up in his mind.'

'Well, it's all because of his feelings for you and ...' He didn't go on to add, the release from his mother, because in a way Stephen had needed that release as much as Don had done, although whereas it had helped the one, it had ... He shut off his thoughts, saying now, 'You look grand the

195

day, you know.'

'I feel grand. You know something, Dad? I've even been able to pull in a long breath.' And he smiled as he demonstrated. But then, the smile disappearing, he said quietly, 'You know, there are days when I wake up and wish I hadn't, but since hearing yesterday about the baby and that Annette is all right, and then the news today that she is sitting up and as chirpy, as Joe said, as a linnet, it's quite amazing the effect on me: I've hardly had a twinge of pain all day. And I've only had one lot of pills, and I'm not taking those—' he pointed to the side table on which were two small white pills on a plate and next to it a medicine glass with brown liquid in it, and he said, 'If I continue to feel like I do now I'm going to go to sleep naturally for once, because that lot makes me so thick-headed in the morning. You know, Dad, feeling like I have today I've had to ask myself if pain can be controlled, because since I heard about the baby and Annette, as I said, I've felt different altogether. In fact, if the pain were to start again I don't think I would resort to the pills. If I can do it one day I can do it another.'

'Oh, I'd take your pills, lad. The thing is, as you get stronger you'll have less pain.'

Don now looked at his father and repeated, 'As I get stronger ... we are kidding each other, aren't we, Dad? Today is only a flash in the pan; tomorrow I'll be in the pan again and all the high thoughts about pain being controlled will, like most of me in the morning, have gone down the drain.'

'Now don't talk like that; miracles do happen.'

'*Oh, Dad.*' Don made an impatient movement

with his shoulders. 'Don't come pious on me, for God's sake. The only miracle that can happen to me is that I live long enough to see my child crawling towards me on the bed here. Oh, now, now, don't you get upset; it's only you and Joe I can open up to. By the way, what made you send him off in your place? I thought you would have loved to see Flo married.'

'Oh, I don't know. A number of things: I wanted to be near you and my grandchild'—he pulled a face now—'and I didn't fancy that journey, and I knew once I got to yon end I'd be kicking my heels to get back again. Anyway, Joe likes travelling.'

'It isn't so much what Joe likes, Dad, it's what he does for others. We're lucky to have Joe. You know that.'

'Yes, I know that.'

'And Maggie.'

Daniel knew that his son was holding his gaze, and he thought, Oh, no no. Then he almost muttered aloud, Oh, my God! when Don said, 'She's a good woman, Maggie. I don't know why she's stayed here all these years, Dad, do you?'

For a moment he felt stumped, then said, 'Well, she hadn't a family of her own; she looks upon us as her family,' as he again held his son's penetrating gaze. But then the head turned slowly away as Don said, 'You know what I'm going to do? I'm going to read myself to sleep just like that big gowk over there.' He thumbed towards Stephen, and Stephen cried, 'You want one of my comics, Don?'

'No, I don't want one of your comics. Get off your lazy backside and hand me that third book down on the table over there.'

197

'This one with the blue cover, Don?'

'That's the one. Fetch it here.'

After Stephen had placed the book on the bed Daniel leant over and looked at the title, then at Don, saying, 'Plato's Socrates? You're going deep, aren't you? What do you want to read that for? But there, that stuff should put you to sleep.'

'You should read it, Dad. I read it in my last year at school. I didn't understand it then, only that there was a lot of truth in it, but now I do. It's the story of a man about to die.'

'*Oh, lad,* for God's sake!' Daniel sprang to his feet, but Don's hand stayed him from moving from the bed as he said, ''Tisn't like that at all; 'tisn't mournful.'

'No? But why are you reading that kind of book?'

'It was among my books upstairs and I used to look at it every now and again because of the man's knowledge of human nature. But then a while ago I got Annette to bring it down because I knew there was something more in it for me. And there was: it's how to die with dignity.'

'Oh, God Almighty! boy.'

'Don't act like that, Dad. Would you rather I was lying here squirming because of my coming end? You must read this book. You'll learn a lot; if nothing else, you'll stop being afraid of the other fellow. I was always afraid of the other fellow, you know, right from when I was small. Everyone of them was cleverer than me, better than me, taller than me, broader than me ... especially Stephen. I loved Stephen, yet at times I hated him. But this book is about a man who is ugly, in no way prepossessing, yet he attracted the greatest respect, even from his enemies. Fear is not the antithesis of liking or of love or of respect; it's really envy of those qualities. Oh, Dad, don't look like that. Look, I'm happier tonight than I've been for a long time, believe me.'

As Daniel looked at him he thought, yes, he is. Strange, but he is. But how altered his son was, still so young and talking like an old man. 'I'm going along to have a hot drink now,' he said. 'And you, Stephen'—he looked across to the smiling figure on the other bed—'don't you go to sleep until I come back. Do you hear?'

'I'll not go to sleep, Dad. I never do when I'm with Don. Do I, Don?'

'No, you don't. You're a good watchdog.'

'There you are, Dad, I'm a good watchdog. And do you think, Dad, that the snow will lie and there'll be enough to play snowballs in the morning?'

'I doubt it. But then you never know, it's cold enough. Well, if you want me you know what to do: ring the bell. I'll be in the kitchen for a little while.'

He had expected to find Maggie still up, but apparently she had already retired, for the kitchen table was set for the breakfast and the fire was damped down. He took an enamel pan from the rack and held it in his hand for a moment, staring down at it. Then thrusting it on to a side table, he went out of the far door and along the short corridor. And after first tapping on Maggie's sitting-room door he pushed it quietly open.

The room was in darkness, although there was a light coming from the bedroom door, which was ajar.

'Maggie.' He was holding on to the handle of the door as he gently pushed it further open and quietly stepped into the room.

She was sitting up in bed and her voice was a whisper as she said, 'Something wrong? You need me?'

He was standing over her now looking down into her face as he said, 'Yes, Maggie; I need you. Let's not have any more talk.'

Swiftly he threw off his dressing-gown and pyjamas and, pulling the clothes aside, he lay down beside her and took her into his arms.

CHAPTER EIGHT

It was barely ten minutes later when the large, white-coated figure emerged from the kitchen garden, groped its way along by the low wall that ended at the beginning of the courtyard. It slunk past the two stables that were now used as spare garages, then turned and crossed the yard towards the door of the glass-fronted store-room. Knowingly, a hand went up on to the low guttering and pushed the snow away until the fingers came in contact with a key. The door was unlocked and pushed gently inwards, and the figure groped forward.

When it tripped over some wellington boots it kicked them to the side and went on until it came to a further door. When it entered the wood-room, the figure put its hand out towards the stacks to the right of it and guided itself towards where a light was showing beneath the bottom of a further door.

Here it stood listening for a moment; then quickly swung round and groped at the top of the wood-pile until it found a longish piece of wood, and then, gripping it tightly, moved towards the streak of light.

With its free hand it flung the door wide, and almost sprang into the room, only to stop dead.

Winifred Coulson surveyed her kitchen. It was as she had seen it day after day, year after year: everything neat and tidy as she had demanded it should be.

She moved swiftly across the room to the green-baize door, opened it, then stood with her back to it for a moment looking through the muted light coming from the standard lamp at the far end of the hall.

For one so big and heavy, for her bulk had not diminished over the past months, she ran up the stairs, past the room that had been hers, to stop outside her husband's room. Slowly she put her hand on the knob of the door, then with a jerk she flung it open and burst into the room, only to come again to a standstill.

The light was on but the room was empty. She took in the fact that his shirt and pants were lying on a chair, his trousers laid over the back of it, and on the floor to the side of the chair were his socks. She took a step forward as if to pick them up, then stopped. She had never been able to stand untidiness; it was a fetish with her: everything had to be straight, even handkerchiefs had to be laid in straight edged piles in the drawers. She stood now, the piece of wood across both hands as if she were weighing it; then, swinging round, she went out on to the landing and made for the stairs. But before she reached them a thought seemed to strike her and she ran quickly back and thrust open her bedroom door. She snapped on the light, thinking perhaps to find him in her bed, but this room was empty too, and tidy. Everything was just as she had left it, except that the cheval-mirror was gone ... She had smashed that.

In the corridor again she made for the stairs; but instead of running down them, she crept slowly and softly, and when she reached the hall she turned in the direction of her son's room.

At the door she stood listening, but when no sound came to her her hand went to the knob and, turning it, she thrust the door open. Then yet once more she was standing still.

Seemingly taken aback that she was not being confronted by Daniel, she stood, her mouth agape, one hand gripping the piece of wood held at shoulder height and for a moment deaf to the silence coming from the two beds in the room; just for the moment, for Don had raised himself on his elbows and exclaimed in a voice no louder than a whisper, 'Oh my God!'

But the cry that Stephen gave was loud. He had jumped from the bed and was standing near Don now, crying, 'Go away, Mam! Go away, Mam!'

She didn't appear to see him as she walked towards the bed, because her eyes were on her son. 'Where is he?' she demanded.

His breath coming in gasps, Don said, 'Mam! Mam! Sit down.'

'Your father; where is he?'

Don was unable to answer, for his breath was choking him, and it was Stephen who said, 'D... ad, is in ... in the kitchen.'

'He's not in the kitchen.'

She was still staring at her son, all the while brandishing the stave.

'He is. He is, Mam. Go on, go away. Get out! Leave Don alone.'

Like a child now he put both hands out to push her away, and the next moment he was screaming as she brought the piece of wood down on his shoulder. She had aimed for his head, and she tried again, but his arms were up. Thwarted and like a wild beast now, she sprang at him, flailing him with the stave. And when he fell to the ground, still covering his head with his arms, she took her foot and kicked him, and he stopped crying out.

She now turned to Don, who was lying back, deep in the pillows, his arms hugging his chest as he fought for breath. His face was contorted with pain, and she stood over him, her eyes boring into his, and after what seemed an age she said, 'You never loved me, did you? You never loved me.'

He made an effort to speak; but finding it impossible, he groped for the pills on the table at the other side of the bed.

Like a flash, her hand went out with the piece of wood held in it and with a swipe she overturned the table, and the pills and the medicine fell almost soundlessly on to the carpet.

'You're dying, aren't you, and in pain? Well, now you can suffer as you made me suffer. *Yes you did. Yes you did.*'

It was as if he had contradicted her. 'And you've got a daughter, they tell me. Well, she's a bastard. You know that? She's a bastard. And she's not yours, she's big Joe's and the daughter of a

203

bastard.' She smiled now, a terrifying smile, as she said, 'You are going to die, you know, and slowly, because there'll be nobody to come to your aid this night, not when I'm finished with them. You've all hated me, all of you, you even made the servants hate me. That Maggie running my house!'

She lifted her head back now as if listening: then she said, 'That Maggie. Yes, that Maggie. John wouldn't take me, would he? He said he didn't know the address. He could have asked her, couldn't he?' She looked down on her son again. Don's eyes were closed, his hands lying limp at each side of him. She pulled herself back from the bed, looked down at the twisted form of Stephen, then turned and left the room.

When she reached the hall the phone was ringing. As if none of the events of the past months had happened, she lifted the receiver and in a quiet tone said, 'Yes?'

A voice at the other end said, 'May I speak to Mr Coulson?'

'He's ... he's not available at present.'

'This is important. Could you please get him or someone in the household. Who's speaking?'

She paused before saying, 'This is the maid.'

'Well, try to find somebody in authority and tell them that Mrs Coulson has got away. We don't know how. She is not in the grounds, so he must be on his guard. Will you tell him that?'

'Yes; yes, I will tell him that at once.'

She put the phone down and kept her hand on it for a moment, and as she looked at it she squared her teeth, and her lips went back from them as if in a snarl, and she said, 'Yes, I'll tell him that at once.'

204

Quietly now, she crossed the hall and went through the door into the corridor leading to the kitchen, stopping outside Maggie's room. Very quietly she turned the handle of this door. There was no light on in the small sitting-room, but there was a light coming from the bedroom, and also a murmur of voices. She went to the partly open door through which, by standing to the side, she could see her husband and her housekeeper in bed.

She had always been light on her feet, but the spring she made from the doorway to the bed could have been likened to that of a panther on to its prey.

They both screamed at the terrible apparition above them, but it was too late for Daniel to escape the blow to the side of his head. It was as if his ear had been wrenched off. In attempting to pull himself out of the bed, his hands went towards his wife and she brought the stave across his arms, all the while her mouth spewing out obscenities. Maggie had jumped from the other side of the bed and, screaming, she made for the door, only to be stopped by a blow on the back of the neck that silenced her screams and brought her to the floor.

Returning now to her main target, Winifred Coulson almost threw herself on to Daniel, who had struggled from the bed, his naked body bent forward, one arm supporting his blood-covered face, the other hanging limply at his side.

When she came at him he brought his hand from his face and flung it around her neck. But when she used her knees and her feet on him he crumpled up by the side of the bed. And now she flailed him with the blood-soaked stave until he lay quiet. Then, her body heaving, she stood over him and turned him on to his back, and, her lips curling at the sight of his nakedness, she lifted the stave again and was about to bring it down on to his loins when she heard a distant voice, crying, 'Dad! Dad!'

Wildly, she gazed around the room as if looking for a way of escape. The next minute she was running through Maggie's sitting-room, pulling the door to as if hiding what she had done, hurrying through the kitchen and out the way she had come...

Stephen was half lying on the bottom step of the stairs. He had stopped calling 'Dad! Dad!' and was now crying, 'Peggie! Peggie!' then changed to 'Maggie!' And his whirling mind hanging on to the name seemed to give him the urge to pull himself up from the stair and to stumble, zig-zagging towards the kitchen door, and when in the room he leant against the table, crying again, 'Maggie! Maggie!' his face awash with tears.

He was about to sit down on a chair when he stopped. Where was his Dad? Maggie would know.

He went from the kitchen into the dark corridor. But there was a dim light streaming out from Maggie's sitting-room.

'Maggie, where's Dad? Maggie?'

He stopped at the bedroom door and stared at the naked, bleeding form of his father and the huddled body of Maggie. He did not move towards either of them, but there escaped from his lips a thin sound that could have come from a weary, pain-filled animal. And now, at a shambling run, he made for the hall again.

In his present state of mind he deduced that, having to climb the attic stairs to Peggie's room and then to waken her, for she slept so soundly, it might be too late to help them all. But there was the phone: yet he didn't know numbers, for he had never tried to ring anyone on the phone; although somewhere in his mind he recalled an adventure story in Children's Hour where the clever boys had caught the thief because they had used the telephone and rung the number nine.

He had the receiver in his hand. He pressed his shaking finger in the dial and turned it to nine. But nothing happened: nobody answered.

It was nine, he told himself; or was it two nines? or three nines? Again he stuck his finger in the dial and turned it to nine twice. Still no voice came to him. Almost angrily now he swung the dial for a third time. There was a silence and then a man's voice said, 'Yes, can I help you?'

Holding the receiver from his face he now cried, 'Will somebody come; my Mam's been here.'

The voice said, 'Speak up, please. Can I help you?'

He brought the receiver close to his mouth and yelled, 'Mam's been here! She's killed them all!'

'Tell me your address.'

He paused a moment before he said, 'Wearcill House.'

And a voice said, 'Wearcill House? Now where is that? Which road?'

'Fellburn.'

'Yes, but which road?'

'Oh, Telford Road runs at the bottom.'

The voice said, 'Wearcill House, Telford Road. Don't worry; somebody will be there very soon.'

He went and sat on the bottom stair again and stared towards the front door. He knew he should open the front door to let them in, but if he did his Mam might come in again.

It seemed a long time that he sat there, but it was only ten minutes before he heard the car draw up outside; yet not until the knock came on the door did he move to open it.

There were two policemen standing on the step, and as they came in he backed from them. They were looking at his blood-stained face and hands. The taller policeman said in a quiet voice, 'Are you the young man who phoned?'

Stephen didn't speak but just nodded his head.

'Well, tell us what happened? You said your mother was here.'

Stephen now shook his head, saying, 'She's gone. She's gone. She hit me with the wood.' He put his hand to his head. 'But she's killed Don and my Dad and Maggie.'

The policemen now exchanged glances; then one said, 'Show us.'

Stephen looked one way, then the other, as if wondering who was most in need, then when he said, 'They've got no clothes on,' the policemen again exchanged glances. Who had they here, a big fellow talking like a child?

It was the shorter policeman who said now, 'Come and show us where your Dad is, lad.' And Stephen moved shakily to obey him.

When the two men entered the room, just as Stephen had done before, they stopped dead for a moment, and one of them muttered, 'God Almighty! Somebody's been busy.

The shorter policeman knelt down by Daniel's side, put his hand on his blood-stained ribs, waited a moment, then said, 'He's still alive. What about

208

her?'

'I don't know if a pulse is there, it's very faint. Go and ring for an ambulance.'

Then rising from his knee, he said to Stephen, 'Is there anyone else in the house?'

'Don. I tried to save him but she hit me.'

'Where is he ... Don?'

'At the other end, in his room. He's bad, he can't move. His legs won't work.'

'What's your name?'

'Stephen.'

'Stephen who?'

'Stephen ... Coulson.'

'Coulson.'

The policeman now raised his eyebrows as if he was recognising some thought, and he said, 'Oh, yes, yes; Coulson. Come and show me where the young man is.'

As they passed through the hall the other policeman had just put the phone down, and he said, 'This is the Coulson place?' And his companion nodded, adding, 'Yes, it's just come to me.'

When they reached Don's room one of them said, 'God! It looks as if she's finished this one off an' all.'

'This is her son; the one that had the accident, remember? on his wedding day.'

'Oh, aye. Aye, yes.'

They turned now and looked at Stephen. 'Is there anyone else in the house?'

'Peggie. But she's asleep.'

'Asleep through all this? Show us where she is.'

Stephen had to be helped up the second flight of stairs; and when Peggie, shaken out of a deep sleep, saw the two policemen staring down at her, she let out a high scream. And one of them said, 'It's all right, miss, it's all right.'

'Wh ... at ... wh ... at do you want?'

'We want you to get up. Come downstairs and see what's happened in the time you've been asleep.'

'Oh, my God!' She was now staring at Stephen and his blood-stained condition and she cried, 'What have you done?'

'It was Mam. It was Mam, not me.'

'All right, old fellow, all right.' The policeman was patting Stephen on the shoulder now.

Looking at the policeman, Peggie said, 'Couldn't be her, she's ... she's in the asylum.'

'Apparently she got out of the asylum, miss. Now will you put something on and come downstairs and prepare yourself; there's one or two nasty sights.'

'Oh, my God!'

They were turning from her when one said, 'Is there any one else about we could get in touch with?'

'There's Lily and Bill in the lodge. But oh'—her head bounced back—'they're in Newcastle. They've gone to a show and that, it being Friday night, their night out. And John ... Dixon, he's a gardener and handyman, he lives out.'

'No other friend of the family?'

'Well'—she blinked her eyes—'Mr Joe is in London at Mrs Jackson's wedding and young Mrs Coulson, she's just had a baby; she's in hospital. That's the lot.'

'Well, get something on and come down.'

They were making for the door when Stephen

210

turned round and in a high voice cried, 'You thought it was me, Peggie. That was nasty. I'll tell Maggie about it.'

'It's all right, son. It's all right.' They both put their hands on his arms and led him out.

A few minutes later, when Peggie entered Maggie's room, she let out a squeal, putting her hand over her mouth and closing her eyes and almost collapsing.

'Come on. Come on.' The tall policeman led her from the room and, seating her on a kitchen chair, he said, 'Now, tell me where we can get in touch with this other member of the family, the one who's gone to London.'

She sat gasping for a moment before she was able to say, 'Mrs Jackson's; it's in the phone book. He'll be there with her. But she's to be married tomorrow.'

'Well, I'm afraid that she'll be one man short. It wasn't him she was marrying, was it?'

'Oh, no, no. She's his aunt. She's marrying a black man. He's nice, though.'

Whatever comment the policeman might have made at this was cut off by his companion saying, 'There's the ambulance. By the way, who's their doctor? I mean, the young man's at the end; who's his doctor?'

'Doctor Peters.'

'Well, come on; be a good lass and go and ring him. No; on second thoughts, just give me the number. I'd better speak to him.'

And now the other policeman said, 'Yes, I think he'd better come and see the damage afore they are lifted.'

When Doctor Peters pulled down the quilt that

211

was now covering Daniel his teeth gritted for a moment before he lifted up the blood-stained hand and felt for the pulse. He then went to Maggie where she too lay covered up, and after feeling her pulse he looked at the ambulance man, saying, 'Get them there quick.'

'What about the young man; the invalid?'

'I'll tell you when I've seen him. But first of all, get these two off.'

'And the young fellow?'

'Oh, Stephen? I'll have a look at him and I'll ring you if you're needed again.'

When the doctor looked down on Don he thought for a moment, as the policeman had done, that he was already dead. But when the pale eyelids flickered, he leant close to the face, saying, 'Don. Come on. Come on. You're all right.'

In raising his head and looking beyond the bed he noticed the pills on the floor and so, turning to the policeman, he said, 'Would you get those pills, please; then help me to raise him up just a bit. Come on, Don. Have this drink.'

The eyes flickered, then opened and now the head moved slightly. After taking in the presence of the policeman, his eyes came to rest on the doctor, and his lips moved a few times before he said, 'Mother. Mother...'

'Yes, yes, we know. Don't worry.'

'Stephen?'

'Stephen's all right. He's all right. Come on, take this drink of water, then swallow your pills.'

Don sipped at the water, then painfully swallowed the pills. And as he lay back again, he said, 'Mother,' then added, 'mad.'

'Yes, Don. Yes, we know. Now, just rest. Go to

sleep; you'll feel better in the morning.'

Don kept his eyes on the doctor for a moment, then he sighed and closed them.

Out in the hall again, the doctor spoke to the policeman. 'She's done a thorough job. Now she's got to be found before she does any more harm, although I don't think she'll be back here again. But then, there are two other members of the family...'

'We've contacted the son in London. He's catching the midnight train back. He seemed in a bit of a state, naturally. But that's one who escaped unharmed, anyway.'

'Oh my God!' The doctor put his hand to his head. 'If she knows about the child she'll make for the hospital, and she's mad enough to act sanely to get what she's after.'

He grabbed up the phone and got through to the hospital and within a minute or so was explaining the situation to the doctor on duty, who assured him that they would be on the look-out and would put a nurse in charge of Mrs Coulson and the baby.

Next, he phoned the superintendent at the asylum, telling him in direct words that he had better get his men out and start looking for her, for she had played havoc in her home and he didn't know if two of her victims would survive the night, only to be told they were already searching.

Following this, he now turned to Stephen, who had been hovering in the background all the while, and said, 'Go upstairs, Stephen, and Peggie will run you a bath. Now get into it, and then I'll have a look at you, because at the moment I can't see where the damage has really been done. That's a good fellow.'

Peggie had him by the arm when he turned and, looking at the doctor and the policeman, he said, 'Will she come back?'

'No, no, she'll not come back. Never.'

'You mean that, Doctor?'

'Yes, I mean that.'

Yet, even as he said this, Doctor Peters wasn't quite sure in his own mind, because it was as if he had been waiting for this call for a long time. What he was sure of was that until she was safely under lock and key, there would be no accounting for the events of this night as having ended here and now...

His examination of Stephen revealed that the main source of blood had come from a three-inch cut in his skull behind his ear. Fortunately it was only surface deep; his thick hair had cushioned the blow; but his arms, back and legs were covered with bruises, which tomorrow would be giving him more pain than they were at present.

When the doctor was making for the door, Stephen said, 'Don't like her. Nobody likes her.'

And the doctor paused, then looked down for a moment, thinking, that's the trouble, nobody likes her. Nobody has ever really liked her. And she knew it.

*   *   *

Joe arrived at half-past seven the next morning and was dazed by the turn of events that had taken place during his short absence, as related by the garbled descriptions coming from both Stephen and Peggie.

Peggie and Lily had taken charge of the house now. A new day nurse had just put in an appearance, because the last thing the doctor had done before leaving early in the morning was to get in touch with Nurse Pringle and ask her to come and take over again in the sick-room...

It had snowed heavily in the night: there was all of three inches lying. Everyone said it had been expected; it was cold enough for it. But here it was, the end of March. Really! it shouldn't happen.

Bill White came up to the house and half apologised to Joe, saying it wouldn't have happened if he had been on duty. But as Joe assured him, there was and could be no blame attached to him for, apart from it being his night off, she hadn't come in by the drive-way but had got in through the wood-room. Naturally she had known where the key was kept.

There had already been men from the asylum asking for exact details of when this and that had happened. But Peggie didn't know anything, and Stephen couldn't tell them how long he had been lying on the floor before he himself came to.

There was now a police guard on the gate, but that hadn't stopped two reporters getting through to the house at half-past six this morning. Bill White, however, had given them short shrift.

Everyone was glad to see Joe back, because now there was someone who could take the responsibility.

And this is what Bill White said to John Dixon as they stood in the warm greenhouse discussing the events of the past night. 'Joe'll see to things. Anyway, at bottom, he always has.'

'This'll put her away for life,' John said.

'Well, it's not afore time, if you ask me, because from what our Lily tells me she was a bitch to him; no wife at all for years. And, you know, our Lily was right about more than one thing. She's been saying for some time now she suspected there was something going on atween Maggie and the boss. Then, of course, there they were found like that, him stark naked, and her an' all. You surprised?'

'No, not at all.' John Dixon shook his head. 'I've known which way the wind was blowing in that direction for a long time. She had him followed, you know, when he used to go to Bowick Road. I tipped him off once or twice.'

'You did? You never said anything to me.'

'Well ... well, you've got a wife an' all, you know'—he grinned now—'and you would have likely told her and it would have been passed on to Peggie, because she's your niece and you know Peggie's got a mouth like a pontoon; and I thought, well, the boss had enough to put up with; it's best to keep a still tongue sometimes. Anyway, I wonder where she got to after she went through the house with her mallet or whatever she had in her hand.' He paused before saying, 'What's the matter with Larry?' and he pointed through the glass door to where a small Scotch terrier was barking furiously. 'What's up with him?'

'Smelt a rat or something. He's always like that when those devils are about.' Bill White opened the door and the dog ran to him and jumped up, then darted back, turned and waited, and Bill said, 'All right, all right. Come and show me.'

'I haven't seen any rats for weeks,' John Dixon said. 'Likely it's rabbits coming in from the fields.'

They both went out, pulling the collars of their

216

duffle-coats up around their necks, and as they crunched over the snow in the wake of the dog, Bill said, 'Who'd believe this, snow at this time of the year? You know it's my opinion it's those atom bombs they're dropping all over the world. It's altering the seasons.'

'Where's he going?' John Dixon now asked.

'He's going for the hen-crees. I bet you what you like a fox is around.'

They passed through an opening in a low hedge and so into a small field, at the end of which were a row of hen-crees; although only one or two hens had come through the hatches.

'They don't like the snow, but I bet if we put the food outside they'd come out fast enough. What's he after?'

They now followed the dog along by the side of the crees to an open shed used for storing boxes and crates. The front ones were partly covered with snow that had fallen during the night. Then they both stopped within yards of the place and looked at the two feet sticking out from among the tumbled boxes.

'*Eeh no!*'

'*God above!*'

At a run now they reached the shed and, pulling the boxes to one side, they exposed the stiff body of their mistress.

'Is she dead?' Bill White was bending over John Dixon as he was tentatively putting his hand inside the crumpled coat; and after a moment he said, 'Can't feel anything. Look; dash back to the house and tell Joe to ring for an ambulance. And you'd better bring a door or something. We could never carry her like this.'

Bill raced up the garden, straight over the frozen herbaceous beds, and made for the front door. He didn't ring but banged on it, and when Peggie opened it, he gasped at her, 'Joe ... Mr Joe, where is he?'

'Along with Mr Don. What's happened now?'

'The missis. She's in the garden.'

'Oh my God!' She put her hand over her mouth. 'Close the door.'

'Stop it!' He pushed her. 'As far as I can tell she's dead. Get Mr Joe. Go on!'

Within seconds Joe was standing before him, saying, 'What! In the garden? Where?'

'In the box house. We must get a door or something; couldn't carry her, the weight she is. And ... and you'd better call the doctor an' all.'

Joe stood for a moment as if dazed; then, looking at Peggie, he said, quietly, 'Ring for the doctor. Tell him it's urgent.'

Peggie ran to the phone, crying, 'He'll know it's urgent if it's anything to do with this house.'

But Joe was already following Bill at a run to the outhouses; and there, Joe said, 'There's no doors here except that big glass one, and that's too heavy as it stands.'

'Aye, you're right, Mr Joe. But there's a sling ... well, it was a hammock, like. It's up in the loft.'

It was a full twenty minutes later when they brought Winifred back into her home in a sling and laid her on the hall floor. The doctor was waiting; then as he knelt down by her side he shook his head slowly. But after a moment he looked up at Joe, saying, 'She's still alive. Phone for an ambulance.'

Sitting by her side in the ambulance, Joe

pondered on the events of the last few days. There was Annette and the baby in one part of the hospital, and his Dad and Maggie would be in another part. And he still didn't know whether they were dead or alive. And now here was his adoptive mother being taken to the same hospital. It now only needed Don and Stephen to go and they'd all be there; and by the look of him Don could soon be joining them. And poor Stephen, black and blue from head to foot and yet still carrying on. He had experienced an awful night; and, as Doctor Peters had just said to him, if it hadn't been for him they could have all lain in their battered condition and would very likely not have survived the night.

What had come upon them? It was like a curse. But it was no curse, it was simply mother-love, twisted mother-love. As he looked down on the dead-white face, the ambulance man who was sitting near him said, 'She's in a bad way. Lying out all night in that; it would kill a horse. It's amazing she's still breathing.'

Yes, it *was* amazing she was still breathing, and some part of him wished fervently that she wasn't, because, after this, what would her life be? They certainly wouldn't send her back to the County but to some other place of high security, especially if either his Dad or Maggie died. And then there was Annette. How to tell her? because she was still weak. The birth had taken it out of her more than somewhat. His talk of her sitting up and being perky had been diplomatic bluff.

There was more bustle at the hospital, and as his mother was being wheeled away he was surprised to see in the hallway a nurse whom he recognised as being from the County Asylum, accompanied by a man. And she, seeing him, approached him immediately, saying, 'Tragic, Mr Coulson, isn't it?'

He nodded. 'Yes, nurse, tragic,' he said.

And as if somewhat apologetically, the man said, 'We searched the garden last night. Although it was dark we went over it thoroughly after we knew she had been to the house.'

'Oh, you wouldn't have thought of looking among those crates and boxes,' excused Joe; 'but how did she get out?'

He turned to the nurse and she replied, 'Apparently with the help of two of her room-mates. They're wily . . . they're all wily. They had done the old trick of packing pillows in her bed, and they did it thoroughly because, as you know, she's a size.'

'But she'd have to get through the gates?'

'Oh, she didn't go that way. She must have had this in mind for some time and had looked around the garden and the strip of woodland. She climbed over the wall. There's a tree grows near the wall and one of the lower branches touches the top of it. How she managed to get up there with her weight, I don't know, I just don't know, but they think that's the only way she could have escaped. She was very agile on her feet, you know, very light. Still, to climb that tree! But in that state they'll do anything, and can achieve anything once they set their mind to it. Do you think she'll live?'

It was on the tip of his tongue to say, 'I hope not,' but he answered, 'I can't tell.' Then, saying, 'Excuse me,' he turned away and went to the desk and said, 'May I see Mr Coulson and Miss Doherty?'

'If you'll just take a seat, I'll enquire,' said the receptionist and lifted the phone. Presently she beckoned to him, saying, 'If you go to number four ward, Sister Bell will see you.'

'Thank you.'

Sister Bell took him into her office and, after offering him a seat, she said, 'What a tragedy. I've just heard that your mother, too, has been brought in.'

He made no answer to this but said, 'How's my father, and Miss Doherty?'

'Well,' she sighed, 'it appears there's little change from last night. Yet they're both alive and we can only hope for the best. But I would say your father is in a much worse state than Miss Doherty.'

'May I see them?'

'Yes; if you stay just a moment and don't start a conversation.' She shrugged her shoulders now, adding, 'Not that it would be of any use.'

When he stood by his father's side he looked down on a face that was swollen and so black and blue as to be unrecognisable. There was a tube up his nostril, one in his arm, as well as what appeared to be wires attached to his arm. He looked much like Don had looked after the accident. He wanted to put his hand out to him and say, 'Oh, Dad. Poor Dad,' for the words were like whimpering inside of him. Stephen had said she had been carrying a lump of wood. Well, it must have been a hefty stave, but then she was a hefty woman, and in her madness she could have wreaked havoc with a hair-brush.

When, next, he stood by Maggie's bed, her eyes were open and peering out from the bandages

221

around her head and face. He said aloud, 'Oh, Maggie.' And she went to raise her hand from the bed cover, but the effort seemed too much.

Looking down on her he felt his throat was full: Maggie of all people, why did she have to suffer like this? But why not? She had, in a way, made his mother suffer, for she couldn't have been unaware of her cook's feelings for her husband. Yet she must have, or else she would have sent her packing years ago. If she hadn't been mad to begin with, that bedroom scene would surely have tipped the scales.

He brought back to mind the sight of Stephen standing there in the corridor that morning, almost before he had got into the house, and gripping the lapels of his coat as he stammered, 'Dad was on the floor, Joe, with no clothes on. And Maggie, she was an' all, with no clothes on. That was bad, wasn't it? Maggie shouldn't have been there, not without her clothes. I haven't told Don, as he's still asleep. Anyway, that new day-nurse wouldn't let me in.'

Joe had shaken him gently, saying, 'Now, be quiet, Stephen. Be a good lad. And from what Peggie tells me you've been a very brave fellow getting the doctor and the ambulance.' He didn't mention the police.

'My head aches, Joe, an' all over. I'm paining, Joe.'

'Well, go upstairs and get into the bath and I'll be with you in a minute or two.'

'But I've had a bath, Joe.'

'Well, go and have another.' He had only just stopped himself from yelling at him, but keeping his voice level he went on, 'Lie in it: it'll help to take the pain away. Then I'll come up shortly. Go on now.'

'You won't go away, Joe, will you?'

'Go away? What are you talking about? Don't be silly. Go on now.'

* * *

He had to cross the hospital yard to get to the Maternity Ward. At one point he stood on the frozen grass verge and pondered what he should say to Annette. It wasn't likely that she'd heard the news already, so he decided he would say nothing until later in the day, and not even then unless either of them died. He didn't include Maggie in his thinking, nor yet Don. He remained standing as he thought: four of the household in this hospital; five, if one counted the baby; and back in the house Don lay as near death as made no odds. There seemed to be only himself and Stephen left whole. What had happened to the family?

When love, all kinds of love, came as the answer, he jerked himself from the verge and hurried towards the Maternity Ward, and strangely, Stephen's words came to the front of his mind: 'You won't go away, Joe, will you?'

Annette was propped up in bed. She showed her surprise immediately by saying, 'You're supposed to be at the wedding.'

'Oh, Dad changed his mind and thought he should be there. So we swapped around again.'

'But you would have liked to go, Joe.'

'Not all that much. Anyway, they'll be coming up this week. How are you feeling?'

He drew up a chair to the side of the bed and

223

took hold of her hand, and after a moment she answered, 'Up and down. I've had an uneasy night, they tell me. Temperature popped sky high around midnight. I felt awful. I couldn't explain it so they made me take a sleeping tablet. You know how I hate sleeping tablets. And then I had sort of nightmares. Oh, I'm glad to see you, Joe.'

But he did not pursue this line; instead, he asked, 'How's her ladyship?'

'Well, I saw her half an hour ago and she said she'd like to stay here with me, but they wouldn't let her. And I told her to put on some weight and then she could defy them, and walk in all on her own.' She smiled wanly, and he said, 'You'll be surprised how soon that'll come about.'

Her eyes tight on his now, her face unsmiling, she asked, 'How is Don?'

He paused a moment before answering: 'Well, he was still asleep when I came out.'

'He's worse? Tell me, tell me the truth, Joe, he's worse?'

'Now, now; don't be silly, he's not worse.'

'You know what, Joe? With that weird feeling I had last night I was sure he had died. I must get home soon. They said it might be ten days or a fortnight but I can't possibly stay that long. And ... and he must see the child. Joe, you understand?'

'Yes, my dear'—he was stroking her hand now—'I understand how you feel, and I'll have a talk with the doctor and find out just how soon they'll let you go. But you must remember this was no ordinary birth, as I think you know. It wasn't plain sailing.' He smiled at her, but her face was straight as she answered, 'Nothing I seem to do is

224

plain sailing, being clever and getting pregnant for a start.' She turned from him now and looked down towards the foot of the bed. 'Getting married and having such a wedding day. And I blame myself for that because if ... if I hadn't been pregnant there would have been no hurry. And what did it do to Don? Killed him slowly.'

'Be quiet. And don't talk like that. What you did, what both of you did, was out of love for each other.' There was that word again. What a lot it had to answer for. He went on, 'Stephen sends his love. I'm going to have to bring him in one day to see you. It's a job to get away from him when he knows I'm coming in and he keeps yammering on about the baby.' How easy it was to create a story; and once started he went on, 'The girls send their love, and ... and Maggie. They keep asking when they'll be allowed to visit. They've all been knitting like mad.' That was true; he had seen them at it in the kitchen.

The nurse entered the room now with a tray and, looking at him, she said briskly and in an exaggerated Northern accent, 'This is chucking out time. Will you go peacefully or shall I have to use force?'

He smiled at her, saying, 'Well, I don't know; I might make a stand for it.' Then bending over Annette, he kissed her on the cheek, saying, 'I'll be in this afternoon.'

As he backed a few steps from the bed she said, 'When will Dad be back? I want to hear all about the wedding.'

'Oh ... oh.' He scratched his brow now, saying, 'Well, I think he might stay on until they come up. I ... I really don't know. But anyway, you'll have

225

to put up with me for a day or so.'

'Give my love to Don, won't you?' Her voice was small and he said, 'Oh, yes, yes, I'll give him your love, dear.'

Once again out in the grounds, he stood breathing deeply of the icy air. He knew he must now go back into the hospital and find out what was happening to his mother, when all he really wanted to do was get into the car and drive, drive away from it all ... from everyone. Yes, even from Annette, because every time he looked at her he was torn between love for Don and desire for her.

Back in the reception area of the hospital he was making his way towards the desk when a sister hailed him; then standing in front of him she looked at him and said quietly, 'I'm afraid, Mr Coulson, we weren't able to save your mother. She ... she didn't regain consciousness. She died from the effects of exposure.'

Was he sorry? Was he glad? He didn't know. But after a moment he asked, 'What is the procedure now?' And she answered, 'Well, she'll go to the mortuary and you'll have to make your own arrangements. They generally lie in the undertaker's chapel, you know.'

'Yes, yes. There's nothing more required of me now?'

'No; unless you would like to see her.'

'*No*.' The word was emphatic. Then he added, 'Thank you. I'll ... I'll be back.' And on that he turned abruptly from her.

The sister went to stop him with a movement of her hand as if she had something more to say. Then, turning towards the desk, she leant on it for a moment as she said to the receptionist, 'He's

226

upset naturally, but if you ask me it's just as well she went. She could have been certified as insane and then she would have spent her life inside. And if she wasn't ... well! by what I understand she did to those other two last night, she would have gone along the line for that. Oh well, it's all in a day's work.' And on a small laugh she said, 'One day I'll write a book and I'll call it, "She Died At Her Post", because I don't know how I'm going to get through this session. My head's lifting off.'

CHAPTER NINE

It was Sunday evening. Flo and Harvey had arrived earlier in the day, and it was Flo who was now standing in the hall talking to Father Ramshaw.

Helping him off with his coat, she said, 'I'm sorry, Father, to get you out at this time of night, and such a night, but I don't think this is a case for the doctor. As I said to you on the phone, he swears she's in the room with him.'

'Well, she might be at that, Flo, because she was a very forceful woman. She's shown that in more ways than one. Dear God! she has that. But who would have thought she would have gone to the lengths she did. But there, human nature is as unpredictable as the weather, for who would have thought we would have snow at this late time of the year. But then again we should have remembered we've had it before as we should also remember that human nature is a very strange mixture of the good, the bad, and the "I can't help

227

it".'

'Will you come in to the dining-room and have a drink first, Father?'

'No, no; later perhaps. What's the latest from the hospital?'

'Daniel has regained consciousness. They think he'll pull through.'

'Thanks be to God for that at least. And Stephen?'

'He's asleep, Father. I gave him a tablet. He's been through it, poor boy.'

'He acted very sensibly by all accounts.'

'Yes, yes, he did. You know, Father, I must confess, if I'm sorry for anyone in this world I'm sorry for Stephen. Just that little something . . . just that tiny little something up here'—she tapped her forehead—'and he'd be a splendid fellow.'

'God picks his children, Flo; they come in all sizes. By the way, I'm forgetting you were married yesterday.'

'Yes, Father, I'm pleased to say.'

'In a registry office?'

They had been walking towards the corridor and Flo stopped, saying, 'No, Father, not in a registry office; we were married in a church by special licence.'

'Oh! Oh! But'—he poked his head towards her—'the other side?'

'Yes, Father, the other side.'

'Oh, well, I've heard He pops in there now and again when He has time.'

'Oh, Father.' She pushed him in the shoulder, and he grinned at her, saying now, 'I'm happy for you anyway. And he's a fine man, what I've seen of him. But you know . . . well, I think you know, that

228

life won't be easy.'

'I'm well aware of that, Father, and he more so; but we'll get through.'

'That's the way to look at it.'

When they entered the sick-room the nurse seemed to be relieved at the sight of them, and she said immediately to Flo, 'He won't take his tablets.'

'Go and have a bite.'

'I've had my supper.'

'Well, go and have another one.' The priest pushed her gently towards Flo, then went towards the bed and, pulling a chair up close, he sat down.

Don was propped up against the pillows, although his eyes were closed and he kept them closed as he said, 'Hello, Father.'

'Hello, son. Misbehaving yourself again?'

'So they tell me, Father.'

It wasn't until the door had been closed for some seconds that Don opened his eyes and, looking at the priest, he said, 'She's here, Father.'

'Now, now, now.'

'Don't say that, Father. My body's in a mess, I'm only too well aware, but my mind isn't affected. She's here. I . . . I said it isn't affected, but how long it will stay that way I don't know.'

'What makes you think she's here?'

'I saw her, Father. She was standing there at the foot of the bed.'

'When was this?'

'Last night. No, no, yesterday, sometime. Can't rightly put the hour to it. I thought I was imagining it at first because she looked just like an outline. And then, towards night-time it got stronger. She stood there looking at me, with no smile on her

229

face, just staring. And I was glad to take the sleeping tablets; but then, in my dreams, she became more lifelike. Oh yes.' He moved his head on the pillow. 'She sat on the edge of the bed where you're sitting now and she talked to me, the same kind of stuff that I'd listened to for years, how she loved me...'

'Well, she did love you, and that's what you must remember.'

'There's love and love, Father. She must have been insane half the time.'

'No, I don't think so.'

'You didn't have to live with her, Father.'

'No; that's true. But she's gone now, only God knows where; she's not here any more.'

'*She's here, Father.*'

'All right, all right, don't get agitated. All right. To you she's here. But I can promise you this, she'll go.'

'When? Tell me that, when?'

The priest paused for a moment, then said quietly, 'Tomorrow morning I'll give you Holy Communion. But in the meantime, should she return, talk to her. Tell her that you understand how she felt. Yes, yes, do that. Don't turn your head away like that, boy.'

'Father, you don't understand, she's waiting for me to die, then she'll have me again wherever I go.'

'She won't. I promise you. Listen to me.' He gripped both of Don's hands now tightly and shook them as he said, 'After tomorrow morning she'll go. You'll never see her again. But your main job now is to give her peace. Send her away in peace. Tell her you forgive her.'

'Forgive her, Father! She doesn't think that she's

done anything to me that needs forgiveness.'

'You know nothing about it, Don. Only she knows how she felt for you, and likely the main reason she's coming back is to ask for your forgiveness. Give it to her.'

It was some time before Don answered; then, his chin on his chest, he murmured, 'I'm frightened, Father.'

'Of her? Is that all?'

'No, no. Of everything. Where I'm going shortly ... Everything. I thought I wasn't, but I am.'

'Well, you needn't worry about the latter; God's got that in hand.'

'And Father, there's something else.'

'Yes?'

'I've ... I've already spoken my mind to Joe about it. I ... I want him to marry Annette. I want him to have the care of her. You could manoeuvre that for me.'

'*I'll do no manoeuvring.* No such thing. If it's so willed that they should come together, they'll come together without any more manoeuvring being done in this house.' He got to his feet. 'I suppose you know you are where you are at this minute because of manoeuvring. You're aware that your Dad manoeuvred you towards Annette. Oh God forgive me.' He put his hand to his brow. 'I don't want to lose me temper at this stage; I'm too old to get worked up about life's foibles.' He stopped here for with some surprise he saw that Don was actually smiling, and so, his voice now taking on a purposely rough note, he said, 'And what are you grinning at? I have a pretty rough time of it. You're not the only one you know.'

'You always do me good, Father. You know,

231

I've always thought you've been wasted as a priest; you would have done much more good on the stage.'

'For your information, boy, I *am* on the stage. What do you think the priesthood is but a stage and all of us enacting a play...?'

The last word trailed away and his head drooped and he said softly, 'I didn't mean that.' Then his chin jerking upwards, he said, 'Yes, I did. God isn't fooled. He's looking down on this stage all the time and watching His lead players. Like a good producer, He's picked us. But He doesn't take on the directing; He's left that to each individual, and some of us find the act harder to play out than others. I'll tell you something.' He leant both hands on the bed now and, bending, brought his face close to Don's, and almost in a whisper he repeated, 'I'll tell you something. You know what I would like to have been if not a priest?'

'A psychiatrist?'

'Psychiatrist, no! A clown, a simple clown. Not a magician; you know, one of the clever clots; just a simple clown. And I would like to have acted solely before children under the age of seven, because it is then we are told they come to the use of reason and reason wipes out wonder. Have you ever thought about wonder? It's a gift that's given only to children, but they lose it so quickly, so quickly.' He sighed now, pulled himself up straight and, his voice changing, he said, 'You know something: you're bad for me. You're like Joe. He's the kind of fellow that makes you go to confession every time you talk to him.' He chuckled now, then said in a deep but soft tone, 'Good-night, my son, and God be with you every minute of it.' And on this he left

232

the room. And Don, pressing his head back into the pillow, said, 'Yes, God be with me every minute of it.'

Joe met the priest in the hall, saying, 'Come in here, Father; I've got a hot drink for you.'

'Don't have a shock, Joe, but I'm going to refuse it. I've got two visits to make and it's getting near me bedtime. See that he takes his tablets early, will you? Do you know, he ... he thinks she's come back and is waiting for him.'

'Yes, Father. I got an inkling of it a while back, and I believe he's right.'

'Oh, now, don't you start, Joe. You with a head on you like a spirit-level.'

'Does that mean, Father, that you're insensitive if you're level-headed?'

'Not a bit of it, not a bit of it. You know what I mean.'

'Harvey sensed something, Father. He didn't know what. But he wasn't in the house very long before he said, "I can't believe she's gone. I've got the feeling she's still upstairs, and not in the ordinary way. I just don't know."'

'Well, coming from his culture, they're nearer the earth than we are.'

'Or the gods.'

'Oh, Joe, don't egg me on to theology at this time of night and in my present state. Still, I know what you mean and although I'm throwing doubt on everybody's opinion, let me tell you I too know she's here. There are more things in heaven and earth than this world dreams of. One more thing and I must be off. How soon can Annette come back? because he wants to see that child and it's only fair that he should.'

'It'll be some days yet, Father, I'm afraid.'

'Oh, well, there's no doubt about it, he'll hang on if at all possible. I'll be round in the morning at eight o'clock for Holy Communion. And it wouldn't do you any harm to take it either. Two for the price of one.'

'I'll buy it, Father. Good-night.'

'Good-night, Joe.'

CHAPTER TEN

Don took Holy Communion the following morning, but his mother remained with him.

They buried her on the Wednesday and it was noticeable how few of her friends attended the funeral, for had she not been insane and tried to murder her husband and other members of the household? Besides Joe, Flo and Harvey, you could have counted another twenty people, half of them Daniel's workmen. Nor did any of these, other than Joe, Harvey and Flo make their way back to the house.

From the talk around him, Stephen had known that his mother was to be buried that day, but he had shown no desire to attend the funeral; in fact, he had remained in his room until Joe had gone up to him. 'It's all right,' Joe had said to him, 'for I want you to stay and look after Don till we get back.' And Stephen had jabbered with relief, 'Yes, yes, Joe, I will, I will. I'll see to Don. Don likes me seeing to him. Yes, I will.'

On arriving back, Joe went immediately to Don's room. Inside, however, he did not approach the bed, but looking towards the nurse, he said, 'Mr and Mrs Rochester are going to have a bite of food; would you like to join them?'

Taking the broad hint, the nurse smiled and left the room; and Joe, now standing close to the bed, looked down on Don but found it most difficult to speak for the moment. It was Don who seemed the more composed, and he said quietly, 'Well, you got it over?'

'Yes, yes, it's over.'

'So now we'll see. But ... but somehow it doesn't matter; I'm not afraid of her any more. I haven't been for the last few days. I think it was after I took Holy Communion I seemed to get quiet inside. It was like Extreme Unction. He hasn't brought that up yet.' He smiled wanly. 'Father Ramshaw, I mean. He's sort of putting it off until the last minute. I've always thought Extreme Unction must be like signing your name to a death warrant. Oh, Joe.' He slowly lifted his hand and caught Joe's wrist. 'Don't look like that, man. Don't you think it's as well I can talk about it? You know, it's like people who are afraid to mention the name of anyone who's just died. I always think that's silly; it's like shutting them out. I don't want to be shut out, Joe. I don't want you to talk about me when I'm gone, behind my back.' He gave a small laugh.

'Oh, for God's sake, Don!' Joe pulled his hand away from the weak grasp. 'You know what? You break my heart at times.'

'Oh, Joe, I'm sorry. Look at me. Come on now. I'll tell you something. You know what the doctor said this morning? He said my heart's steadier than it's been in weeks. Now why is that? And I said to

235

him, I'm going to get better; I'm sick of paying your bills. Come on, Joe. Joe, please.'

Joe did not turn round, but muttered, 'I'll . . . I'll be back in a minute.' And with that he went into the sitting-room, and he was about to ring the bell that could be heard in the dining-room and the kitchen and which would summon someone back here, when he heard Don's door open and Stephen's voice say, 'Oh, I thought Joe was here. He said we could play billiards.'

'Come and sit beside me for a while.' Don's voice came as if from a far distance. 'Joe'll be back in a minute; he's gone on an errand for me.'

Joe slipped out through the conservatory, along the corridor, and so to his own apartment. And there he sat down and drooped his head into his hands. He couldn't stand much more of this; the turmoil inside him was tearing him apart. Again he wished he was miles away. At one time he had loved this house for itself, now he hated it. He, too, was certain that although her body might be in the grave her spirit was still here.

After a moment or so he rose to his feet and stood looking out of the window on to the garden. The sun was shining brightly. The week-end winter had gone; it was even warm. That unfailing announcer of spring, the bed of crocus just below the window, was pushing through, and a border of daffodils, their buds now showing but still pointing straight up, on the other side of the path. The garden was beginning to smile. He drew in a long breath.

But down to earth again: in an hour's time he would be going from one to the other in the hospital. And yet, did he need to? They all knew she had been buried today.

Annette had had to be told of her father-in-law's and Maggie's sojourn quite near her. When he told her what had happened to them she had become fearful, saying, 'She'll come here and try to get the baby.' And so, to calm her he had been obliged to tell her that her mother-in-law was already dead.

It had also lain with him to break this news to Daniel, and that had come about only yesterday. The doctor had advised against it, and when he had received this advice he had wanted to say, 'He won't be shocked. He'll be glad to hear it.'

His father had spoken to him for the first time two days ago: 'She did it at last, Joe,' he had said.

What Maggie had said was, 'I think I would have done the same in her place.'

Well, Joe told himself as he gazed down on the spring flowers, it would be over once Don was gone.

But what then?

Well, he'd just wait and see. But did he want to wait and see? There was a change taking place inside him: it was as if he too had been battered, and into insensibility, for it came to him that once Don died he would be free, and being free he knew what he would do.

CHAPTER ELEVEN

Inside the hospital they separated, Flo and Harvey visiting Annette while Joe made straight for Daniel's room.

Daniel was sitting up in bed. It was as if he was

237

waiting for him.

'Well, Joe?' he said.

'How are you feeling?'

'Relieved, in a way. I'm all right inside apparently, so the X-rays say. And they've stitched me up here and there ... she was always methodical. What happened this morning?'

'What could happen, Dad? We buried her.'

'Well, don't look at me like that, expecting me to say I'm sorry or I feel any guilt, or poor soul, or what have you. What I've been feeling over the past few days is deep bitterness and regret for the wasted years in having to put up with her. Forgive and forget, they say. Let them try it after living with someone like her for half your lifetime.'

'She's dead, Dad. And the past is dead with her. You've got to look at it like that.'

Daniel made no reply to this, only cast a sidelong glance at Joe before he did say, 'How's Don?'

'About the same. But I think Annette should try to come home as soon as possible. I'll see the doctor before I leave.'

'Maggie will be home tomorrow. She was in just a little while ago ... I'm going to marry her, Joe.'

'Yes, yes. Of course, I understand that you'll marry her.'

'But we won't go on living there. That's one thing sure. She doesn't want it and I certainly don't.'

'I can understand that an' all. What about Stephen? Where does he go?'

'He'll come with us. He's my responsibility, after all.'

Joe felt the urge to speak his thoughts by saying,

238

I'm glad you see it that way; you've practically made him mine over the years.

What was the matter with him? He was tired. He must be careful of his tongue. Yet the next moment he was saying, 'Have you worked out what's going to happen to Annette and the baby?'

'Why are you using that tone to me, Joe? That doesn't need any working out. Once she's ... left alone'—he paused—'she'll go to the home that was intended for them. That only leaves you. What do you intend to do? Would you like to stay there? I mean, I can pass the place over.'

'*Thank you very much.* Stay in that house! Me? Alone?'

'Well, you've always said you liked the place, loved it even. Apart from ... her who wanted it in the first place, you considered it the best house in the town, not only from your architectural point of view, but because of the house itself.'

'Things change. People change. I don't want the house. As soon as you're on your feet I'm off.'

'Off? Where?'

'It doesn't matter much where.' He moved a step from the bed; then turned and said, 'Perhaps I'll try to find my own people ... me ain folk, you know.'

He was going out of the door when Daniel called to him, 'Joe! Joe!' But he took no notice. He found he was sweating. He took out a handkerchief and wiped his face, the while chastising himself: Daniel was still in a bad way and he had gone for him like that. Well, Daniel's body might have been knocked about but his mind was just the same. And at this moment he was seeing him as a man who had gone his own way all his life. Perhaps he had bowed to duty once or twice by staying with his wife, but for the rest he had lived on the side, whereas he himself had never tasted that kind of life. He had wanted one girl, one woman, from when he had first held her hand and taken her across a road. And he would have had her, he felt sure of that, if the man behind that door who had acted as father to him, and whom he had thought of lovingly for years, had not had the urge to get back on his wife in some way. And so he had made plans. And his son unsuspectingly had carried them out.

Well, here he was, twenty-six years old, and he could have been the virgin that his adoptive mother had desired in her own son, for, as yet, he hadn't known a woman. Not that he hadn't wanted to. My God! Yes, he had wanted to. Then why hadn't he? Hadn't he told himself that once Don and Annette were married that would be that? And then if he never married he would certainly taste the fruits of it. But what had happened? Well, the result of what had happened was all about him. And now he was waiting for his brother's dying.

No, *he wasn't*.

Once again his thoughts were spurting him forward and along the corridor and into the new ward to which Maggie had been moved.

She was sitting in the chair by the side of the window when he entered, and she turned to him, her face and voice eager as she said, 'Oh, hello, Joe. I am pleased to see you. I'm coming home tomorrow.'

'So I understand.'

He sat down opposite her and, after a moment while she looked at him, she said, 'I called it home, but, you know, I'm afraid to enter that door. I want to be away from there as soon as ever I can. Do you understand that, Joe?'

'Yes, Maggie, I understand that.'

She pressed her head back, looking hard at him for a moment; then she said, 'You understand most things, Joe. Somehow you've been forced to understand. I've sometimes thought that it was a good thing for the family when you came into it but a bad thing for yourself.'

'That's life, Maggie. And isn't that the most trite remark in the English language? Yet, like many another, it's true. I had no say in it, had I, whatever power that ordained my life, and I often think there's more than one on that committee up there and that some are blind and others cynical.'

'Don't be bitter, Joe. That's not like you. What's the matter?'

'Aw, Maggie.' He waved his hand at her and then laughed. 'Fancy you saying that; what's the matter?'

'Well, I mean'—she bridled a little—'I know what's happened only too well. Dear God! I know what's happened. But as long as I've known you you haven't had an acid tongue.'

'That's because I swallowed my thoughts before they slipped out of my mouth.'

Sadly now she shook her head; then she asked, 'Has ... has something happened that I don't yet know about?'

'No, Maggie, I think you know about everything, except that Dad has suggested that I take on the house when he leaves. I think that stopped me swallowing my thoughts.'

'Oh. Oh.' She nodded now before saying, 'That was a damn silly thing to say.'

241

'Well, I suppose, as he says, I'd always appeared to like the house when everybody else was trying to get away from it. But under the circumstances, me there ... and who else? Eh? Who else? Oh, I'm sorry.' He took her hand, saying, 'Don't look so troubled.'

'Did you have words with him?'

'No, no; no words. Well, not really. Anyway, I'm glad you're coming back tomorrow, for however long or short.'

'I'll have to stay until Don goes.'

'Yes, yes.' He rose to his feet and sighed now. 'We'll all have to stay until Don goes. Poor Don. We're praying that he won't die, yet all of us are waiting for him to go.'

'You *are* upset, aren't you, Joe?'

'Perhaps. Anyway, I'll see you tomorrow, Maggie. Goodbye.'

'Goodbye, Joe. Joe.' He turned as he was opening the door for she was saying, 'If I hadn't been in love with your father I would certainly have fallen for you and said so, no matter what the age gap.'

He jerked his chin up and laughed as he said, 'Thanks, Maggie. That's nice to know. And I'd have been honoured to have you.'

When he reached the Maternity Ward and Annette's room, Flo greeted him with, 'It's about time you came and talked some sense into this one here; she's for discharging herself against the doctor's wishes.'

'Oh?' He stood by Harvey now and looked at Annette, and he said, 'Well, by the look of her she seems fit enough to me. Do you feel fit, Mrs Coulson?'

242

'Yes, Mr Coulson, I feel fit. And the baby's fit. We want to come home.'

'Well, I think we'd better see the doctor, hadn't we, and leave the decision to him?'

'May a man of the law speak?' They looked at Harvey now, who was smiling widely, and it was Flo who answered, 'It wouldn't be any use trying to stop you, would it, sir?'

'Well, as I see it, I think the person in question should be regarded as her own doctor. Put the said person in a wheelchair, transfer her to an automobile, carry her and the said child into the house and put them straight into bed. What could be simpler?'

Annette smiled at Harvey and said, 'That sounds sensible. Well, what do you say, Joe?'

'I still say we should leave it in the doctor's hands. Anyway, I'll go and have a word with someone in charge and I'll be back.'

After he had left the room Harvey and Flo exchanged glances and looked at Annette, and she said, 'I've never known Joe to be in a temper. But ... but what do you think? He's in a temper, isn't he?'

'He's in something.' Flo pursed her lips and turned to Harvey, saying, 'Don't you think so too?'

'Well, if you want to know what I think, ladies, I think that everybody, I mean everybody, puts on Joe. As far as I can gather, he's been a dustbin for everybody's woes, the sorter out of troubles. Oh, Joe'll do this and Joe'll do that. And something must have happened that's made Joe think that he's tired of being a dustbin. Perhaps I'm wrong; it might be something else. I don't know. But in my short acquaintance with him, this present Joe is not

243

the Joe that I had come to know.'

Getting up from where she was sitting on the side of the bed, Flo said, 'I wish I wasn't going, that we weren't going.' She looked across at her husband, and he said, 'Well, we made a decision.'

'Oh ... oh, yes, yes, I know, and I'm looking forward to it, and although I said I wish I wasn't going, it's because I just want to see Annette settled.' She put her hand out and stroked Annette's hair back from her forehead, adding, 'But once you're in your own home you can start a new life.' Her voice trailed off; then jerking herself away from the bed, she said, 'Oh my God! the things I say.'

'Flo, I'm not upset. Things like that don't upset me. I faced up to it a long time ago. Don will soon go. That's why I want to get back. And you must go too and be happy in your new life. And who couldn't help but be happy with this big handsome fellow here.' She put out her hand and Harvey gripped it. 'Write to me every week, won't you? And perhaps in a little while I ... I could come out for a holiday with young Flo.'

They were both standing over her, silent now, until her arms came up and went round their necks and Flo's tears mingled with hers and, brokenly, they said their goodbyes. And the last words Harvey spoke before leaving her were, 'I'll always be grateful to you, Annette, for being prepared to give your son—had he been a son—my name. You'll never know how much that means to me.'

Left alone, Annette gulped over the lump in her throat, telling herself she mustn't give way, for if she got upset it would stop her going home. And yet, in another way, she was dreading going back to that house, even though it still held Don. But she wouldn't be able to leave until he left it too. And Joe. What was the matter with Joe? She had never seen him as he had appeared a short while ago; distant. He wasn't the Joe she could rely on, the Joe that was always there. What if he too wanted to leave? Everything was changing. It was natural, she supposed, yet she had thought that Joe was the kind of person who would never change: he was there, stable, someone you could rely on. But he had his own life to lead. She recalled that only a few weeks ago she had seen him in the town talking to Mary Carter. She was a very smart girl, about his own age. She was a Protestant, though. But then she couldn't see religion standing in Joe's way if he really wanted her. Then there was Irene Shilton. She had trailed him for years, and she was a Catholic. She was very pretty, younger than him. Strangely, she had never liked her.

The door opened and the nurse entered carrying the baby, and when the child was laid in her arms and the nurse said, 'She's putting on weight every day. Isn't she lovely?' she looked up at her and said, 'I'd like to see Sister as soon as possible, please. I...'

'Is something wrong?'

'No, no, nurse; nothing's wrong. And you've been so kind, but I want to go home. My husband, you know, is very ill. I want him to see the baby.'

'Yes, yes, of course. I'll tell Sister.'

CHAPTER TWELVE

It was eight o'clock the following morning. Flo and Harvey were ready for leaving: they had said their goodbyes to Don and the staff, and now they were standing outside by the car, with Joe and Harvey shaking hands.

'You'll come and see us, Joe? You promised. And you will?'

'I will. I will. Don't worry about that.' Then he laughed as he added, 'For two pins I'd pack my bags and come along with you now except that, at this time, two's company.'

Flo didn't laugh; but now, putting her arms around Joe's neck, she kissed him and, looking into his face, she said softly, 'Everything comes to him who waits, Joe.' And she jerked her head back to where Harvey was standing, the car door in his hand. 'Look what happened to me.' Again she kissed him, and he returned her kiss.

He watched the car moving down the drive, Flo's arm out of the window and, for a moment, Harvey's hand out of the other. And then they were gone and he doubted if he'd ever see them again.

Slowly he went back into the house. Everything comes to him who waits.

Waits for what?

When he entered Don's room the nurse had just finished washing her patient and was stroking a thick quiff of hair back from his brow as she piped, 'Who's a pretty boy then?'

The sound grated on Joe's ears. What effect it

was having on Don's didn't show. But he, looking up at Joe, said, 'They've gone then?'

'Yes, they've gone.'

'She doesn't know it'—he drew in a gasping breath—'but things aren't going to be easy out there.' Another gasp at the air. 'I ... I shouldn't wonder to see them back in ... in no time.'

'Oh, I think they know what they're up against. They've got through it here so they'll manage.'

'You're ... you're all dressed for out.'

'Yes, I have to go to work sometimes, you know'—Joe smiled—'if it's only to put in an appearance.'

'Nurse said your ... your light was ... on at half-past two ... this morning.'

'She's a Nosey Parker, like all nurses.' He glanced towards Nurse Porter and she turned, smiling, towards him, saying, 'I'll tell her tonight what you said. She's a hefty piece; you'd find your match.'

'That would be nice.' He returned her smile; then looking at Don again, he said, 'Well, I'm off. I'll be back at lunch-time. Behave yourself, mind. Do you hear?'

'Joe.' Don's voice was a thin whisper now. 'When ... when is she ... coming? I mean...'

'Any time now. I'm going in this afternoon; I'll likely bring her back with me then.'

'Do. Please do, Joe.'

'I will.' He patted the thin shoulder. 'Don't you worry, just behave yourself.' And with this, he turned and went out and along the corridor to his own cottage.

Having thrown some papers into his case, he stood looking down at it for a moment and

247

repeated to himself and grimly, 'Everything comes to him who waits.' My God! Flo must have thought he was hanging on for that ... Well, wasn't he?

No, No! He wasn't going to have that said of him.

★　　★　　★

He entered the hall at dinner time to see Maggie coming slowly down the stairs. She stopped, and he stood at the foot smiling up at her, saying, 'You've made it then?'

'Yes, I've made it. But I hadn't realised just how much it had taken out of me until I stepped outside the hospital. I would prepare yourself before you go along there'—she thumbed towards the sick room—'there's visitors.'

He glanced in the direction she had indicated, then said, 'Who do you mean? Annette?'

'Yes, Annette.'

'But how?'

'Oh, quite easily. She phoned Lily. Lily brought her clothes and mine in a taxi, and Bob's your uncle, here we are. Now, now; don't look like that; it's all right.'

'And the child too?'

'Yes, and she's doing fine. She's put on a pound or more in a week.'

Maggie descended the rest of the stairs and stood in front of him, saying, quietly now, 'Oh, you should have seen his face when he took the child from her. You know, it's sort of given him a new lease of life. I shouldn't be surprised if'—she shook her head now as if denying her thoughts.

248

'Anyway, it's given him a reprieve, I know that.'

He made no comment on this but turned from her and walked towards Don's room. His step was not hurried nor yet slow and he prepared himself for the tableau before opening the door. And there it was: father, mother, and child, close together.

It was Annette who spoke first. Getting to her feet, she said, 'Now don't be annoyed with me, Joe; I just couldn't stand that room a minute longer. And I'm fine. We're both fine. Look at her!' She pointed to where the child was held in the hollow of Don's arm, a finger of his other hand stroking the wisps of hair. And Don looked at him, saying, 'This is ... the happiest day of my ... my life, Joe. Isn't ... isn't she beautiful?'

'She is that, she's beautiful.' He was bending over them now, and when he put his hand out towards the tiny one groping at the air and it hung on to his thumb the restriction in his throat seemed to expand and cover his chest, making his own breathing difficult for a moment.

It was the nurse who broke the tension by saying, 'Not that all babies don't do that, but, there you are, she's claimed you straight away. So look out! If she howls in the night you know what to expect.'

'She doesn't cry at night,' Annette said. 'They told me she sleeps soundly.'

'And that's what she's going to do now,' said the nurse. 'So here! Give her to me. And you'—she nodded towards Annette—'go and have something to eat and then it's bed for you this afternoon. Now do what you're told. I've had my orders and I'm giving them to you.'

When the nurse had taken the baby from Don's

249

arms Annette leant over him and, after looking
into his face for a moment, she kissed him. And his
arms came around her and held her close. Then he
was lying back with the tears oozing slowly from
beneath his lids.

Joe, taking hold of Annette's arm, drew her from
the bed and out of the room. They didn't speak
until they reached the dining-room; and there she
sat down before, looking up at him, she said,
'You're vexed with me?'

'No. What makes you think that?'

'Because ... because I came home on my own
and didn't wait another day or so as I promised.
But I'm all right and I felt I must be here near him.
You understand?'

'Of course I understand.' He sat down beside
her. 'I was going by what the doctor said was best
for you; but if there had been any noticeable
change in Don you know I would have brought
you home immediately.'

'He looks dreadful, Joe.'

'Do you think so? I thought ... well, I thought
he was even looking better?' he lied firmly.

'No, no. And it's not just because I haven't seen
him for a week or so. But now, seeing the baby,
perhaps he'll rally. What do you think?'

'I think just that, he will rally, he'll go on.'

She shook her head as she looked away from
him. 'You don't believe that. Neither do I. I looked
in on father-in-law ... or Dan, as he insists I call
him. He says he's coming home too, but he still
looks awful. He ... he told me he's selling the
house: he's already told his secretary to put it on
the market. I'm glad of that. I hate this place; I
wish I could take Don and the baby straight to the
250

cottage. Oh, it's all right, it's all right.' She closed
her eyes and put out her hand towards him. 'I
know I can't but ... but I did think Dad might
have waited until ... well—' She shook her head.
Then looking at him again, she said, 'What will
you do?'

'Oh, don't worry about me; I have it all worked
out.'

'You won't leave the town?' There was a note of
anxiety in her voice, and he answered, 'No. No, of
course not; my work's here.'

'You could set up your work anywhere.
Newcastle for instance. Durham, anywhere ... or
even Canada.'

Her head drooping on to her chest now, she
murmured, 'I felt so lost in there, Joe. I ... I
thought perhaps Mother might come and see me.
Father I knew would never come, but ... but
somehow ... But there, she didn't. When the
papers were full of it last week one of the new
nurses said to me, "It's a good job your parents
weren't in the same house when your
mother-in-law got going. I bet they were relieved
that you were in here at the time." And when I
burst out crying she patted me, saying, "They'll
likely be in soon. Don't worry. Don't worry."'

Her face flooded with tears and he steeled
himself not to draw her near to him, but just took
her hand and patted it, saying, 'There now. There
now. Don't cry like that, please. If he sees you
upset it'll only make him worse. And ... and
you've got the baby to think about.'

'By the way'—she was drying her face
now—'where's Stephen? I haven't seen him.'

'Oh, he's been in bed these last few days. He's
251

been having accidents again, you know. I think he heard Lily and Peggie talking about the likelihood of this place being sold and the old fear about being put in a home has erupted again. He's been threatened with that so many times. I've tried to tell him that wherever Dad and Maggie go, he'll go with them. You understand about them, don't you, Annette?'

'Well, I do now, Joe, if I didn't before. I must admit I was a bit surprised, but I don't blame him, either of them. Oh, no, I don't blame them, Joe.' She squeezed his hand tightly and paused before she said, 'Do ... do you think Don's mind is becoming affected too?'

'His mind? What makes you think that?'

'Well, it happened as soon as I put the baby into his arms that ... that he held it up as if showing it to somebody, and he looked towards the foot of the bed and said, "And this is the result." It ... it was as if he was seeing someone. You don't think ... ?'

He took her other hand now and pressed them between his two large ones, and he shook them gently as he said, 'He's not going off his head, dear; it's just that he imagines his mother has come back. And it isn't just imagination, you know, for at times I too feel she is here. Now don't ... don't. Please ... please don't shake like that. You have nothing to fear. She's gone. She's dead. But you know how she felt about him, and these things happen whether we like to believe them or not. I wouldn't have believed it a few months ago. In fact, I wouldn't have believed any of this.' His voice was harsh now. 'But I know as well as he does that she's there in that room. And that's

252

what's troubling poor Stephen as well. We try to put it down to the fact that he doesn't know what's going to happen to him, but whereas once he wouldn't leave Don's side, he now seems afraid to go into the room. The last time he was there he actually wet his pants on the spot. Now, that's never happened before. Did you feel anything strange when you went in?'

'No. No, I didn't. Perhaps I hadn't been in the room long enough. I was only so pleased to see him.'

'Well, if he does mention it to you don't let him see that you're afraid. Just tell him that she can do him no harm. And you know, it's odd, but I'm sure she doesn't want to do him any harm; she just wants him. There's one thing, though, I know, and I've got to say this, that once death comes to him she'll be gone too, because it's mostly in his mind.'

'But if it's mostly in his mind how do you too feel that she's there?'

'Because it's in my mind as well, I suppose. Love and hate can create a sort of ethereal body. At least, that's how I've explained it to myself: there's the three of us, three men. Don's love, or any feeling he had for her, turned to hate because of her abnormal obsession with him. As for me, her attitude towards me over the years created dislike. And yes, that could have bordered on hate too. But in Stephen's case it's fear: fear has created her for him. Well'—he sighed—'that's the only explanation I can give. But what the three of us know is that her presence is still in that room. But the strongest emotion is between her and Don, and through this he almost sees her, if he doesn't *actually* see her. But as I said, once he goes ... and

253

he'll go in peace, she'll no longer be there. Nor, I imagine, will she be able to hold him, for there'll be no coming together.'

'That's an odd thing to say, Joe.' Her voice was quiet. 'It's against all the tenets of our religion, isn't it? The coming together, the meeting up with the loved ones, the forgiveness of sins, life everlasting, the mansions of God. What do you say to all that?'

'That it's mostly myth. Don't look surprised. Yes, I know I attend Mass, I go to Confession, I say the Rosary. But I'm protesting all the time. I've talked it out with Father Ramshaw and in his kindly, God-like way he tells me the doubts will pass. Every true Christian goes through this stage, he says. Well, I've been through it for some time now and all that has happened is the doubts have become almost certainties. Still, it takes strength to throw over God, to do away with him altogether, and I doubt if I'm all that strong. But, don't look so worried.'

'I'm not worried, Joe, I'm only surprised, because you've put into words the feelings I had in the convent. Some of those nuns were like angels, some like devils. And if it hadn't been for Father Ramshaw I would have rebelled openly some time ago; especially after a rating from Father Cody. And do you know, that man tackled me about my sin, Don's and my sin together, and he told me I should do a long penance and berate my flesh.'

'He didn't! You should have told Father Ramshaw about him.'

'Oh, I don't think Father Ramshaw needs to be told about him. Odd, isn't it?' She smiled now. 'I know that those two hate each other like poison.

Disciples of God and living in the same house and can't stand the sight of each other. Oh, but what does it matter? That's all beside the point really.'

'Yes, dear. Yes, it is. Now come on, have something to eat, then as the nurse said, you go back and you feed Flo. ... They went off this morning, you know.'

'Yes, I know. They called in at the hospital again.'

'They didn't!'

'Yes. Yes, they did.'

'That was nice of them. I thought they were going straight on. Anyway, you're going to have a rest, but not in that room. You're going upstairs. Peggie had already fitted up a guest-room with a dressing-room attached, and now she's fixed that up as a kind of nursery. So it's all ready for you.'

'Oh, that *is* nice.' She rose now and went towards the dining table; then quietly she asked, 'Have you been along to the cottage lately, Joe?'

'Yes, I've looked in at least every other day. I had business with a client up that way, so it was easy. And I don't know why it's called a cottage, with nine rooms set in an acre and a half of land. It's like a little manor house. You'll be happy there, dear.'

She looked at him for a long, long moment, but said nothing; nor did he, for he felt it had been a tactless remark to make: happy in a nine-roomed house on your own with a baby.

CHAPTER THIRTEEN

From the moment of Annette's and the baby's return Don seemed to blossom, inasmuch as his breathing became easier. He complained less of pain; the doctor seemed pleased with him; and he exchanged quips with Father Ramshaw. And a fortnight after Annette's arrival home his father stepped into the room and he held out both arms to him and returned the hug that Daniel gave him.

One side of Daniel's face was still discoloured, he walked with a slight limp and it was evident that he had lost some weight.

They talked about everything that didn't matter until the day wore on and it was time to say good-night; then, appertaining to nothing that had gone before, Daniel, from where he was sitting at the side of the bed, leant his elbows on the coverlet, took hold of his son's hand and said, 'She's not here. Get it into your head, lad, she's not here. She's gone forever.'

'You don't feel her, Dad?'

'No ... no, I don't feel her; except where she's left the bruises all over me body. That's where I feel her. But not anywhere else.'

'She's here, Dad. She's been here from the minute she died.'

'Now, Don.'

'It's no good talking, Dad. And I'm not the only one. Why do you think Stephen isn't down here chatting away? He hasn't been near the room for days. He's in bed, supposedly with a cold. He knew she was here; and so does Joe.'

'Oh, not Joe. Joe's too level...'

'Joe's not too level-headed, Dad. He feels her almost as much as I do. And I know one thing for sure: she won't go till I go. But I'm not afraid, I mean, of her. I've become so that I pity her. But she knows she can't hold me. I've told her that and she knows it. It is as if knowing it she's determined to see the last of me here.'

'Don't talk like that, lad.'

'Dad ... you grew to hate her. You hated her for a long time, and the more you hated her the more she loved me. And in the end, you know, I've come to think that love is stronger than hate because it's her love, or whatever name you could put to it, that's keeping her here. I don't mind her now. I was petrified at first, sick at the thought of her being here, but not any more. And even her appearance is altered. She's sort of pathetic. I'm sorry for her. And don't look like that, Dad, as if you were scared; my mind's not affected, it's the only place that's been left whole. I know it's whole.'

'Have you talked to Father Ramshaw about it?'

'Yes; yes, we've discussed it openly and often. He understands. As he says, there's more things in heaven and earth than this world dreams of, and he's right. Have you had any takers for the house yet?'

'Yes ... yes, I understand there's been takers.'

'Well, they'll have to wait a while, won't they?'

'I hope they have to wait for years, lad.'

'Oh, no, not as long as that, Dad, not as long as that. It'll be funny, this house breaking up; it seemed so solid at one time. Dad ... ?'

'Yes, son?'

257

'You and Maggie will get together, I know that, and Stephen will go with you. Well, let it rest there; don't interfere in any other way, will you? Will you not?'

'What do you mean, interfere?'

'Just that. Let ... let the rest of them run their own lives.'

'The rest of them? Who do you mean? There's only Joe and Annette.'

'Yes ... well, I know, there's only Joe and Annette. But whatever happens, Dad, let things take their course.'

Daniel got to his feet and, looking down on his son, he said sadly, 'I don't like that, Don, not the way you're saying that. Whatever I did in the past was for your good.'

'Yes, yes, I know, Dad, but that is what most people say, you know: I did it for ... for somebody's good.'

Daniel narrowed his eyes as he looked down on the thin pale face with the sunken eyes, the face that a year ago had appeared like that of a young boy ... well, at most, a young man about to enter his twenties. But the eyes, as they gazed back at him from the deep-set sockets, could have been those of an old man and one who had lived a life and had experienced many things. He said quietly, 'Good-night, son. Sleep well.'

'Good-night, Dad. You too.'

*   *   *

It was a fortnight later and around seven o'clock in the evening. Father Ramshaw was sitting in the library with Joe. Each was drinking a cup of coffee

258

and the priest was saying, 'I'm sorry I missed Daniel, I wanted a word with him. You say he's gone to look at his old place at the foot of Brampton Hill?'

Yes. It's odd, isn't it, that it should become vacant at this time? He never wanted to leave that house really. It was one of the smallest on the hill and one of the oldest. I think it was the first one built before the élite of the town got started with their mansions.'

'Yes, so I understand. And he's going to set up house there with Maggie and Stephen? Well, that's one part of the family that'll be settled. What about you?'

'Oh, I'm settled too.'

'What do you mean? Have you got a flat?'

'Yes, sort of. It'll all be settled soon.'

'Well, I don't think you have very long to wait. He's near his end; I feel that he should have the last rites tomorrow.'

'But ... but he seems bright, Father. I thought he could go on for some time yet.'

'It's a forced brightness, Joe. I thought you would have seen that. But he knows that his time is running out and fast. The doctor said to me when we had a crack the other day, he's amazed that he's lasted so long. It's Annette and the child that's kept him going, and he's happy. It's strange but he's happy and quite ready to go. If I were you I'd sit up with him for some part of the next few nights. By the way, what's going to happen to the staff, Bill, John, Peggie, and Lily?'

'Well, Peggie is going to stay with Annette, and John is going with Dad. Bill and Lily will stay in the lodge, and if the new people, whoever takes the

259

house, want to keep them on, well and good, if not, Dad's going to see to them in some way. So they are all going to be accounted for.'

'Well, that's good to know. And you, are you going to live in this flat of yours alone?'

'Well, what do you suggest, Father?' Joe pursed his lips now as he waited for an answer. And the priest, raising his eyebrows, said, 'Well, from what I gather you wouldn't have far to look for a partner. There's two in the church I know of and one outside.'

'How do you know about Miss Carter?'

'Oh, I know lots of things, lad. It's amazing the news I get and where it comes from. Well, are you going to pick one of them?'

'I may.'

'So you've been thinking about it?'

'Yes, Father, I've thought about it a lot; in fact, I've already made a choice. I made it some time ago.'

Father Ramshaw's eyes widened. 'Well, well! That's news. No inkling to who it is?'

'Not as yet, Father. I'll tell you when the time comes.'

'Inside or out?'

'I'll tell you that too when the time comes.'

'Well, that's something to look forward to. Now I must be on my way. I enjoyed that meal. It was always a good meat house this. And it's sad, you know.' He stood up and looked about him. 'It's a beautiful house, especially this room and all those books. What'll you do with them? Send them to auction?'

'Some of them, but I'll keep most of them.'

'For your flat?'

'For my flat that could be a house.'

'Oh, oh, we're getting somewhere now. The flat that could be a house. Well, well! You know me, Joe: once I get my teeth into anything I hang on until I know whom I'm biting. But it's going to be a surprise to me. I know that, because I thought I knew all about you both inside and out.'

'There's always a depth, Father, in all of us that only the owner can plumb.'

'Yes, yes, you're right there, Joe, you're right there. Nevertheless—' He chuckled now and shook his head, turned away and went down the room and out into the hall and to the front door. And there he stopped and, looking back towards the stairs, he said, 'If your Dad doesn't sell this place to one of the tribe then my visits here will be cut short pretty soon. Good-night, Joe.'

'Good-night, Father. And Father, you're a great believer in the efficacy of prayer, so you should see what it'll do about the new occupants.'

The priest threw his head back now and laughed, saying, 'That's good advice, Joe. Yes, I'll do that. Yes, I'll do that.'

*   *   *

At ten o'clock Annette said good-night to Don and when he took her face between his hands and said, 'I love you,' she answered brokenly, 'And I you, Don. Oh yes, and I you.' And when he added, 'Be happy,' she drew herself from him, and going to the nurse who was at the other end of the room, she said, 'I . . . I think I'll sleep down here tonight.'

'There's no need, Mrs Coulson. If there was any change at all I'd call you immediately.'

'I'd rather.'

'Annette.'

From the bed, Don said, 'Go to bed upstairs, please. I'm going to sleep. I feel fine, really fine.'

She went back to the bed again. 'I'd rather, Don, if you ...'

He took her hand, 'Do as you're told, Mrs Coulson. Go to bed. If you are lying on that hard mattress I'll be aware of you all night and I won't rest. Moreover, I want my daughter seen to.' He continued to look at her long and hard, then said, 'Please.'

To hide her emotions she turned and hurried from the room. But instead of going to her own room she went along to Joe's apartment.

When there was no answer she went in and called softly, 'Joe.' And when there was still no reply, she turned about and went hastily along the corridor, through the hall and towards the kitchen. He'd likely be there talking to Maggie. Strange, she thought, that Maggie should still be carrying on what duties she could in the kitchen and sleeping in her own room while her father-in-law slept upstairs: the proprieties must not only be kept, but be seen to be kept. And after all they had gone through it seemed silly to her.

However, Maggie was not in the kitchen. Peggie said she was in her room and she had last seen Mr Joe in the library.

She found Joe in the library. He was at the table thumbing through some books, and at the sight of her he raised his head and rose to his feet, saying, 'What is it?'

'I don't know.' She gave her head a little shake. 'He seems all right, but ... but it was the way he acted. I wanted to sleep there but he won't let me.'

'Well, I'll be staying up, and if there's any change whatever you know I'll come for you.'

'Yes, yes, I suppose so. But he seemed different, sort of very calm and, in a strange way, happy. It ... it was puzzling, even weird.'

'Now, now. He's in a weak state and he's bound to react like that at times. Go on, get yourself to bed. I promise you, at the slightest change I'll come and fetch you post haste.'

'Promise?'

'I've said so, haven't I?'

Turning abruptly, she made for the door; but there she stopped and, looking back towards him, she said, 'Odd, isn't it, that Dad's going back to the house that he first lived in? It seems that everything is falling into place for everybody, even you; I heard Dad say that you had told him you had got a place, a house of some sort. Is that right?'

'Yes. Yes, it's right, Annette.'

'Are you going to furnish it from here?'

'No, no. The only things I'll take from here are my books and papers, because there's nothing here that really belongs to me.'

'It's all settled then?'

'Yes, it's all settled. For once in my life I'm going to please myself and do something that I know I should have done a long time ago.'

'Yes. Yes, I understand, Joe. You've never been able to please yourself. As I said the other night you've been at the beck and call of everybody, even of me of late. Well, I'm happy for you. Good-night. And ... and you'll call me?'

'Yes, I'll call you. Good-night.'

He returned to the desk, gathered up his papers,

263

put the books into their respective places on the shelves, then left the room and made his way to his own quarters. There, he took a quick shower, got into his dressing-gown and slippers, then went along to the sick-room.

He had hardly closed the door before the nurse greeted him with, 'We've got a naughty boy here; he refuses to take his pills. What are we going to do about it, Mr Coulson?'

'Hold his nose. I think that's the only way.'

'He's not going to like that.' She was looking towards the bed and smiling. And Joe said, 'We've got to do lots of things in life we don't like.'

Joe took his seat beside the bed and Don looked at him and said, 'All right, then; let's have them. You look very fresh and handsome tonight, Joe.'

'I don't know about handsome; fresh, yes, because I've just had a shower.'

'Yes, your hair's still wet. Funny, I could never stand my hair being wet; I always had to dry it with the electric drier. Remember?'

'Yes, I remember.'

'What's the weather like?'

'Oh, it's a very nice night: calm, not even a breeze, and quite warm.'

'That's nice. I feel very calm, Joe, very calm. Nurse!' He now looked towards the nurse. 'Do you think I could have a cup of hot cocoa?'

'A cup of hot cocoa? Why, of course. But you've never asked for cocoa before at this time of night.'

'That's what I would like, nurse.'

'Well, that's what you'll have.'

She went out smiling.

'Hot cocoa?' Joe gave a small chuckle. 'What's this, hot cocoa?'

264

'I just wanted to say something to you, Joe. Time's up. She's gone. I told you she would stay until I was ready to go. Oh ... oh, dear fellow, dear dear friend, and yes, dear brother, don't look like that but be pleased that I'm going this way. Do you know, I haven't got an ache or pain in my body: in fact, you would think I hadn't got a body. I haven't said anything about this, but I haven't had a pain, nor an ache, for two or three days now. I seem to have got lighter and lighter. And I have no fear, not of Mother, or death, or the hereafter. It all seems so settled. Oh, please, Joe, be happy for me. Be happy that I'm going like this. I want you to stay with me tonight. Sit just where you are.'

Joe's voice was breaking as he said, 'I should bring Annette down.'

'No, no. I said my goodbyes to Annette. She knows it too. I couldn't bear to see her weep. I wouldn't go easy then. But with you, Joe, it's different. You're the only one I've ever been able to talk to, properly that is, to say what I think. I'm going to close my eyes now, Joe, and when the nurse comes back you can tell her that I've fallen asleep. In a short while she'll sit in her chair over there and she'll drop off. She does it every night.'

'But ... but I thought you've just taken your pills?'

'I've become very clever at that, Joe. You know, you can hold things under your tongue for a long time.'

'Oh, Don, Don.'

'You know I want to laugh when I hear you say my name like that. You sound just like Father Ramshaw. There's a man for you. He knew, too, that I don't often take my pills at night, the

265

sleeping ones. The other one and ... and the brown stuff ... oh yes, yes; I've had to take them sometimes. But, as I said, for the last three or four days I haven't needed them. You know, Joe, when I was first put into this bed I was bitter. Oh dear God, I was bitter, and when they let me up out of the drugged sleep, I wanted to scream. And I can't look back and tell you when that time changed. You know, Joe, I've lived a longer life these past few months than I ever did in all the years before. And I know that if I had lived to be ninety or a hundred I wouldn't have understood half as much as I've come to understand in these past days. I've learned so much lying here, so I'm not sorry all this happened. Strange that, isn't it? for me to say that I'm not sorry that all this happened. And here I am leaving a beautiful young wife and a child. But I'm not worrying about them either. It's all right, Joe, it's all right, I won't go on. What will be will be. I hold you to nothing; you have your own life to live. And Father Ramshaw let it slip the other night that you had your eye on somebody. He was quizzing me to find out which one it was, but I couldn't tell him and I'm not asking you now, Joe, either. Every man has a right to change his mind, and Annette and the child are in God's hands. He'll take care of them. Don't look so worried, Joe, and don't say anything. Please, don't say anything. I understand everything.'

'You don't, you don't. Who do you think you are anyway? God, already?'

'Oh, Joe, Joe, don't make me laugh. That's funny, you know. I ache when I try to laugh. Oh, she's coming. She's heavy-footed, that one; she thumps the carpet. Hold my hand, Joe, and keep holding it, will you?'

Joe took the hand extended to him and when the door opened it was all he could do to turn and look at the nurse as she entered with the steaming cup of cocoa on a tray. He couldn't speak to her but he signalled to her that the patient was asleep, and she shrugged her shoulders, smiled, laid the cocoa down on a side table, then settled herself in an armchair.

★　　　★　　　★

At what time Don died, Joe didn't know. He had sat wide-eyed for a long period, the pale hand held in his. Once, he glanced at the clock, which showed a quarter past one. And it was at about this time that the nurse roused herself and apologetically said, 'I must have dropped off. He's sleeping quietly?'

He nodded at her. She didn't come towards the bed but busied herself at a table for a little while; then sat down again, wrote something in a notebook, and within a short while, if not quite snoring, was emitting quite heavy nasal sounds.

His arm and wrist were in a cramp but still he didn't move. What he did do was try to edge his chair a little nearer to the side of the bed to relieve the tension on his shoulder. It was some time after this that he closed his eyes and some time again before a voice said, 'Oh! Mr Coulson. Mr Coulson!'

His eyes sprang wide open and he stared at the nurse on the other side of the bed as she had Don's other wrist between her fingers.

'I'm afraid ... I'm afraid, Mr Coulson...'

267

He looked at the face on the pillow. It appeared to be warm and alive, yet stiff, as if it had been set into a mould. It could have been a sleeping face, but it wasn't.

'He's ... he's gone, Mr Coulson.'

'Yes, yes, I know.' Slowly, he lifted the thin white hand and unwound his fingers until they were straight, then just as slowly eased his cramped arm from the bed.

'I'd ... I'd better phone the doctor.'

'Yes. Yes, nurse.'

'And ... and call his father and his wife.'

'Leave that to me.'

Why was he so calm? It was as if he had imbibed the feelings that Don had expressed a short while ago: he was feeling no sorrow, no remorse, just a quietness that was expressed in the face on the pillow and that seemed to fill the whole room, for, it was true, she had gone too. Definitely she had gone.

He flexed his arms and went towards the door; but he found he couldn't grip the handle with his right hand, so opened it with his left.

Instead of making for the hall and up the stairs to alert both Annette and his father, he turned the other way and towards his quarters. And from his sitting-room he opened his door into the conservatory; then he opened the conservatory door and stepped out into the night, which was bright with moonlight: the full moon was hanging like an enormous yellow cheese in a pale blue sky. The air was cool and there was just the slightest breeze. He felt it through the sweat on his brow. He put his head back and took in the great expanse of nothingness in which just the moon floated and the stars twinkled and into which Don and his mother had gone, but in their separate ways.

CHAPTER FOURTEEN

Within seven weeks the house had been sold and almost completely denuded of furniture. Daniel had furnished his new home with the better pieces, and Maggie and Stephen were already installed there.

The new owners of the house agreed to keep on Bill and Lily in the lodge. All that remained was for Annette, the baby, and Peggie to be moved into the cottage. And it was strange that, although it was weeks since Don had been buried from the house, Annette still seemed hesitant to move permanently away from it. She had driven backwards and forwards to the cottage almost every day, returning to the house at night to sleep. Today, however, was her final day here; as it was Joe's. And where was Joe going?

Only this morning he had filled his car with cases holding his clothes and boxes holding his books, and had driven them to his new home. Where was this? As yet no-one knew, and the question was now being put to him by Daniel. They were standing in the empty drawing-room, and when Joe told him where he was to live Daniel didn't speak for a moment; then he said, 'You can't do that, man.'

'Why can't I?'

'Well, there'll be talk.'

'My God! Dad, for you to say that to me: there'll
269

be talk.'

'Oh, I know, I know, but my life's mine and I'll have to stand the racket for it, I always have. But you're different. Here you are twenty-six years of age and no-one could raise a finger to you.'

'Dear God! I just can't believe it.'

'I'm only speaking for your own good. There'll be talk.'

'Yes, there'll be talk. And what the hell does it matter to me who talks? What is amazing to me at this moment is the way *you're* talking.'

'All right, all right. I don't want to argue with you, Joe. I'm past arguing in all ways.'

'I wouldn't have thought so.'

'I'm only thinking of you.'

'Only thinking of me? and Father Cody? and Father Ramshaw? Well, let me tell you, you can cut Father Ramshaw out.'

'I would doubt it in this case.'

'We can wait and see then, can't we?'

As Joe turned away Daniel said, 'Joe. Joe, we are breaking up. It's as if a bomb had hit us, a time bomb left over from the war, and it's knocking us to blazes one way or another. You and me, we don't want to part like this. You're all I've got in the way of a son, and it's because of that I've said what I've said.'

'Well, you've still got a son, Dad, if you want one, but he's got to live his own life, as you've lived yours. And don't forget it, you have lived it, and right to the full. I haven't sipped at mine yet, but I'm going to. But don't worry, I'll be along to see you later, perhaps tonight or tomorrow. So goodbye Dad, for the present.'

In the hall Annette was standing with the baby

270

in her arms and he said, 'Are you ready, then?'

'Yes, Joe. But ... but there's no need for you to drop me off; Peggie will be back with the car at any time. She's just slipped into the town to see her mother. I can wait.'

'Well, I've got nothing else to do at the moment.'

'Is your place all fixed up?' Her voice was stiff as she asked the question, and he said, 'Yes. Yes, all fixed up and very nicely.'

'You've been very secretive about it; why?'

'Oh, you'll soon know the reason. It'll be all out shortly.'

She cast him a sidelong glance, then went towards the front door. But there she turned and looked around the hall and towards the stairs and, her voice grim now, she said, 'If ever there was an unlucky house, this is it. Pray God I'll never know such again.'

'Pray God you never will.'

He opened the rear door for her and settled the baby on her knee; then took his seat behind the wheel. And they had gone some distance before she said, 'Wherever this place of yours is, will you be near enough to drop in now and again?'

'Oh, yes, yes, definitely.'

'Joe.'

'Yes, Annette?'

'Can't you tell me? Why have you kept this place secret?'

'Well, Annette'—he paused, for they were approaching a corner—'I thought it the best policy. And, you see, there is this young woman concerned, and I felt I've dallied with her long enough; I wanted to bring things to a head sort of

271

abruptly.'

'I don't understand you, Joe, not lately I don't.'

'Well, Annette, for a long time I didn't understand myself, but now I do and I know what I'm about.'

'Well, that's all that matters, isn't it?'

'Yes, that's all that matters, Annette.'

There was nothing more said between them as the car sped the rest of the journey through pleasant countryside. And then there they were bowling up the short drive and stopping in front of the long, grey-stoned two-storey house.

He opened the front door into the small hallway and she went in before him, then stopped abruptly and looked down at the four suitcases standing side by side near the telephone table. Swinging round, she looked up at him, and he said, 'Yes, yes, they're mine. There are a number of boxes, too, books you know, but I've put them in the loft.'

She took three steps back from him, and he said, 'Look out! you'll fall over the chair. Come and sit down.'

He pushed open the door of the sitting-room, then took the baby from her and, entering the room he laid it on a deep-cushioned armchair.

She hadn't followed but was still standing at the door, and so he walked back to her, took her hand and brought her to the couch. And here, pressing her down into it, he sat beside her and said, 'This is my new flat; I'm staying here. I've already picked my rooms at the end of the corridor upstairs. They'll do for a time. What do you think about it?' His hand spread out, taking in the room with the gesture. 'Quite a nice place?'

'*Stop it! Joe. Stop it!*'

'No, I'm not going to stop it.' His own voice had changed now, all the banter gone. 'I'm doing what I should have done many years ago. I shouldn't have been pressed aside. You know it, and I know it. And Don knew it. Oh, yes, Don knew it. You were mine long before you were his. We both knew that. I don't know where you come in in that part, but I knew that if I had spoken before Dad started his manoeuvres, I would have had a wife by now, and a family. You grew to love Don. I'll not deny that. And he loved you. Oh, yes, he loved you. You loved each other. But it was an interlude. As I see it now, that's all it was, an interlude. In looking back, you belonged to me right from the beginning. Can you imagine what I felt like when I was forced to take on the big brother role? Can you? Oh, don't cry, my dear. Don't cry. I want to talk to you. I've got a lot more to say and it's this: I've waited so long now I can go on waiting until you're ready, but I've got to be near you, and I've got to know that you are mine, and that one day we will marry. And I can't help but add I hope it will be soon. But you know something? Dad warned me just before I left the house that there'd be talk. He was upset when I told him what I was going to do. He of all people to tell me that there would be talk. Can you imagine it? Now, the point is this, Annette. The talk could have substance, or it couldn't. I leave that to you and in your own time. Just know this. I love you ... I've always loved you, and I can't see myself, after all this long time, ever stopping. And because I love you so much I feel that it would be impossible for you not to love me in some way, some time.'

'Joe. Joe.' Her eyes were tightly closed. Her head

273

fell against him and rested on his shoulder as she muttered, 'I do love you. I love you now. I've been full of guilt with the feeling. I loved Don. Yes, I did. But I loved you too. All through I've known I loved you, and not just as a brother. Oh, Joe. Joe.'

His chin lay on top of her head, his eyes were screwed up tight, his teeth biting into his lower lip. Then pressing her face upwards from his shoulder, he brought his lips gently down on hers. And when she clung to him Flo's words sprang into his mind: 'Everything comes to him who waits.' Then his eyes twinkling, he said quietly, 'You know there'll be a field-day. Are you prepared for that?'

'Yes, Joe.' Her face still wet, the tears still running, she repeated again, 'Yes, Joe. And the stalls and the coconut shies.'

'With Father Cody pelting us?'

Once more they were enfolded in each other's arms and Joe added, 'And by God! he will that. Even if we get no further than this'—he kissed her on the tip of her nose—'he'll flay us as only he can flay with his tongue...'

She looked at him steadily now as she said, 'Well, we'll have to see that we are flayed for something, won't we, Joe?'

'Oh, my dear. My dear.'

Gently now they enfolded each other and lay back against the couch. But when a small cry came from the chair, their mouths opened wide and they laughed aloud. Then, springing up, Joe picked up the baby and, rocking it widely from side to side, he cried, 'Listen to me, Flo Coulson, your mother loves me. Do you hear that? Your mother loves me. Everything comes to him who waits. Your mother loves me.'